BREEZE

Her father, Omar Blackwell, a jazz musician who felt music through his skin pores, nurtured and adored her. Her mother, Lillian Blackwell, who had enough of musicians and their bohemian lifestyle, discouraged and deceived her. Her first love, Alexander "Lex" Franklin, a hit-making record producer whom she lost through trickery, would return to teach her the rapture and dangers of sexual desire. She is a beautiful singer with an incredible, soulful voice that catapulted her to super-stardom.

Her name is Breeze.

Reunited with Lex Franklin, their separate lives finally come together. But in the entertainment world, where love is an everyday casualty, will their love survive?

BREEZE

ROBIN LYNETTE HAMPTON

Genesis Press, Inc.

F

Indigo Love Stories

An imprint of Genesis Press, Inc.
Publishing Company

Genesis Press, Inc.
P.O. Box 101
Columbus, MS 39703

ISBN-13: 978-1-58571-308-0
ISBN-10: 1-58571-308-2
Manufactured in the United States of America

First Edition 1994
Second Edition 2008

Visit us at www.genesis-press.com or call at 1-888-Indigo-1

DEDICATION

*Dedicated with much love
to my daughters
Cara Diandra Allen and Cassidy Milan Allen*

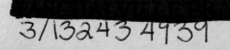

PROLOGUE

"More! More! More!" The crowd of thousands roared from the stands of the Omni Coliseum in Atlanta, demanding that Breeze Blackwell return to the stage. Eighteen thousand hands clapped thunderously, beckoning Breeze to continue the magic of her razzle-dazzle concert.

The spell Breeze cast on stage was powerful. The mixed audience—young and old, black and white, rich and poor—was spellbound by seventy minutes of what the *Atlanta Journal* called "the most entertaining performance since Michael Jackson."

"The Breezing Tour" was a huge success nationwide, selling out 20,000-seat arenas in record time. Her fans had anxiously waited three years to see Breeze Blackwell perform hit after hit from her history-making debut and current albums. Every song on both albums became number-one hits, phenomenally scoring twenty number-one hits, eclipsing singles by Michael Jackson, Madonna, and Whitney Houston. Breeze's success was like Niagara Falls: immeasurable and spectacular.

On stage, Breeze didn't perform, she mesmerized. She had the power to entrance thousands with her music, to possess their senses with the sheer versatility of her soulful voice.

The audience screamed, "B.B.!" "B.B.!" in a two-beat rhythm. "B.B.!" followed by two short claps. "B.B.!" Clap, clap!

Backstage in her dressing room, Breeze felt high. Hearing the booming thunder of the applause was a rush. The audience chanting her name was a shot of adrenaline that could match no other feeling. The chorus of voices echoing her name electrified, energized, and thrilled her. It was the reality of her dreams, the only drug she needed.

Breeze looked at her reflection in the mirror, but did not see her face. Instead, she envisioned flashes of her life whirling around like a kaleidoscope: the first time she nervously sang in front of an audience and discovered that she had been blessed with a beautiful singing voice; her father playing the saxophone and his huge record collection; the sound of music that always filled her ears and spoke to her soul; and Lex smiling encouragingly, "You can sing, Sunshine, you can sing!"

Rohan, her musical director, poked his head through the door, interrupting Breeze's trance. "Hey, Breeze! You ready?" he asked, returning Breeze to the present. The audience's screams, sounding louder and louder, were rising like a mystical incantation.

The sound of her name recharging her energy, she nodded. "Let's do this!" It was time to give the screaming audience what they demanded.

Dressed in a form-fitting, gold-studded black leather jumpsuit with deep V's in the front and back, Breeze ran back on stage. Two hours before the show, her hair had been curled, combed, brushed, gelled, and spritzed. After performing two funky, fast-paced songs, her hair had wilted like a rain-drenched flower from dancing and sweating under the bright, hot lights. For her final number, Breeze's hair had been brushed into a ponytail. Sweat glistened against her caramel-colored skin.

It was dark except for the single flames from the sea of lighters held high, glowing like twinkling stars lighting up the midnight sky. The audience went wild when they saw Breeze back on stage. Their screams grew even louder as they chanted, "B.B.! B.B.!"

Breeze rushed to the front of the stage. The musicians, dancers and back-up singers took their designated places.

"You want some more?" Breeze screamed into the mouthpiece of the headset microphone. "What do you want to hear?"

The audience replied, "Imitation of Love," her latest hit.

Breeze moved to the left of the stage. "What do you want to hear?"

"Imitation of Love," the audience screamed.

Breeze moved to the right of the stage and sang, "Tell me, umh, umh, what do you want to hear?"

The audience chanted, " 'Imitation of Love!' 'Imitation of Love!' "

Breeze screamed, "I'm going to give you what you want!"

She moved to the center of the stage, lights flashing, spotlighting her movements. She signaled her band, the music came in soft and mellow. The audience was breathlessly silent.

In a seductive voice, Breeze whispered, "I like to start this song real slow." She sang the first verse of the song a cappella.

Quickly, the tempo of the music changed—it was fast, it was upbeat, it was kicking.

In full accord, the dancers started imitating the rhythm of an African tribal dance. They whirled and twirled, gyrating their lithe bodies frenetically around the stage, as Breeze's powerful voice permeated the Omni Coliseum.

Breeze's first verse of "Imitation of Love" was loud and strong, sultry and deep. But when she sang the chorus, accompanied by the back-up singers, she sounded strangely off-key. By the second verse, her voice was quivery and strained. Suddenly, Breeze slumped to the floor, and a soft wailing sound echoed through the coliseum.

Breeze had fainted.

After a minute of confusion, the audience realized that Breeze's sudden drop to the floor was not part of the act. She wasn't moving, nor was she singing. The music suddenly stopped, and the back-up singers and dancers were too stunned to move.

Rohan was the first to react: He rushed to Breeze's side. He listened to her chest and was relieved to hear faint heartbeats. Pandemonium broke loose when everyone scrambled around the stage to help the unconscious Breeze.

The audience watched with concern and disappointment as Breeze was carried off the stage on a stretcher.

Unexpectedly, the show was over.

CHAPTER ONE

"You really don't know Miss Abbot, so why should you go to her wedding, anyway," Rayna said. Only sixteen, Rayna had a grown woman's voluptuous body: big breasts, small waistline, full hips, and protruding behind. There was nothing sweet sixteen in Rayna's attitude or actions.

"Don't forget who you're talking to, Miss Think-You-Grown," Lillian scolded, glaring at her eldest daughter. "I told you before about that mouth of yours. It's going to get you in trouble. You better learn to keep it shut before I knock you to kingdom come!" Lillian sat on the edge of her bed, soaking her aching feet in a bucket of warm water.

"But we want to go by ourselves like everybody else," Breeze said distressfully. She moved out from behind Rayna, and stood directly before her mother, wearing her most beguiling, I'll-get-my-way smile.

Weary from a busy day working as a legal secretary, Lillian had looked forward to coming home to peace and quiet. After dinner she planned to soak her feet to ease away the tensions of the day, and then go to bed. Instead of ringing telephones and banging typewriter keys, the girls were beating her eardrums with their insistent pleas.

In a firm voice, Lillian said, "I've already talked to Miss Abbot. She knows I'm coming to the wedding."

"Ma!" Rayna huffed, sucking in her breath. "How could you do that? How could you embarrass me? Treating me like a baby." She rolled her eyes and poked out her lips.

Lillian gave Rayna a don't-try-me look.

"Dag, Ma," Rayna mumbled under her breath and stomped out of the room, leaving Breeze and India to plead their case.

"Pretty please!" Breeze pleaded, bouncing up and down, but not leaving the floor.

"We'll be good. We'll be home by nine o'clock," India promised, the tallest and thinnest of the three. She had jet black hair that hung straight down the middle of her back and a fudge-brown complexion that was a gift of her Caribbean heritage.

India was adopted into the Blackwell family after Lillian had divorced her musician husband and had moved back to her hometown, Philadelphia. India had lived next door with her grandmother on a street that had no children, other than the Blackwell girls. The little girls had become an inseparable trio. They walked to school together, and got into trouble together. When India's grandmother died, her mother could not be found. So, Lillian took care of India, and after two years had passed and no one called to claim her, Lillian legally adopted her.

"There's gonna be mostly grown folks there, drinking, dancing, and carrying on," Lillian explained. "You ought to be glad that I'm letting you go at all."

"But all the other kids are going by themselves," Breeze insisted. She removed the bucket of water from under her mother's feet, and handed Lillian a thick towel.

"How many times do I have to tell you that I make my own decisions? I don't care how other people raise their kids," she said irritably, drying her feet with the green towel. "Well, I'm going to be there too. Case closed," Lillian pronounced. She stood up, the sound of her feet hitting the floor as final as a judge banging a gavel.

A petite, reddish-brown woman with a massive head of thick black hair that seemed to overpower her small frame, Lillian was noticeably attractive, with striking features: large brown eyes, a short, broad nose, and heart-shaped lips. She often wore her hair in a long, single braid that traveled past her shoulders. At times, Lillian would braid and wrap her hair, crowning her head as if she were an Indian priestess.

"I've got to get up early, so you all go on out of my room so I can get some sleep."

With frowns on their frustrated faces, Breeze and India kissed their mother on the forehead and bid her good-night.

Lillian took off her tattered terry cloth robe and hung it on the back of the closet door before climbing into the queen-size bed. The lights were out, the television was off, but her mind was on, racing away with thoughts of the past.

Closing her eyes, waiting for sleep to come, Lillian thought back to the years when her girls were younger, when their demands were much simpler.

Rayna and Breeze, the treasures of my broken marriage, she smiled wistfully in the dark bedroom, recalling memories from long ago.

There were many mornings, back then, when Lillian Blackwell had found her two daughters crowded together in the same bed, even though she had tucked them into their own beds. And some mornings, she rose early to go into Rayna and Breeze's bedroom to stare at them before waking them from their perfect repose.

They're beautiful, she would muse. *I'm truly blessed to have such healthy children.* Smiling down at them, she had thought, *My daughters will have better choices when they become young women. The world is changing, I can feel it and see it. Just in time for my babies. Dr. Martin Luther King is sure causing a commotion. Thank God, Negro children can now dream with hope.*

When they were young, the morning ritual was always the same.

"Hey, you two sleeping birds, rise and shine. It's time to wake up," Lillian used to say with a lilt in her voice. She greeted them with a smile, no matter how much her marital problems burdened her heart.

Rayna was always the easiest to awaken. She would pop up her head and greet Lillian with a hug and kiss, and then Rayna would shake her sister, who'd be busy feigning sleep. Breeze would lie, twitching eyes closed tight, until Lillian bent over and kissed her. Then Breeze would lift her head with an angelic smile.

"Good morning, Mommy," chorused Breeze and Rayna.

Lillian returned their cheerful greeting, cherishing those precious moments. "I want you to go wash up. Your clothes are laid out on my bed."

Rayna and Breeze nodded their heads, but they didn't budge.

"Is Daddy coming home today?" Rayna asked anxiously.

A pained look would cross Lillian's face. She tried to hide her feelings, but her daughters sometimes noticed the sadness in her smile.

"Mommy, what's wrong?" Rayna asked, seven years old, the older of the two.

"Nothing. You know your father is on the road with his band." She paused momentarily before delivering the disappointing news. "He won't be back for a month."

Lillian had angrily slammed the phone down when Omar Blackwell told her that he was going directly to another gig instead of coming home. Tears of disappointment welled in Lillian's eyes. She was so tired of the same old line. She didn't even look forward to his phone calls anymore. More and more often, their conversations ended with, "I don't know if I'll be home Sunday" or "We've got another gig."

Every time she heard those inevitable words her heart felt like a sinking ship. She listened closely to Omar's voice when she answered the phone, trying vainly to prepare herself for the defensive tone in his voice whenever he had some change in plans. But the sinking sensation was always the same. Lillian wanted to see Omar, she needed her husband, but music always came between them. Lillian could never steel herself for the inevitable letdown that always felt like he was drilling a hollow in her heart.

In her mind she'd whisper urgently to herself. *Don't miss him too much. Don't need him so much. Don't love him anymore.*

"A month?" Rayna and Breeze had cried. "That's a long time."

"I know, babies," Lillian had replied. Seeing the disappointment reflected in their cocoa and copper-brown gazes intensified her sense of loss.

"He was only gonna be gone for a week," Rayna moaned.

Breeze whimpered softly, rubbing her eyes. "I hate it when Daddy's gone. It's forever."

"It's not forever. You have to understand, baby, he's a musician and that's what musicians do," Lillian bitterly explained.

Tears streaming down her chubby cheeks, five-year-old Breeze had cried, "We'll never see Daddy!"

"Breeze, don't be such a baby," Rayna chided.

"He'll be here before you know it. We'll cross out days on the calendar until he's back," Lillian had said, her voice coated in cheerfulness.

Breeze's sad face had lit up. "I want to make the X's!"

"Okay, now you girls get dressed or you'll be late for school."

The huge hotel ballroom, lavishly decorated in wedding motif, was packed with friends, family, and guests of the bride and groom. Breeze, Rayna, and India huddled in the back of the ballroom with the rest of their schoolmates, thankful for the crowd so they couldn't be seen by their protective mother.

Dressed in brand new dresses and shoes, the girls were excited to be at such an adult affair. The previous Saturday, they spent the entire day at the mall looking for special dresses to wear to Miss Abbot's wedding. When they got home that evening, even though they were exhausted from going to every store in the mall, they modeled their dresses for Lillian.

Rayna strutted into the living room in a low-cut yellow dress, outlining her hourglass figure. The plunging neckline boldly exposed her breasts. Lillian raised her thinly-arched eyebrows and shook her head at her daring daughter's all-too-revealing dress.

"Rayna, you know that dress shows off too much. up too fast," Lillian said, shaking her head in dismay.

"But Ma, I think it's pretty," Rayna said. She knew her mother wouldn't approve, but she bought the dress anyway.fv

"It's pretty revealing, that's what it is. Don't you know that you're supposed to leave a man wondering? A little mystery keeps them interested and wanting to know more."

"Ma, that sounds old-fashioned," Rayna replied. She ran into the hallway to look at herself in the full-length mirror. Rayna had a long face, small lips and eyes, and was the exact same reddish-brown as her mother. She smiled in the mirror, pleased with her selection.

"I won't tell you what you look like," Lillian said, standing behind Rayna, looking in the mirror at her difficult daughter. She felt Rayna's thick hair, adorned in corn-rows.

"I hope you get rid of all those ridiculous braids you got twisted in your hair. That's not appropriate for a wedding."

"I know, Ma," Rayna said, defensively jerking her head away.

"I don't know why you wear your hair like that. You have such a pretty face."

She turned around when Breeze and India came into the hall wearing their dresses: India had on an ankle-length, southern belle floral number, and Breeze modeled a purple dress with criss-cross straps in the back and a large bow at the waist.

"Ah, that's more like it," Lillian said. "You see, Rayna, these dresses are more befitting a high school girl."

"Since I'm older than them, I figured I could wear a more grown-up dress," Rayna replied.

"The next time, I'll go shopping with you and make sure you get the right kind of dress," Lillian said. "Now go take it off. I'm still not sure if you are going to wear it."

"Oh, Ma!" Rayna steamed, stomping up the carpeted stairs.

On the morning of the wedding, the trio went to the beauty salon for fresh hairdos to go with their brand new outfits.

At the reception, the first thing they did after escaping from their mother's watchful eye was to go into the bath-room to finish putting on makeup. Rayna and India put on the works: thick mascara, heavy eye shadow, blush, and lipstick. Breeze put on blush for the first time, and added a generous dose of shiny red gloss to her lips. Rayna removed the safety pin Lillian had used to close up her breast-baring dress.

They peeked out of the bathroom door, searching for Lillian before coming out. India and Rayna ran off to meet their boyfriends, leaving Breeze at the table.

"Remember, if Ma comes looking for us, tell her we had to help with the wedding," Rayna said before strutting away.

Breeze watched the dancing, drinking, smoking, and talking. There was something different, she noticed, in how the adults talked and laughed. It was as if they knew something that she didn't know. She couldn't wait to find out, to know what they knew. She wanted to go to parties and do all the things she was told that she was too young to do.

In three years when I graduate, she thought, *I'll do whatever I want to do. I'll be grown.*

Breeze felt somebody watching her. It was a strange, sudden feeling. She turned to her right, but didn't see anyone looking her way. But when she turned to look in the other direction, she found herself looking into Alexander "Lex" Franklin's handsome face. He was sitting in the chair beside her.

"Hi, Breeze," he said, with an ear-to-ear grin.

Shyly, Breeze said, "Hello." She hoped her face didn't betray what was happening to her body—her stomach was a nest of butterflies. She couldn't believe that she was actually sitting next to *the* Alexander Franklin. He was the best-looking boy in school, the one who made her heart skip a beat. Lex was tall and had the lean, muscular body of an athlete, even though he never participated in high school sports. All the girls in school were drawn to his friendly manner and charming personality.

In school, Breeze saw him between the third and fourth periods, on the way to gym class. Some days she would walk slowly down the halls, take long drinks at the water fountain or lollygag by her locker just so she could get a glimpse of him.

He would always smile at her, and sometimes he'd even say "Hi." Other times he would compliment her outfit or tease her about the "hole in her chin." No matter what he did, seeing Lex was the highlight of Breeze's day.

"You know Miss Abbot?" Lex inquired. He stared at Breeze as if she were a beautiful and rare painting on display.

Breeze had large, copper-brown eyes, high cheekbones, full lips, and a mega-watt smile.

"She lives on our street, and Rayna's in her home-room."

"I know. I'm in the same class."

"Those flowers are so pretty," Breeze said, pointing to the flower arrangement in the center of the table. "What kind are they?"

What a stupid thing to say, thought Breeze. *I know what they are. Wow! I can't believe he's sitting next to me. He came over to talk to me!*

She felt shy and awkward in his presence, but she didn't want him to leave. Her eyes were cast downward, and her hands were clasped tightly together on her lap.

"They're orchids." He reached across the table and took an orchid from the centerpiece that decorated every table in the ballroom. Lex delicately placed the flower in Breeze's hair over her right ear.

Alexander's touch sent chills up, down, and around her body. Every nerve was singed at his touch. Breeze didn't understand what was happening to her, but she knew she liked the feeling.

"You are so beautiful," Lex complimented, his eyes never leaving her face.

She looked away, not wanting to look into his deep, dark brown eyes. Blushing, Breeze demurely whispered, "Thank you."

"I've got to go, Breeze. It's time for the next set." Alexander touched her hands. "Save a dance for me, okay?"

"I will," she eagerly promised, returning his smile.

Lex left Breeze rooted to her chair. She was in a daze of inexplicable joy. She wanted to jump on the table and announce to the world that Lex had sat beside her, that he had talked to her, that Lex had touched her.

"What's wrong with you?" Rayna asked when she returned to the table. "You look strange."

"Alexander was here," Breeze whispered.

"So?" Rayna said, digging in her purse for a safety pin.

Touching the flower in her hair, Breeze said, "He put this flower in my hair."

"Oh…so, you finally got to *talk* to Lex," Rayna teased.

"He sat right beside me." Breeze closed her eyes. "He's so fine! One day, he's going to be mine."

"You're silly! Where's India?" Rayna inquired, her eyes roaming the room.

Shrugging her shoulders, she replied, "I don't know." Breeze's eyes were still closed, imagining Lex sitting beside her.

"Wake up, Breeze!" Rayna chided, pinning together the front of her dress.

Rayna and Breeze sat at the table and waited for India. They sipped on their soft drinks, wondering why it was taking so long for the band to get started.

"Rayna, do you remember the last time we were at a wedding reception?"

Rayna tilted her head back and drank the last of her soda. "Umm-huh," she said, nodding. "Daddy was playing with his band. I think it was Daddy's cousin who got married."

"Yep, and it was a very pretty wedding. Remember, we wore identical dresses!"

"Ugh," Rayna responded. "I'm glad we don't dress like that anymore." She paused before flatly saying, "That was before we left."

"Do you still miss Daddy? I mean living with him."

An angry shadow crossed Rayna's face. Glaring at her sister, she said, "He was never around, Breeze."

"I know. But, I miss him a whole lot. Even when he wasn't around I could always feel him. Not anymore."

"Breeze, I've got a big favor to ask you," Lex interrupted their conversation, leaning over her, his hands resting on the back of her chair.

It must be important, she thought, *because Lex looks terribly upset.*

"What?" she asked, her copper-brown eyes enlarged.

"I need you to sing for me. Our singer hasn't shown up and I don't know where she is. All I know is that we are supposed to be performing right now," Lex anxiously explained. "Right this minute."

"I can't sing!" Breeze exclaimed.

"Don't even try it," Rayna challenged. "You can sing. Everybody knows it but you."

"Don't you sing at church?" Lex asked.

"I'm in the choir. But I never sing solo."

"Rayna says you can sing like Chaka Khan," he insisted.

"Pleezze! I don't sound nothing like her."

"You can do it, Breeze," Rayna encouraged. "You sing your little heart out around the house like you have an audience. Just pretend you're at home."

"I can't. Ma would kill me." Breeze's arms flung outward.

"She'd understand that you were helping out a friend," countered Rayna.

"Come on, Breeze," Lex insisted. "I really need your help."

"Can't you get somebody else?" Breeze suggested.

"Not here. Not right now. Clarice is on her way. So I'm not asking you to sing for the night. Just one set," Lex implored, his hands gesturing wildly.

"What's a set?" Breeze asked, her thick eyebrows crinkled together.

"Five songs. I just need you to sing five songs that you know."

"She knows the words to all the latest songs," Rayna added.

Breeze shot Rayna an exasperated glare. But when Breeze looked into Alexander's face, she couldn't refuse him.

She went with him to meet the members of his band. She told them the songs she knew and what key she sang in, and they cued her on how to signal them. Before Breeze knew what was happening, she was on stage, staring into a sea of eyes. Lex had introduced her and she was supposed to open her mouth and sing.

She stood frozen by all the eyes. Her mouth wouldn't move. She wished she could shrink into the floor and disappear. She heard the beginning melody of a song she had selected, but missed her cue. The band played the music again, and this time she opened her mouth and sang one of her favorite songs.

She sang with a vocal range and power that got the audience's attention, singing the songs of Chaka Khan, Patrice Rushen, and Teena Marie. The audience was impressed and applauded as if she were a professional singer.

Breeze sang five songs and even though she was starting to relax under the scrutiny of eyes, she was immensely relieved when the music stopped.

"You were born to sing. No doubt about it." Smiling, Lex handed Breeze a glass of water.

She was flabbergasted at Lex's praise. "You're just saying that," she said while gulping down the water to soothe her dry, scratchy throat. "Singing really makes you thirsty."

"No, I mean it. You're a natural. You should hear yourself. I mean really hear yourself."

"I don't want to be a singer. I'm going to be a lawyer."

"You were born to sing. That's all I can say. Do you like it?"

"I love it," she said, admitting it aloud for the first time. "I just don't take it seriously."

"You should." Grabbing her hands and moving closer to her, Lex said, "Thank you for helping us out, Breeze. I could strangle Clarice for being late, but you're a better singer anyway. Way better."

"Did she get here?"

"She came in on the last song. Now she's upset that I let you stand in for her."

"Good. I just don't want to get back on that stage." She wiped the beads of perspiration from her brow with the palm of her hand. "I better go find my sisters so we can go home. I'll see you in school on Monday." She smiled sweetly at Lex before turning away.

"Wait!" Lex called. Breeze turned back around.

"Breeze, would you go to a movie with me?" he asked in a rush of words, his eyes smiling directly into her eyes.

Her head dipped before she softly replied, "I can't," and nervously rubbed her elbow.

Shifting his feet, Lex asked, "Why?" before gently placing his hand on her shoulder.

She didn't want to tell him why, but couldn't think of an excuse fast enough.

"Do you have a boyfriend?"

Breeze shook her head no, her eyes on the floor. Embarrassed, she explained in a small voice, "I'm not allowed to date until I'm sixteen."

"Oh!" Bending low, he whispered in her ear, "When will that be?"

"In two months. I'll be sixteen on July sixteenth."

"Breeze, would you go out with me on July sixteenth?"

Breeze lifted her head and looked directly at Lex. "Yes," shot out of her mouth like a cannon.

"Then, Sunshine, I'll see you on July sixteenth," promised Lex.

Breeze searched for her sisters, anxious to tell them about her encounter with Lex. People stopped her along the way to praise her singing abilities. Folks that knew Breeze were quite surprised that she sang so well, and they couldn't believe Breeze didn't realize what a gift she had. One woman who went to their church told her that she had a "gift from God."

Never before had so many people told Breeze that she could sing. She enjoyed singing with the choir at church, but never took it seriously because Lillian constantly preached against "the sinful life of musicians, singers, and actors."

A dour-faced woman with protruding lips and huge glasses that covered her face encouraged Breeze. "I'm going to the choir director about you, child. You should have been the one singing solos instead of her tin-voiced daughter. And I think I'll tell the Reverend, too." The old woman stared at Breeze, with beady eyes that behind the ultra-thick glasses looked like a rat's. "And you're cute as a button," she laughed while pinching Breeze's cheeks.

Breeze smiled tightly. "Thank you, Miss Winfrey."

"And I'm going to talk to your mother. She's been hiding you."

Breeze didn't know what to say. She let Miss Winfrey speak her mind, and simply nodded. Breeze was relieved when India interrupted their conversation, and politely excused herself from Miss Winfrey's grumblings.

"You were bad, Breeze. I never heard you sing like that before," India praised.

"Everyone keeps telling me that," Breeze said. She grabbed India's hand and pulled her into the hotel lobby. "Guess what Lex told me?"

"What?"

"He said that I was born to sing, and that I sound like Chaka Khan."

"You do kind of sound like her."

"And you know what else?" Breeze was so happy, she wanted to jump into the clouds. "I think I want to be a star like her."

India's eyebrows furrowed together. "Honey chile, you're crazy. I thought you wanted to be a lawyer."

"Well, I changed my mind," Breeze claimed, folding her arms across her chest.

Rayna rushed over to them. "Ma is so mad at us. She's been lookin' for us for an hour. And she is really upset with Breeze for singing with a band."

Breeze ignored her. "Lex is going to take me out for my birthday."

Rayna and India said together, "You bad!"

CHAPTER TWO

It was July sixteenth and Breeze was in a panic. There were clothes scattered on the bed, on the floor, and hanging out of half-opened drawers. Breeze searched through the pile on her bed, frantically looking for her red blouse. She couldn't find it, so she wriggled out of her jeans, muttering that she didn't want to wear that outfit anyway. She looked in the mirror at her frizzy, untamed hair and screamed. When India peeked into the room, she saw Breeze on the bed buried underneath her clothes.

"What's the matter with you?" India screamed from the doorway over the blasting radio.

Breeze poked her head out from under blouses, pants, dresses, skirts, and underwear. "I don't have anything to wear, and Lex is picking me up in an hour," she said, her voice a call of distress.

Shaking her head, India said, "You are crazy. It's your birthday. You're not supposed to be hiding under your clothes, crying like the world is coming to an end." India couldn't stop herself from laughing. Breeze wiggled herself from under the clothes. "You gotta help me, India. Please!" she begged. "Pretty please?"

"Okay, where are you going?" India asked as she strolled into Breeze's bedroom filled with a full-size white

French provincial canopy bed, dresser, chest, desk and bookcase. The shaggy pink carpet was matched by pink-painted walls. Pictures of her father playing the saxophone in jazz clubs and on album covers hung above her cluttered desk.

"To dinner and a movie," she boasted. "Lex is taking me to the Ponderosa Steakhouse!"

India shrugged her shoulders. "Easy. You need a dress."

"I don't have any casual dresses. All my dresses are for church and I don't want to wear those things," complained Breeze.

"A skirt and a blouse."

"I hate my skirts," Breeze fussed.

Ever resourceful, India began sorting through Breeze's clothes, separating them into piles. She matched up a few outfits and showed them to a disinterested Breeze.

Pointing thumbs downward, Breeze grumbled, "I hate my clothes."

"You got to pick something," urged India, feeling frustrated.

Suddenly, Breeze's face lit up and she disappeared into Rayna's room and returned with a turquoise blue spaghetti-strapped cotton dress with the price tag dangling from it.

"Rayna will kill you," India warned. "She just got that dress!"

"If she doesn't see me, I'll just put it back in her closet."

Flippantly, India said, "Are you going to wear it with the price tag still on?"

"Oh, I didn't think about that," Breeze nonchalantly replied. She stared at the dress for a minute before saying, "She knows I want to impress Lex."

Sitting on the bed, India said, "She won't care about that. And don't say I didn't warn you when Rayna gets on a set with you."

"She won't stay mad for long," Breeze predicted, looking at India for support.

Holding the dress in front of her, Breeze insisted, "We've been through all my clothes. I've got to wear this dress." She ripped off the price tag.

Breeze rummaged through the bottom of her closet and found some multi-colored sandals, and happily showed them to India.

"Look, these are perfect!" Breeze whirled around and bounced to the Motown song playing on the radio, happily snapping her fingers. "Ooh, baby! I've got something to wear!" she sang, making up the words.

She stopped in front of the dresser mirror, and when she spotted her limp hair, she spun towards India. "Would you curl my hair?"

India nodded her head, laughter bubbling out from between her lips.

"And can I wear your red lipstick?"

Alexander Franklin arrived with a bouquet of orchids, his heart throbbing with anticipation. They hadn't seen each other since the school let out over a month ago. He had thought about her every day and had a hard time waiting for July sixteenth. Breeze had marked red X's on her calendar to July sixteenth, counting the days until her date with Lex.

Peeking out her bedroom window, Breeze saw Lex drive up. She jumped on the bed screaming, "He's here! He's here!"

With a finger over her pursed lips, India murmured, "Be quiet or he's going to hear you."

Lex was disappointed when Breeze didn't greet him at the door. He waited in the living room, his eyes darting to the stairs, and talked with Mrs. Blackwell He was respectful and politely answered Lillian's questions about his family and his future. When he told her that he planned to be a musician and a record producer, Lex thought she was going to have a stroke.

"A musician!" Lillian said. The words rolled out of her mouth with distaste and displeasure; it was as if she had bitten into a sour pomegranate.

"I've been playing the piano since I was seven, and I taught myself how to play the drums and guitar."

"That's a hard business to be in," Lillian remarked, wearing a deep frown. "Not everyone makes it. And then you have to travel all the time. You don't want that kind of life," Lillian bluntly advised, her fists tightly folded around the arms of the chair.

"Everybody tells me that, but that's all I want to do, Mrs. Blackwell. And, I practice every day."

"Breeze's father is a musician. He plays the sax. But Breeze grew up without him because he was always with the band. The band was his family." Bitterly, Lillian added, "She might as well have been fatherless."

A deadly chill settled over Lillian's body. *If I had known she was going out with a damn musician I would have forbidden it! Even if it meant going back on my word. Please, baby girl, don't fall in love with this boy. We don't need that kind of trouble.*

Lillian hoped that Lex would not affect Breeze the way Omar had affected her. She remembered all too well the way Omar Blackwell had made her feel.

The bus stopped on Main Street in front of the ever-green-tall skyscrapers that lined the downtown streets the way that maple and oak trees line a residential street. The doors of the bus opened, squeaking and squealing their welcome to the passengers waiting to board.

Lillian dropped a quarter into the fare box and smiled sympathetically at the bus driver, who was wiping his brow with a sweat drenched handkerchief.

"Is it hot enough for you, Lily?" he asked, his eyes indiscreetly inspecting Lillian's fine figure. Lillian pretended not to notice the bus driver's roaming eye. After all, he was old enough to be her father.

"Too hot! And this bus seems to get more crowded. Where do all these people come from?" Lillian asked, perspiration shining on her face.

"Those skyscrapers sure do hold a lot of people. The problem is everybody gets off work at the same time."

"Ain't that the truth," Lillian said while squeezing pass passengers crowded together like sardines in a tin can. She moved to the back of the bus and grabbed onto a bar just as the bus lurched forward.

The first thing she noticed about the man she stood in front of was his polished, brown wing-tipped shoes. They were so shiny she could see reflections shimmering in their water-like surfaces. Sitting on top of the shoes were cuffed, brown pants with crisp pleats. The gabardine pants had a matching double-breasted jacket, topped by a bright white, starched shirt and narrow brown tie.

When Lillian looked into the man's face, she thought she was going to cry out. She had expected an older, gray-haired man to be wearing the expensive suit, not a hand-some young man with a thick moustache, copper-brown eyes, and full, expressive mouth. The man's straw hat, slightly tilted over his face, gave him an air of recklessness.

Umm, umm, Lillian thought *Where did he come from?*

"Miss?" he said.

Lillian kept her gaze outside the window, staring dispassionately at the people rushing out of the buildings and onto the street into congested traffic. ft was the same scene she saw every day at five o'clock when she left work. She stared out of the window to keep from staring at the unbelievably handsome man sitting down in front of her.

Again, the man called out, "Miss!"

Lillian realized that he was talking to her. She looked at him, praying that her makeup wasn't smeared, and replied, "Yes?" She looked directly into his eyes, and felt a sudden movement in her chest.

"Would you like to sit down?"

She started to say no since she was used to standing part of the way home. But then, she changed her mind. Smiling brightly, she replied, "Why, yes, I would."

He stood up and they switched places. Lillian stammered, "Thank you," while her attention focused on the long, rectangular-shaped steel case he was holding. "Would you like me to hold that for you?"

He nodded his head and sat the box on her lap. "It's my sax."

Lillian wanted to ask him about the instrument, but she decided that he probably didn't want to be bothered, for he had such a serious, preoccupied frown on his face. She tensely hoped that he would say something—anything—but he remained rigidly silent, so she was silent. Finally, after the first few minutes of uncomfortable quiet, she drew her own conclusions about the well-dressed man standing before her:

He was a musician from out of town. Maybe he's famous, but I just don't know him.

When her stop came, she gingerly handed the stranger his saxophone and quickly thanked him for the seat, her gaze lingering on his eyes. Moving to the front she slowly stepped off the bus.

Walking down the street towards the house where she had lived all her life, she heard someone from behind her shout, "Miss! Miss!"

Lillian turned and spotted the handsome stranger from the bus who was quickly moving towards her. "Oh God!" she thought.

Her heart began to pound. She desperately wanted to pull out her compact mirror to see if she looked presentable, but realized there wasn't enough time.

"Hello," the mystery man said. "My name is Omar. Omar Blackwell."

"Hello!" Lillian greeted. She didn't know whether to be excited or frightened. The stranger looked like the type of man her mother warned her about. Suave, cunning, worldly, a heart stealer.

"I wanted to meet you and I knew if I didn't get off the bus, I might never see you again."

"Probably wouldn't," she agreed, nervously clutching her handbag.

"What's your name?"

"Lillian."

"Your name is pretty, but you are even prettier," Omar complimented, flashing a seductive smile.

Lillian's reddish-brown skin flushed with heat. "Thank you."

"Do you live around here, Lillian?"

"Around the corner."

"And you work downtown?"

"I'm a secretary for U.S. Steel," she said proudly.

"And you ride the bus everyday?"

"Everyday. Twice a day."

"I just got into town. I don't know many folks here, but I sure would like to get to know you. Would you go out with me?"

"I don't know," Lillian answered, clutching her handbag tighter.

"Are you married or do you have a boyfriend?"

Looking away, she said, "No."

"Would you go out with me?" Omar smiled enticingly, and, in that instant, Lillian couldn't think of one reason why she shouldn't have a little fun for a change.

Three days later, Omar arrived at Lillian's front door with a dozen red roses. It was the first time anyone had ever given Lillian roses. Omar took her out to a fancy restaurant, and later to the jazz club where he played with his band.

After their first enjoyable evening together, much to Lillian's parents' dismay, they shared many evenings together.

Omar took a sheltered, nineteen-year-old Lillian to places she had never been before. For the first time, she had something to look forward to after work besides having dinner with her family, watching television, and going to bed.

To Camille and Charles Douglas, Omar's presence in Lillian's life was an unwelcome intrusion. Her conservative, church-going parents did not approve of Omar's bohemian lifestyle.

"I don't understand what's happening to you," Camille said as Lillian hurriedly combed her hair in the hall mirror. "You don't have time for a decent breakfast anymore, running around with that man."

Lillian ignored her mother's words and concentrated on applying her makeup. Camille went into the hall so her daughter could not pretend not to hear her.

"This man is no good for you," Camille said.

"What's wrong with him?"

"It's not that there's anything wrong with him personally. It's what he has to offer you. Musicians live like a feather in the wind. You're too good for that, Lily. All your sisters have married stable, hard-working men like your father. That's the kind of man you need. What's wrong with Myron?"

"Oh, Mama," Lillian said, turning to face her mother standing in the kitchen doorway, "He's…he's boring. He doesn't excite me."

"That's because you've known him all your life."

"It's not just that I just don't have the same feelings for Myron. I never have."

"You two have been together a long time. Everybody expects you to get…"

"Married. But I don't want to many him, Mama. I didn't know why until now."

"Why?" Camille probed, a brown-skinned woman who had become progressively bigger after giving birth to eight children. Her face was still attractive, just rounder. Her black hair was brushed back into a bun.

"I don't have that special feeling for Myron. That spark."

"Sparks don't last very long, baby."

"Mama, what we have is special. He's real good to me. He makes me feel like a queen," Lillian explained, light gleaming from her eyes.

"Your father will never approve, Lillian, and neither do I. I know this is what you want, but it's not what you need. You need someone who will always be there for you.

if not Myron, then someone else who can provide a stable life."

"I don't know, Mama. There's something about the way he makes me feel. I don't want to let go of it."

Lillian thought about her mother's words on the bus ride to work. But when Omar called her at work and made plans to meet her for lunch, her mother's warnings flew out of her mind.

Her father had made his feelings painfully clear. When they watched television together, he now said very little to her. He warned her "not to be foolish."

For the first time in her life Lillian didn't listen to her parents. She hated that they didn't like Omar. She wished there was some way she could make them change their minds about him, but she knew they would never understand. In spite of their objections, she couldn't stop seeing Omar.

She didn't want to.

In thirty days, Omar and Lillian were married. They didn't have an elaborate ceremony in the church where her five sisters were married. Lillian became Mrs. Omar Blackwell in a small chapel in Las Vegas.

When Lillian called home to tell her parents that she was in Las Vegas and that she had eloped, there was silence on the other end of the phone.

"Daddy? Daddy?" Lillian spoke anxiously.

Sternly, her father had said, "I didn't raise you to marry no musician. What kind of life are you going to have? You had your pick of the boys in church. Fine young men who could take proper care of you." His disapproving voice added, "But you made your bed, so now you gotta lie in it," just before he hung up.

Lex's voice returned Lillian to the present

"I do plan to go to college, Mrs. Blackwell," he said.

"Really? What do you plan to study?" Lillian smiled for the first time since meeting her daughter's date.

"Music. I'm trying to get into the Boston School of Music. I'll be graduating from high school next year."

"What about something to fall back on in case you don't get to do what you want? It's hard making a living in that business unless you get real lucky. Luck isn't too much to depend on."

With youthful zeal, Lex said, "I'll make it. I'm going to study business, but I'm gonna make it with my music." Grinning he added, "My mother says I can do anything if I set my mind to it and I believe her."

Breeze came into the living room wearing a smile as bright and warm as the morning sun. Lex couldn't believe that in just one month, she could grow more beautiful, but she had. She was coming into her beauty, blossoming like spring flowers. Her shoulder-length hair was curled back, elegantly framing her face. The turquoise sundress showed off her glazed caramel-colored skin and highlighted her copper-brown eyes. When Lex looked into her sparkling, happy-to-see-you eyes, he was mesmerized.

"I'm ready."

Lex stood up and handed Breeze a bouquet of orchids. "Happy birthday!"

July sixteenth was a memorable day for Breeze and Lex. It was the day they discovered the crazy emotions they were feeling had a name: Love.

Over the summer their young love grew with Saturday visits and daily telephone calls. But Lillian was firm about her dating rules: Breeze could only date once a week. On Saturday afternoons, Lex would pick Breeze up, and they'd spend time together, returning by curfew, nine o'clock.

They talked on the phone, sharing their every thought and experience. But when Lillian discovered Breeze talking on the phone with Lex at three in the morning, she took the phone out of Breeze's room for a month.

So, Lex and Breeze found other ways to communicate. He'd leave flowers in the mailbox for her or slip a love letter or poem under the door for the evenings when they couldn't talk. He affectionately called her "Sunshine" because her Colgate smile glowed like the sun and warmed his heart.

They found ways to be together. India was friends with Catrina, the sister of the drummer in Lex's band, so Breeze had good reason to go with India when she visited Catrina. Lex was usually practicing with the band. Sometimes, Breeze would even sing.

On one of these occasions, Lex taped her singing. A few days later, he played the tape and Breeze innocently listened to herself sing, but didn't recognize her own voice.

Lex chuckled, "Okay, now listen to these other tapes."

Lex played the audition tapes of three singers, but Breeze wasn't impressed.

"I like the first one you played. That girl can blow!"

"That's your voice, Sunshine!" Lex said, laughing smugly. Breeze eyed him suspiciously. "Lex, I don't sound like that!"

"Yes, you do. That's your voice."

"I didn't know I sounded like that," Breeze spoke thoughtfully. "Play it again."

"That's you, Sunshine. You should think about it."

"Think about what?"

"Singing professionally."

"I'm not that good."

"Yes, you are! Believe me, I wouldn't lie to you!"

"Well, I don't know. I mean, I never thought about it. I've always wanted to be a lawyer."

"Is that what you want or is that what your mother wants?"

"Wow!" Breeze exclaimed when she saw Lex's record collection. They were in the basement of his house, and every wall had a floor-to-ceiling stack of albums, eight-tracks, and cassettes, neatly organized in colored plastic milk-crates.

There was a long, well-worn couch, with a coffee table and a couple of bean bags. One wall held an inexpensive wall unit with a stereo system like Breeze had never seen.

Breeze stood in the center of the room, amazed at the massive record collection surrounding her.

"You have more records than a record store. And I thought my father had a huge record collection," uttered Breeze. "This is serious."

Lex was slouched on a bean bag, his long legs sprawled out in front of him. His face was handsome, with magnificent dark brows that curved neatly above his deep, dark brown eyes. His nose was long and sloping, his mouth firm and full. He was the color of wet coffee, deep brown and luscious.

Breeze walked over to the albums, running her fingers across them, reading the various artists, "Sly and the Family Stone, The Temptations, Ohio Players, Earth, Wind & Fire, The O'Jays, Delfonics, Minnie Ripperton, Jackson Five, James Brown, Funkadelic, Stevie Wonder. You have everybody. Some of these people I've never heard of."

She moved over to the next stack of albums. "Rock! You buy rock albums?" Breeze questioned. "Alice Cooper, Led Zeppelin, Rod Stewart, David Bowie, The Beatles. I can't believe you have all these albums by white artists!"

"I like all kinds of music," Lex shrugged.

"But I've never heard you play rock."

"Yes, you have."

Breeze looked at Lex quizzically.

"What you hear on the radio everyday is rock. A lot of R&B music is a form of rock-and-roll. We brought it to this country. White folks took it to one level, and we play it on another level. But we created it."

"Seriously?" Breeze questioned.

"Yeah, I'm serious. You been listening to rock-and-roll ever since you were a little girl, and you didn't know it."

Breeze wrapped her arms around her shoulders, shivering, and said, "And this stereo system. It looks too complicated."

"I'll show you how to work it," Lex offered, while wrapping a blanket around Breeze's shoulders. "It's always cold down here. I'm used to it. I have my room upstairs in the attic, but I'm mostly down here."

Breeze pulled out a Dee Dee Bridgewater album. "Play this. I want to hear 'Just Family.'"

"Okay, but first I want you to hear this Jimi Hendrix album."

"Jimi Hendrix?"

"I told you he was the best guitar player that ever lived. I want you to listen to him, and then listen to me."

Lex played Jimi Hendrix's signature song "Purple Haze." It sounded like psychedelic craziness to Breeze. When she listened to Lex's version of "Purple Haze," she couldn't distinguish one from the other.

Breeze told Lex that they "sounded the same," but she didn't understand what she was hearing.

"Jimi was left-handed, but he used right-handed guitars, and played them upside down. You have to be really good to do that," Lex explained.

"I couldn't tell the difference."

"I wish I could play like Jimi. He could play the guitar and make it sound like two guitar players were playing at the same time. That's what you call a master musician." Strumming his fingers on his guitar, Lex claimed, "I'm going to be bad like Jimi! One day, I'm even goin' to own one of his guitars."

Breeze didn't know much about Jimi Hendrix, but by the end of the summer she'd know all about his tragic life.

"Doesn't your mother ever get mad at the loud music?" Breeze asked one afternoon, screaming over the music.

"She's used to it. And she tries to stay on the second floor so she won't have to hear it. My old man, he's the one who complains. But he's at work, on the four-to-twelve shift, so I don't worry about disturbing him."

"What does your father think of you being a musician?"

"He bought my first guitar when I was five," Lex smiled. Pointing across the room, he continued, "and you see those drums over there? They were my brother's."

They walked over to the dark corner of the room where a drum, piano, and guitar idly sat.

Lex sat down behind the drums. He picked up the drumsticks, beating the drums and tapping the cymbals for a few minutes, creating a series of unrelated sounds.

"I was the guitar player and Darryl was the drummer, and we were supposed to have a big time band together one day."

"What happened?" Breeze asked, sensing from Lex's faraway look that the story had an unhappy ending.

Stumbling over his words, Lex said, "My brother died…. He died of an overdose," sadness and pain resonant in his voice.

"I'm sorry," Breeze said, gently rubbing his shoulders.

Darryl's drug use was something the family never understood. It was never openly discussed, but whispered about behind closed doors. Mrs. Franklin's badge of guilt was not getting Darryl to a rehabilitation clinic, and Mr. Franklin felt that it was the music business that had introduced his son to hard-core drugs; it was the norm in that world. He worked hard to protect his family from the fringe elements of society, but drugs had penetrated their inner sanctum. He hoped that Lex wouldn't surrender to the influence of drugs. Mr. Franklin tried to dissuade his son from music, but it was difficult to erase thirteen years of encouragement

But Lex was affected by his brother's death in the most brutal way. To get involved with drugs would be to betray his brother. He vividly remembered Darryl's last words to him:

"Don't do it, man. Stay away from drugs. Or you'll become like a dog chasing his tail."

Lex thought back to the eighth grade, to the end of the school year when his brother had died. That summer was the quietest time of his life—it brought a brief end to music.

His family jam sessions had been silenced forever, no one played the radio or stereo. When Lex returned to high school that fall, he picked up his guitar, and played away his pain, listening to Jimi Hendrix.

"When Darryl died, my father didn't want me to be a musician anymore. But I couldn't turn my back on it. The piano used to be upstairs, but now all the instruments are down here in the basement where he doesn't have to see them any more. I can't stop doing what I love because of what happened. I think Darryl would want me to do it, to do what we dreamed about. So even though my old man stays mad at me, I've got to do it, I've got to play."

"I understand," Breeze said, rubbing her hands in Lex's wavy black hair.

"The only time my father comes down here is when he's been drinking and wants to hear Billy Eckstine and Arthur Pry sock."

"My father has worked with them."

"They're his two favorite singers, and he plays them all night long. Over and over he plays 'My Funny Valentine,' 'I Apologize,' and 'Caravan.' Those three songs over and over."

For the first time in Breeze's life, she went to concerts featuring white performers. She knew that Lex liked all kinds of music, but she was surprised when he took her see Elton John and Queen. She felt out of place in her dress and stockings, while everyone wore jeans and sneakers.

No matter what concert they attended, Lex managed to get front row seats. Breeze enjoyed the concerts—the theatrics of the performers, the billowy smoke, the choreographed dancing, and the pulsating energy of live music. Lex studied the guitarist, the way he played, and how he sounded. He'd rate every concert on how well the guitarist performed.

"Nobody notices these things but you," commented Breeze.

"That's why I'm going to be a great guitar player," said Lex, flashing an even-toothed smile. "Wait and see."

One summer evening, with a blanket wrapped around them, Lex and Breeze were watching television and eating popcorn in Lex's chilly basement. Breeze moved to scoop out a handful of popcorn and felt something hard in the bowl.

"There's something in this popcorn," Breeze said.

"What are you talking about?"

Breeze dug her hands into the popcorn until she found what she was seeking and brought it toward her face, studying it in the dim light from the television. "Oh!" she gasped.

"It's your ring."

"I want you to wear it," Lex said, while placing the bowl of popcorn on the floor next to the sofa.

"Really?"

"You're my girl, right?" he smiled, throwing his arms wide.

"Right!" Breeze smiled as Lex gently kissed her and wrapped her in his arms.

The next morning, Lillian noticed Lex's high school ring dangling on the gold chain around Breeze's neck.

"What's that supposed to mean?" Lillian asked, a scowl of disapproval on her face. It was the end of the summer and she knew that Lex had indeed cast the same spell on Breeze that Omar had on her. Each night she prayed that it was a teenage infatuation.

Happily, Breeze said, "You know, Ma. We're going together," while plastering grape jelly on her toast.

"Aren't you kind of young for that?"

"No!" Breeze saucily replied.

"Why'd you have to get serious with the first boy you went out with? You should shop around first."

"Yeah, Breeze," Rayna said, sitting across the kitchen table. "Like me. I don't have time to be bothered with that boyfriend, girlfriend stuff."

"That's why I'm me and you're you," Breeze said.

"You're still a child, Breeze," Lillian frowned. "Remember that!"

CHAPTER THREE

"Keep your hands to yourself at all times, young lady, and keep your skirt down and panties on," Lillian said after telling Breeze that her dating privileges were increased to two nights a week. It was the morning after Breeze's seventeenth birthday party, and Lillian reluctantly conceded to the dating rules she had established when the girls were preteens.

"Did you hear me, Breeze? I said, keep your panties on and your skirt down," repeated Lillian, wishing that she had said nineteen instead of seventeen, and that she had power to protect Breeze from her desires. She knew the dangers of young love and saw Breeze heading for the same trap: love's wicked, blinding trap.

Breeze was embarrassed, but she didn't say a word. Her eyes were glued to the green-and-white tiled floor.

Lillian stood at the kitchen sink with her back to Breeze, washing dishes with an unleashed flurry of tense movements. Bright sunlight flooded through the small window above the sink. She turned off the water, moved away from the sink, and approached Breeze, standing in the kitchen doorway. "You know why, don't you?" asked Lillian. She cupped her wet soapy hand underneath Breeze's chin, tilting her face upward, peering directly into

Breeze's face, probing for signs that she had already succumbed to adolescent desires. Water dripped down Breeze's colorful pajamas.

Avoiding her mother's intense gaze, Breeze quietly replied, "I know," wiggling her leg, impatient for the conversation to end.

"I don't want you pregnant," Lillian warned, shaking her finger at Breeze.

Sighing irritably, she said, "Ma, I'm not going to get pregnant." Hoping to end the conversation, Breeze said, "Ma, I've got to get dressed or I'm going to be late." She turned into the hallway and headed toward the stairs.

"You need to stop spending so much time with that Lex. Why don't you go out with some of the other boys who call here for you?" When Breeze didn't respond, Lillian yelled, "Do you hear me?"

I hear you, Ma, but I don't want anyone else, thought Breeze. This is our last summer together before Lex goes to college and we're going to be together everyday. Everyday!

Omar Blackwell had a party to celebrate Breeze's seventeenth birthday at the same hotel where, the previous month, he had hosted a high school graduation party for Rayna. Breeze was excited to mail out invitations for her friends to come to the Hilton Hotel to celebrate her birthday. It made her feel truly grown up; her birthday parties were usually at her grandmother's or aunt's house and consisted of cake and ice cream.

Lillian complained that Omar was being "too extravagant for a seventeen-year-old." But, as was the norm, Omar ignored his ex-wife and indulged his daughters.

Lex's band, The Funky Boys, provided the music along with the school's most popular disc jockey. The teenagers danced to the latest songs by Earth, Wind, & Fire, the Commodores, Funkadelic, Rick James, Stephanie Mills, and Cameo. Breeze even sang a couple of songs with The Funky Boys and was thrilled by boisterous applause.

Her mother and father stood side by side, watching their youngest daughter sing, their expressions mirroring the faces of theatrical masks: Lillian's characterized by a deep frown while Omar's broad smile took over his face.

Lillian cast a sidelong glance at Omar, and in spite of herself, felt the stirrings of buried emotions. Her attraction to Omar mystified her. Innocence and naiveté was the excuse nineteen years ago, but something was still smoldering there, and it angered Lillian that she still had feelings for Omar—the man who had betrayed and abandoned her. She suppressed those feelings and kept her contact with Omar to a minimum. Lillian preferred no contact because she was afraid that she would give herself away, that Omar would see through her charade of disinterest.

Omar looked forward to the rare occasions when he saw Lillian. He always hoped that she wouldn't be wearing that stern, unforgiving face. He remembered how pretty her smile was, how it would light up her beautiful face. He would try to coax a smile out of her with a teasing remark, but she usually ignored him if their conversation didn't center around Rayna or Breeze. She had made it clear that she didn't approve of his lavish spending on their daughters, but Omar didn't care. His daughters enjoyed their parties, and that's what mattered most to Omar.

Omar rushed over to tell Breeze, "You were wonderful," and while he hugged his talented daughter, pride beamed from his eyes. "My little girl is growing up. And she can sing! Yes indeed, she can sing."

"See, I told you, Sunshine, you can sing," Lex laughed. "Your father's been in the business all his life, and he knows talent when he sees it"

Grinning, Breeze nodded, "Now, I guess I know for sure."

Breeze happily observed her father and Lex talking about what they knew best—music. She was glad that Omar and Lex liked each other. She smiled as the two most important men in her life passionately discussed jazz greats such as Dizzy Gillespie, Duke Ellington, Eddie "Clean Head" Vinson, Louis Armstrong, and other jazz musicians from her father's era. Omar reveled in the conversation; it was rare for a youngster to even know what jazz was, let alone the names of the best jazz musicians whose talents had shaped its history.

When it was time to open her birthday presents, Breeze saved the little box from Lex for last. "It's beautiful," she screamed with joy. She pulled out a gold I.D. bracelet with her name elegantly spelled out in script. She clumsily tried to fasten the bracelet, but her hands were shaking, so Lex fastened the bracelet and sweetly kissed her hand when he was finished. "Thank you," she whispered and hugged him, mesmerized by the charged message in his eyes. She laughed softly to break the intensity of the spell.

The party ended with the only slow song of the night, a love ballad that Breeze and Lex claimed to be their song. Diana Ross and Lionel Richie singing "Endless Love" blasted from the speakers. Lex clasped his fingers together around her waist, and Breeze put her arms around his neck, and they swayed to the music, believing the song was an anthem about their love.

Later that evening, Lillian coldly told Breeze that she shouldn't accept such an expensive gift from Lex.

Her eyes flashing with anger, Breeze strongly stated, "I'm keeping this bracelet, Ma."

"You're too young. You're not supposed to accept jewelry from a man unless you're engaged to him."

"Ma, I'm seventeen now, and I don't think there's anything wrong with accepting this gift. Lex bought this for me and there's no way I can give it back to him," explained Breeze with stubborn resolve.

Breeze and Lex were allowed to date twice a week— one weeknight and a Friday or Saturday, but never Friday and Saturday.

Some of their Saturday dates started with a trip to the grocery store whenever Lex had to take his mother shopping. Breeze helped Mrs. Franklin select groceries, enjoying the time they spent together. They became close, developing an older-younger woman friendship without the strain and conflict inherent in a mother-daughter relationship.

It was a summer of fun, love, and passion. They went to movies and concerts, shopped at the malls, cavorted at the amusement park, and danced at parties. Their unrestrained love was in full bloom, growing deeper by the day, bonding them closer together.

It was the summer Breeze lost her virginity.

As Breeze and Lex's love for each other grew, so did their desire. They were no longer satisfied with hugging, touching, and French-kissing. Lex's kisses sent indescribable, incredible sensations all through Breeze's body. She wanted him to touch her breasts, to caress her everywhere, and to satisfy the gnawing ache between her legs.

Lex struggled with the obvious presence of an erection every time he even kissed Breeze, sometimes when she just brushed against him. He had wanted her from the very beginning of their relationship, but knew she wasn't emotionally ready for sex. But now that the slightest touch, a soft embrace or subtle caress was like a strike of a match, it was hard to resist. Desire taunted their caution; they could wait no longer. Breeze was ready for Lex to make love to her. She didn't feel afraid or ashamed. Her mother's constant warnings became a whisper in the face of surging sexual need. She no longer even heard them.

After a heated encounter on the couch in Lex's basement, Breeze asked Rayna and India to take her to the free clinic for birth control pills. All the girls in her high school knew about the health clinic a few blocks away from the school. They didn't charge for examinations or for the birth control pills. Some of her schoolmates kept their pills in their lockers at school because they didn't want their mothers to know.

"After all this time, I can't believe you haven't had sex," Rayna exclaimed, lighting a cigarette.

"Ma would kill me if I got pregnant," Breeze said, slightly embarrassed. "And, she's going to kill you if she catches you smoking."

"She sure would," India agreed, sitting on the floor in front of the television in Breeze's bedroom.

"By the time she comes home, the smoke will be gone," Rayna reasoned cockily, blowing circles of smoke out of her mouth.

"Have you all done it?" Breeze asked her sisters, her eyes intense with curiosity.

India and Rayna glanced at each other, and then back at Breeze, but didn't respond.

Putting her hands on her hips, "Well?" Breeze asked, then fanned the smoke from her face.

India was the first to confess: "I've only had sex once, and I was scared I was gonna get pregnant so I didn't do it again."

"Did you like it?" Breeze probed, sitting on her bed next to Rayna.

"I guess," India replied, crossing her long skinny legs in front of her, watching the show on television. The foggy memory of her fumbled sexual encounter was mostly forgotten.

"What about you, Rayna?" Breeze inquired.

Rayna giggled mischievously, "I've been having sex since I was fourteen."

"Fourteen!" Breeze shrieked. She knew her sister was kind of wild, but not that wild.

"It feels good," Rayna shrugged. "And I like to feel good."

"Have you done it with Stevie?" India asked.

"Yeah!" was Rayna's nonchalant response.

"But he's so much older than you," Breeze said about the college senior who came around when Lillian wasn't home.

"I like older men, honey. They know what to do."

"What?" Breeze exclaimed, not understanding what Rayna meant. She was mystified at her older sister's attitude.

She couldn't understand how Rayna could have sex with boys she wasn't in love with. Rayna had a new boyfriend every month.

"I got birth control pills so I don't worry about getting pregnant," Rayna explained.

"I never see you taking anything," Breeze observed. "Does Ma know?"

"Get with it, Breeze. You don't have to have your mother's permission to get them. I keep them hidden, and I take them every day. You're supposed to take them every day or you'll get pregnant"

"Do you think I can get some?" Breeze asked.

"Yeah, I'll take you to the clinic. The doctor will examine you and then he'll give you a box of pills. I'll take both of you. And then you won't have nothing to worry about."

"Okay," Breeze said, feeling nervous about sneaking into the health clinic. Turning to India, she asked, "When do you want to go?"

Hesitantly, India replied, "An...I don't want to go."

"Why not?" Rayna asked, inhaling her cigarette.

"Because I don't want to," India said.

"Look, India, nothing's going to happen to you," Rayna assured.

"I don't have a boyfriend right now." Her eyes averted, India mumbled, "and maybe I want to save myself for my husband."

Glaring, Rayna scolded, "Get with it. This ain't the 1800s."

"Well, I'm...just...not...loose...like you, Rayna."

"Forget you then," Rayna fumed. "And when you get pregnant don't come running to me," she muttered before storming out of the room, her silver bracelets jingling as she walked.

India pushed herself to a standing position. "I'm going back to my room."

After a few moments alone Breeze followed India to her room, concern and uneasiness leading her on. Pushing the door aside after no response came to her knocking, Breeze saw India sprawled across the bed, crying.

The walls and carpet in India's small bedroom were bright blue; a pair of striped curtains in blue, green, and yellow hung from the window near her bed. A mahogany dresser, small chest, and desk were kept neat and orderly like everything else in her room. A poster of the Caribbean islands hung above her desk beside posters of Michael Jackson and Earth, Wind & Fire.

Gently sitting on the bed, Breeze quietly asked, "India, what's the matter?"

"Rayna doesn't understand, but I don't want to have an illegitimate child like me."

"You're not illegitimate!" Breeze exclaimed.

"I must be. Why else would my mother leave me and never come back?" Tears flowed down her fudge-colored cheeks.

"I don't know, India, but you have us. You're our family now," Breeze sighed, rubbing the back of India's shoulders.

"It's not the same. My last name isn't Blackwell. And if I had a baby out of wedlock, Mother might throw me out."

"Ma wouldn't do that!"

"I don't know that. She took me in and took care of me. I would feel so ashamed if I had to tell her I was pregnant. She would be so disappointed. I couldn't do that to her."

"Oh, India, don't cry. We love you no matter what." Breeze removed the box of tissues from the dresser and handed it to India.

"I love you all too," India sobbed, dabbing her eyes with a tissue. "I want to show you something," India whispered after blowing her nose delicately. She scrambled out of bed to her closet, and searched inside for an old shoebox.

"What's in there?" Breeze asked, staring curiously at the ragged shoebox on the patterned quilt that her grandmother had made.

India slowly lifted the box's lid and pulled out a picture that was lying on top. "This is my mother," whispered India as she stared at the picture for several minutes before handing it to Breeze.

Breeze looked at the aging black-and-white photo taken years before India's birth. "She's pretty!"

"Yes, and one day, I'm going to find her."

❧

"I won!" Breeze cried joyfully, laying down two spreads of straight jacks and queens.

They were playing five hundred, a card game, at Lex's house, upstairs in the kitchen. A small television sat on the table; its volume was low.

Lex peeked at the score written on the back of an envelope, and then glanced at the cards he was holding. He made a quick calculation and confirmed he had lost by fifty points. Admitting defeat he threw his cards down, and said, "Okay, you won."

Breeze gathered the cards into a pile and reshuffled them. "You want to play another game?"

"Maybe later," he answered, rising from the table. "Let's go downstairs."

She picked up two glasses from the table, and placed them in the sink before following Lex down into the basement.

Lex sat on the end of the sofa, his long legs stretched out in front of him. Breeze assumed her usual position: head resting on Lex's lap, body extended across the couch. They quietly watched an episode of "Sanford and Son" on television.

Lex softy stroked Breeze's cheek and twirled her hair around his fingers. He bent over and kissed her on the cheek.

"I love you, Breeze."

She looked up at him, her copper eyes glowing. "And I love you."

Lex smiled back, staring into the eyes that mesmerized him. "Cat eyes," he teased, and lightly tickled her stomach.

"Stop," she giggled, and pulled her legs to her stomach. After a few minutes, Lex stopped tickling her and hypnotized her with a stare of sexual longing. She turned away, breaking the spell of desire that was getting harder and harder to resist.

Breeze and Lex were kissing in the front seat of The Green Machine, Lex's pet name for his old 1968 Monte Carlo. In between kisses, they were watching a "B" horror movie at the drive-in theatre. Lex lifted Breeze's blouse and loosened her bra strap. While pausing to gently gaze into her face, he slid his hands under her bra and softly stroked her breasts, worshipping their fullness before touching her nipples. She shuddered as Lex rubbed the tips of his fingers delicately across her tender skin.

Breeze tried to watch the movie, but couldn't keep her eyes open. Lex's pressing hands on her tender breasts were causing a commotion inside of her. She leaned back, cramped awkwardly in the car, her head touching the passenger door, and closed her eyes to shut out the world from the wonder of the moment.

After hesitantly pulling her bra up, Lex openly kissed Breeze on the lips and neck, and then started to lick her nipples. She groaned softly as Lex licked one nipple, and then the other. He moved back and forth between nipples, licking one with his tongue and caressing the other with his hand.

Lex's hands touched her stomach, stroking her soft skin as he unbuttoned her jeans. Gently sliding his hands underneath her panties, he felt her soft pubic hair—warm and moist with desire. He was touching, feeling, exploring and finding the soft spot between her legs. Breeze gasped. "Oooh, oooh," when he finally probed possessively between her thighs. Lex rubbed the spot, causing Breeze to writhe. She was overwhelmed by sensations she'd never felt before. Breeze whispered, "It's okay, Lex. I'm on the pill now."

Releasing his passion, Lex unzipped her pants, and then moved up to her breasts. He suckled Breeze's nipples, causing waves of pleasure to ripple through her body.

Lex leaned back, and struggled to unbuckle his belt and unzip his pants. Suddenly, he stopped.

Eyes glazed with passion, "Lex...Lex...why are you stopping?" Breeze asked breathlessly as her body pulsed with sexual tension.

Lex straightened himself up, and between ragged breaths, explained, "I don't want it to be like this. I want it to be special."

Breeze whispered "Okay," and looked away to hide her disappointment. She untwisted her bra from around her neck, and pulled her blouse down over her chest.

Lex raised Breeze's face to his. "I love you and want to show you how much I love you, but it's got to be right."

Breeze went to bed that night with one thought: making love with Lex. Cuddled in bed with all her stuffed animals, she maintained a stranglehold on a favorite teddy bear. Her mind would not rest, filled to the brim with wonderment about sex.

If it feels that good just to be touched and kissed on my breasts, she thought, *what would it feel like to have him inside of me?*

Breeze was wide awake when Rayna came home from partying at two o'clock in the morning.

"B.B., are you asleep?" Rayna whispered, not wanting to wake up their mother sleeping in the next room.

"No." Breeze sat up and turned on the light. "What's wrong with you?" she asked. Rayna's eyes were red and she couldn't stand without wobbling. Finally, she gave up the fight to stay upright and flopped on the bottom of Breeze's bed, smelling of beer and cigarettes.

"I'm drunk." Shaking her head, Rayna groaned at the movement, "Sometimes, Sis, you...can be so naive..."

"You smell just the way Daddy used to when he came home late," Breeze sniffed, sitting up in the bed with the covers wrapped around her. "Ma's going to kill you."

"Ma doesn't run me. I've graduated from high school and I'll be gone in six weeks. Off to college. I'm a grown woman, hoonee."

"I wish you didn't have to leave," Breeze said sadly.

"Hoow else am I goin' to be a *acctresss?"* Rayna slurred, clumsily kicking off her shoes. "Did you and Lex screw yet?"

"Rayna, don't say it like that. And no, we didn't 'DO it!' " Breeze said disappointedly.

"Youu *telll* him you on the *pill!?"* Rayna slurred.

"I told him," Breeze frowned. "But he didn't want to make love in the car."

"The *saaint* and the *virggin,"* Rayna said disgustedly. *"Moove* over, Saint Breeze. I'm sleepin' with you *toonight.* Can't make it to my *room…"*

Breeze and Lex couldn't look at each other without thinking about making love. They sat across the table at their favorite restaurant, Sadie's Soul Food Delights, and halfheartedly ordered their favorite meals. Normally, they would talk about something that happened that morning or share an anecdote about their family or their dreams for the future. But this afternoon, their minds were only on each other, and there was no conversation. Lex simply held Breeze's hands.

"I'll pick you up at seven," Lex said as he kissed Breeze lightly on the lips before leaving the restaurant.

She was ready when Lex came to pick her up. Lillian was in the kitchen picking collard greens when Breeze told her she was leaving. Lillian looked up and flashed a warning glance. "Don't be late."

They went straight to Mookie's apartment, a friend of Lex. It felt strange to be in someone's apartment, but Breeze didn't care because all she wanted was to be with Lex.

He led her directly to the bedroom, walking slowly down the narrow hall. Breeze barely noticed the inexpensive, donated furnishings in the small one-bedroom apartment. The mismatched bedroom furniture, wobbly dinette set, and pictureless walls, signs of a first apartment, were unnoticed by the teenage lovers. The place was clean, and they would be undisturbed. That was all that mattered to Breeze and Lex.

Now that she was there, at the moment of truth, her stomach was infested with wild, maniac butterflies. Breeze didn't know what to do. Lex saw the fear in her eyes, and offered reassuringly, "It will be all right"

He took her hand as she moved in front of the bed, and kissed away her fears. It took only one searing kiss, and Breeze was no longer afraid.

Lex pulled her closer and caressed her mouth tenderly with his own. Hungrily, his lips slid down her neck and shoulders. Slowly and teasingly, he began to undress Breeze, as if she were a gift that he had to savor unwrapping. First he reached under her dress and pulled off her panties. His fingers explored inside her soft thighs, traveling to her calves, and flickering over the soles of her feet.

Breeze sighed and whispered, "Oh, Lex." He unhooked her bra, his feverish hands grazing her breasts and warming her nipples, pulling the straps of her clothing over her shoulders to her waist and then to the floor.

Breeze was naked. Self-consciously, she reached for the blanket to cover her body, but Lex webbed her slender fingers with his. Groaning in embarrassment, Breeze tried to cross her hands over her chest to hide her breasts.

"No, Breeze…I want to look at you as I undress," Lex said huskily, and pushed Breeze's arms away from her chest. Hungrily, he enjoyed the sight of her firm breasts with their jutting brown centers. "You are incredible, Sunshine. You're music in the flesh."

Breeze lowered her eyes, but watched with curiosity as Lex stood to remove his clothes. His eyes never left Breeze's body as he unbuttoned his shirt, removed it and tossed it to the floor. He took his feet out of his shoes while unzipping his pants, and stepped out of them. Breeze shuddered with nervousness when she glimpsed his erection for the first time.

"Relax, Sunshine. I won't hurt you. I promise."

Lex eased Breeze down on the bed, his exploring hands traveling over her body. "I want you, Breeze," he whispered, and smothered her lips with a kiss that was warm and hard, tender and probing. Feeling the hardness of his tongue inside her mouth and the naked smoothness of his body sent a flood of sensations throughout her body, a tidal wave of longing. She experienced the heat, the yearning, and the desperation of sexual need for the first time in her sheltered life.

Lex's probing tongue moved to her full, ripe breasts. Capturing one in his mouth, he suckled from its fullness to its tender tip. The steady motion—licking, rubbing, and nibbling—was an overwhelmingly sensual sensation for Breeze. She moaned softly, her body temperature rising. She reached out and grabbed Lex's arm, holding on, enjoying the delicious feeling of her fingers buried in his resilient flesh. "I love your breasts," Lex murmured, his hands kneading them.

Breeze ran her fingers up and down Lex's hairy chest and stomach, but pulled her restless hands away to avoid touching his sex. "Touch me," he groaned. "Let me feel your hands on me."

Rubbing his body sensually against hers, Lex could sense Breeze's arousal. Eagerly she moved her hips against his, her hands pressing his buttocks in urgent need. Lex wanted to be inside her, to feel all the pleasures of her body closing, encompassing his own in loving heat He eased himself between her legs, but paused as Breeze stiffened.

"It will hurt for just a minute, Sunshine, but afterwards…," he spoke softy, tenderly looking into her eyes, "just let me show you."

At the peak of her desire, Breeze anticipated the pain by closing her eyes, and in a display of implicit trust, wrapped her aims around his shoulders.

Lex lowered his mouth to warm her ear, "I love you, Breeze," and probed inside her, setting off a force of motions they never knew before.

Feelings Breeze had never before experienced sponsored tears which trickled down her face. Softy, slowly, Lex moved deeper within her, stirring a sweet melody of pleasure, and when her body finally released its spiraling tension, Breeze was incinerated with an icy heat.

Lex literally wrapped himself around Breeze as his body shuddered above her own, their limbs entwined in clutching accord. The softness of her sweat-drenched skin was a soothing balm to his hot body. Looking into Lex's eyes, she saw herself reflected in their dark pools, and felt brand new. She had loved him before, but now it was as if they had gone into each other's being and left some of themselves behind.

"Breeze," Lex whispered in her ear.

"I love you, Lex. I'll love you forever."

"And I will always love you, Sunshine. We'll always be together."

Snuggled in each other's arms, the two slipped into a deep, lover's sleep.

Breeze was the first to awaken, her eyes flying open with a jolt of fear. Glancing at the clock on the bedside table, she knew why she had awakened with her heart in her throat. Breeze's panicked voice woke up Lex. "Oh God! It's one o'clock and my mother is going to kill me," she screamed.

They rushed around frantically, putting on their clothes, and locking up the apartment As Lex sped through the wide inner streets of Philadelphia, he could almost cut through the thickness of Breeze's fear. It hurt him to see her so upset.

As soon as they pulled up the driveway, Lillian stormed from the house, uncaring of the curtains being gently pushed aside in the surrounding houses of the tightly knit neighborhood. The two young lovers jumped out of the car and rushed up the sidewalk.

"Where have you been? I've been worried to death," Lillian screamed, panic written all over her face, pink curlers dancing around her head.

"Ma, I'm sorry I'm late, but we went to this party and took some of Lex's friends home and got lost," came Breeze's rush of words.

"For two hours? Two hours?" Lillian asked, eyes narrowed, both hands firmly on her hips. "And I'm a horse's behind. Right? What have you really been doing? You don't look dressed for a party to me."

"Mrs. Blackwell, I apologize for bringing Breeze home late," Lex interrupted, shifting nervously on his feet "We left the party late, and my friend said they lived nearby but they actually lived thirty minutes away...and uh...we got lost."

Her arms folded across her chest, Lillian said, "It won't happen again, I tell you that. Alexander, I don't want you coming around her for the next two weeks."

"Ma!" Breeze exploded, "He's going to be leaving for school in four weeks."

"Come in this house, now," Lillian commanded, while grabbing Breeze's arm. With a tone of finality, she said, "Good night, Alexander."

As she slammed the door, she hollered, "You better not be pregnant, young lady," sniffing Breeze's clothes.

Lex stood motionless outside for a few minutes staring at the unyielding presence of the Blackwell front door before finally moving to his car. Breeze's voice, sounding more distressed than he had ever heard, acted like cymbals in his head, echoing in the chambers of his mind. He wanted to go inside, to protect her from Lillian's angry tirade, but he knew this was not the time.

Inside Lillian railed on. "I'm glad he's going away to college. You two have been spending entirely too much time together and that could lead to nothing but trouble." She repeated, "Nothing but trouble."

Breeze slowly began to walk up the stairs, attempting to remember with every step the extent of her love for Lillian. *Ignore her,* her mind urged, *she's your mother. Remember. She doesn't mean it.*

But she couldn't keep her pain in check. Midway up the stairs, she turned and cried, "Ma, how could you be so mean? You know I love Lex. Why won't you understand?"

Lillian looked up at her distraught daughter, she straightened her back and softened her tone. "He's no good for you, baby. I've been trying to tell you that I don't want you to make the same mistakes I did. You got a lot to learn about life before you know anything about love."

Breeze defiantly hurled back, "I'm not going to stop seeing him."

"You're grounded for two weeks, Miss. I want you to come straight home from work."

"I'm not a child," Breeze argued. "I'm seventeen."

"That boy got you thinking you're a woman, that's your problem. I'm your mother and as a woman I know," she said, poking an angry finger to her heaving chest, "that you still got a lot of growing up to do."

"I don't know everything, but I know what I feel," Breeze insisted as tears fell from her eyes. Only moments ago, lying in Lex's arms, she had felt so good, so safe, so loved.

"And you may not feel that way forever," Lillian predicted.

"We'll always love each other and there's nothing you can do to stop us," Breeze warned. "Nothing!"

"You better watch your mouth, girl. Just go on up to bed," she said sternly. Lillian's face was a mask of absolute conviction; The heart-shaped mouth was hard and set, her eyes narrowed in annoyance. But deep inside, she knew how her daughter felt. Oh yes, she was very afraid of what Breeze was feeling. *Lord, no,* she prayed. *Not this boy. Don't let her feel that way for this musician.*

Breeze stared at Lillian, stunned at her insensitivity. She wanted to explain; wanted her mother to understand how she felt.

If only she would understand, Breeze thought, *she wouldn't be so mean. Wasn't she in love once? Doesn't she know what it's like? Maybe I should tell her how I feel...*

Breeze glared at the stubborn look on her mother's face, and shaking her head firmly, she realized that her mother would never understand. Slowly, climbing the stairs to her room, her heart solidified into a cold tight fist, replacing the warm love of hours ago.

Twenty-four hours ago, when Breeze had stepped into Sadie's Soul Food Delights, her eyes had sparkled and her face had glowed with love and anticipation. The owner, Delilah, was concerned when Breeze walked in bearing the face of gloom.

"What's wrong, chile? Did somethin' happen wid your family?"

Breeze shook her head. "Nothing like that"

"So you want your usual table?"

"Yes," Breeze replied, following Delilah to a window table where she could spot Lex the moment he arrived.

"Did somethin' happen 'tween you and Lex?" Delilah probed while placing a glass of Coca-Cola in front of Breeze. With the most forlorn eyes Delilah had ever seen, Breeze explained, "My mother doesn't want us to see each other for two weeks."

"She jus trying' to protect you, honey." Delilah's round face matched her Pillsbury Doughboy body. Close to three hundred pounds was spread out thickly on her small frame. A high-yellow woman with a close-cropped Afro, she always greeted her customers with a smile. Something about the warmth in her black eyes and friendly smile attracted many people to the restaurant. She sat down at the table.

"She's too protective," Breeze said angrily. "She thinks we spend too much time together." She put her elbows on the table. "She doesn't want me to see Lex, but I know what I feel inside."

"You loves him?"

"Yes, Miss Delilah," Breeze responded fervently. "I would die if I didn't see Lex. It's bad enough that he's going away to college in a few weeks."

"I'd heed my heart, chile," Delilah advised. "When I was young I fell in love with Martin Jones. Boy, did I love that boy. Umh, umh, umh. But my Mama hated his people. She thought dey was bad people. She wouldn't let me see him, but we snuck and did it anyways. But that didn't change nothin'. Our folks hated each other and we didn't dare tell them what we was doin' behind der backs. After 'while his family moved on. But I still think of him. Lord, yes I do, umh, umh, umh." Delilah shook her head while patting her ample rear proportions after standing.

"I'll bring ya some hot apple pie wid some ice cream on top. That'll fix ya."

"I'm really not hungry," Breeze said.

"I know that eatin' makes you feel heaps better. Yup, when I got somethin' on my mind, I fix me somethin' real good to eat. Oh, you don't have to say it. I know I is big as a house," Delilah chuckled, her deep, rich voice vibrating in her chest. "But I knows how to make myself feel good when somethin's wrong." Delilah mumbled as her head jerked towards the door, "Ho…I'll be back in a minute. Yes, I'll just have to eat some myself…"

Lex paused at the door, scanning the restaurant for Breeze before rushing over to the table. They hugged and kissed as if twenty-four hours had been twenty-four days. A rush of words echoed their emotional release.

"I was so worried about you, Sunshine, I couldn't sleep."

"I love you, Lex. I cried the whole night."

"I love you, Breeze. And I wanted to call you and talk to you."

"You can't call me and you can't come over," Breeze miserably complained.

After they sat down, Lex reached across the table to hold Breeze's hands. "That means we'll only see each other at lunch."

"I thought about that," Breeze said, releasing a sigh and plunging back into the booth. "So, I'm going to work half a day," she explained with a half smile, "in the mornings, so we can be together in the afternoons."

Lex's tense face relaxed. He would still see his Sunshine. Breeze felt guilty for disobeying and deceiving her mother, but her love for Lex would not be denied.

Breeze spent the mornings working at the YWCA and the afternoons with Lex. Many days, she watched Lex practice with his band, learning about the technicalities of singing. She began to understand Lex's passion for music and began to unravel the reasons why her father was so inexplicably drawn to music. But as her appreciation for music deepened, she became even more baffled by her mother's disdain. Watching the band rehearse, she wondered what it would be like to be a professional singer. She avidly bought albums featuring female singers: Chaka Khan, Patrice Rushen, Dee Dee Bridgewater, and even old albums by Eartha Kitt, Nancy Wilson, and Billie Holiday, and experimented with their singing techniques.

Lillian couldn't help noticing that Breeze had been stricken with her father's passion. To her disapproval, Breeze listened to music all day and all night; if the radio wasn't on, she was playing albums.

"That music business is evil. I've seen it destroy people," Lillian said, shaking her head at the litter of albums covering her daughter's bed.

"But Daddy loves the business, Ma. How bad can it be?"

"It's not for everybody," Lillian replied vehemently. "You're too good for it."

On their last evening together, Lex took Breeze downtown to a fancy restaurant. The two made a striking couple: Lex dressed in a double-breasted, pin-striped blue suit and tie, and Breeze attired in a red silk wrap dress that emphasized her figure. Her hair was pulled up in a french roll and loose tendrils surrounded her face.

"Baby, baby, baby," breathed Lex as Breeze walked down the stairs. "I've never seen you with your hair up. You are gorgeous."

After dinner, they drove to Mookie's apartment, their special meeting place when they wanted to be alone. On the trip over, they were quiet in the car, their impending separation weighing heavily on their minds.

Inside the apartment, Lex opened a bottle of wine and poured two glasses. As they sat on the living room sofa, he proposed a toast, "To my Sunshine."

"Lex," Breeze said, and sipped on the wine, trying to gain control of her emotions. "I love you."

Lex took the glass from Breeze's hand and placed it on the table. Silently, they stared at each other as if they were permanently memorizing each other's face in their memories. The songs of Stephanie Mills soulfully filtered through the air.

Lex touched Breeze's face, rubbing the back of his hands against the softness of her cheek and running the tips of his fingers across her lips as if to imprint their texture onto his mind. Breeze watched him, breathing softly.

Breaking the silence, Lex said, "I've got something for you." He stood up, fished in his jacket pocket, pulled out a small box, and handed it to her. "Open it."

Breeze stared at the box for a few minutes, before slowly pulling on the ribbon and unraveling the bow. She tore off the gift wrapping paper. "Lex, it's beautiful!" oozed from her lips, as she lifted the box's lid and saw a gold and ruby pendant. She picked up the pendant, fingering the delicate gold chain, and fighting the urge to cry.

"I thought you would like it It's your birthstone, and there's an inscription inside."

Breeze opened the pendant, and saw the words "Forever Yours, Lex" etched on the inside. "Thank you, Lex…I wish you didn't have to go."

"I know," he said soothingly, "but it doesn't mean the end, Breeze."

When Breeze looked at him with tears dancing in her eyes and sadness painting her features, Lex pressed his mouth against hers, hungrily, desperately. Breeze pulled him close, her mouth greeting his in urgency, her tongue delving, reaching.

Groaning, Lex tore his demanding mouth from hers and pressed a hard kiss against her cheek, and then her neck. He wanted more. He stood, placed an arm around her shoulders and under her knees, and lifted Breeze into his arms. Holding her high against his chest, Lex carried his precious package into the dimly lit bedroom where they quickly shed their clothes, discarding them in a disheveled pile on the floor.

Their naked bodies touching, pressing, he kissed Breeze again, gently at first, but the softness of her naked body and the aroma of her musky perfume overwhelmed him. Kisses soon became hard, probing demands, and Breeze eagerly accepted every deep stroke of his tongue.

His hands worked their way from the top of her shoulders to the brown tips of her sensitive nipples. He stroked her body, caressing her breasts, and probing her petal-like folds with an urgency that left her feeling on fire. Moaning and writhing at his heated touch, Breeze ran her finger over his hairy chest, all the way down to his legs.

Lex's heated hands played with the petal-like flower between Breeze's legs. "Lex, oh Lex,…" she called out, arching her body against his.

Lex slipped inside of Breeze, thrusting deep, his moan lost in her open, panting mouth. He had wanted to make love to her slowly, completely, to make the moment last but desire was fierce, and he hastened the tempo; the pleasure building, increasing, until they both exploded in a fury of ecstasy.

Breeze spent the entire night with Lex because she had told Lillian that she was staying over at a girlfriend's house. It was going to be their last night together, and she didn't care if her mother believed her or not. She had to be with Lex every hour of their last day and night. Oh, how she wished he wasn't leaving, but she knew this was the beginning of his future, and resolved to be strong.

"When you graduate, you can come to Boston to go to school. Then we'll be together again," Lex whispered eagerly.

"A year is a long time," Breeze lamented, her head pressed against Lex's damp shoulder.

"We're not going to break up. I'll love you forever. I mean it, Breeze. We have an endless love," Lex proclaimed, his fingers running through Breeze's soft hair.

Breeze felt his declaration inside her soul, letting the words echo through her as truth. She knew he loved her and they were always going to be together.

"I'll be home every holiday and we'll write to each other," Lex promised.

"Promise me you won't forget me!" Breeze begged, burying her face against his solid chest to hide her tears.

"How can I? You are a part of me!" Lex confessed, his arms tightening around her, loosening when she fell into a fitful sleep.

The next morning, Breeze stared out of the living room window, looking for his car, waiting for Lex to come by the house to officially say good-bye. When Lex pulled up, Breeze slowly opened the door and walked out to the street. Lex's car was all packed for the drive to Boston. She got inside.

Lex and Breeze held each other for a long time in silence until finally, pulling away, Lex whispered, "I've got to get going." He kissed Breeze one more time—an urgent, pressing kiss. "I love you and take care of yourself," Lex said.

"And I love you." Breeze spoke the words from the deepest part of her heart.

Breeze watched Lex back out of the driveway and pull away with tears streaming down her face. It was going to be a long time before she saw The Green Machine again.

After a half hour, India came outside and walked down to the end of the driveway, to check on her. "Breeze, are you all right?"

Breeze didn't answer for several minutes, then she looked at India and whispered with tears in her eyes, "He's gone."

"I know," India said, putting her arms around Breeze's waist. "Let's go inside."

CHAPTER FOUR

The first few months that Lex was in college, he wrote letters to Breeze every week, sometimes every other day. On Saturdays, Breeze mailed out long letters, chronicling her thoughts and activities each day of that week.

High school was not the same for Breeze without Lex or Rayna around. She was in the eleventh grade, and India was a senior, and even though they went to all the high school football and basketball games and parties, Breeze deeply missed her older sister and boyfriend.

Lex surprised Breeze by coming home for Thanksgiving. They were inseparable for five days. Breeze ignored her curfew times, and Lex didn't once pick up his guitar. When Lex went back to college, Breeze felt as if her heart had been torn out even though she knew he would be back in a few weeks.

Christmas was special and exciting. It was Breeze's favorite time of the year, and life felt normal again with Rayna and Lex around. Breeze wished that time could stand still, that the moment of everyone being together, happy and loving, would never end. But when the morning light arrived to announce a new day, she knew that another day had passed, and soon Lex would once again be leaving.

The long periods apart intensified Breeze and Lex's love and passion for each other. Their lovemaking was full of fire, dynamic, and explosive. They couldn't get enough of each other—always touching and teasing, arousing their flames of desire again and again.

"Oh, Breeze," Lex breathed, lying beside Breeze, sweat pouring down his heated body. "I can't seem to get enough of you."

Gasping for air, Breeze gushed, "I know." She reached for the glass of water on the nightstand, and gulped down the entire glassful.

They came down from the high of their lovemaking and fell asleep, arms wrapped around each other. Later, when Breeze opened her eyes, she found Lex staring at her. She smiled at him, and tenderly touched his face.

"I love you more and more," Lex confessed.

"I think about you everyday, Lex. I wonder what you're doing, if you had a good day in school. If you're happy without me."

"I know this may be hard for you to understand, Breeze, but I really like it up there. I mean, I thought I knew everything there was to know about music, but I don't, I'm learning and growing. One of my professors really likes me. Professor Quick. He thinks I've got a special way with a guitar."

"Are those his words?" Breeze smiled.

"His exact words!" Lex bragged.

Lex didn't tell her that Professor Quick told him that to take his talent to its maximum, he would have to make some sacrifices; he would have to concentrate on his music, and let nothing else distract him.

"You must become obsessed with your instrument. You must love only your guitar," Professor Quick admonished. "Are you willing to do that?"

Lex's face was blank, but his thoughts were on Breeze. A pang of guilt overtook him with the thought of betraying her. The professor banged his fist on the desk to get Lex's attention.

"Alexander, are you willing to put nothing and no one else before your music?"

"I don't know, Professor," Lex stammered. He didn't want to lose Breeze. Everyone was telling him that his music must come first. But what about love? wondered Lex. What's wrong with being in love?

"Do you have a special lady friend?" Professor Quick asked, noticing the pain in his young student's eyes.

"Yes, and I love her very much..."

"I'm not saying that you must never love anyone. I'm saying that to achieve the greatness you desire, you must practice, practice, practice. Later in life, you can have more than one love. But right now, you can only love your guitar."

Winter was long, cold, and dreary, and by spring Lex's letters were sporadic. Breeze checked the mailbox in the mornings before going to school even though the mailman didn't usually come until afternoon. Every evening she asked her mother if she had received any mail. Lillian would look away, not wanting to see her daughter's troubled face, and mumble under her breath, "Nothing for you."

After months went by and Breeze hadn't heard from Lex, she tried calling him at his dorm, but an annoyed voice told her that Lex was no longer living there. She continued to write, but her letters became fewer and shorter in length—it was hard to communicate with a wall of silence.

Lex didn't come home that summer, and Breeze began to believe her mother's prediction: Alexander Franklin had forgotten her. Breeze was not consoled when Rayna frankly explained, on one of her visits home, that "college kids don't hang out with high school kids." Breeze burst into tears and wallowed in grief upstairs in her room.

The summer Breeze turned eighteen was the worst summer of her life. Through her connections, Lillian was able to get Breeze a job working for a judge. At first Breeze hated it because she was tired of Lillian's constant nagging. Every other day it seemed she would hear her mother say something about "how respectable being a lawyer is" or "your cousin is in law school" or "your grandfather would be so proud." But she was fascinated by the field of law, sometimes she enjoyed searching through the book stacks for precedent-setting legal cases. She socialized with her sister and friends, but never went out with anyone.

Breeze thought constantly about Lex, but he never called or responded to her letters. She played "Endless Love" over and over until she could no longer bear to hear the lyrics that had become lies. So, she stopped playing music. Her stereo system collected dust underneath the pile of albums she no longer played. Slowly, she accepted the fact that Lex had forgotten her. She tried to forget him, but he was always lurking in her thoughts, a pain in her heart that wouldn't go away. She stopped wearing his pendant and bracelet, as the feel of the gold against her flesh reminded her of the coldness lurking in her heart.

Her senior year flew by. She went to school in the morning and worked for the judge in the afternoon. Sometimes she would go to a party or a movie, but she would forever recall her senior year as uneventful. Breeze couldn't wait for graduation. She looked forward to going to college, to somewhere far away, to a place where she didn't have burning memories of Lex stalking every nook and cranny that served as a backdrop for her daily existence.

On the morning of her high school graduation, Breeze told India that she had "a feeling" Lex was going to be at the graduation ceremony. She hadn't spoken to him or heard from him in a year. After two hundred days had passed, Breeze stopped marking X's on her calendar. Instead, it felt like there was a permanent X on her heart.

"Do you want to see him?" India asked.

"At this point, all I want to know is why he stopped calling me!" Breeze fumed angrily.

"You might not like the answer," India forewarned.

"I still want to know."

Breeze's intuition was right. Lex came to her graduation. After the ceremonies, Lex greeted her with a wide grin, reminding Breeze of their first conversation at Miss Abbot's wedding reception. Sporting a moustache, he looked even more handsome, though older than she remembered. The pace of her heart quickened as he approached, but now that the moment of truth was upon her, she considered walking away from him. She didn't think she was ready to face the truth.

Lex encircled his arms around her waist, his eyes closed, savoring the closeness of her body. *How I've missed you so much, baby,* he thought. Absorbed in the smell and feel of her, he didn't even realize that Breeze wasn't responding to him, that she held her body still and firm, unyielding like a statue.

Lex brushed his lips against hers, and then kissed her sweet lips with a hungering need. The kiss was electric, recharging the love lying dormant in their hearts.

Breeze stepped back to distance herself from Lex, from the feelings she had hidden away. For a moment, she had forgotten that he had forgotten her, that he had abandoned her for someone or something else. But the reality of the moment returned and her anguish surfaced. Anger blazed from her copper-brown eyes.

"What's the matter?" he asked, puzzled by her cold response.

Breeze glared at him. He seemed really pleased with himself. She was furious, but there was a part of her that was glad to see him. She had so many questions to ask, but didn't know where to begin.

"I brought you something from Europe," Lex said tentatively.

Her eyes grew wide. "When did you go to Europe?"

"Last summer. I got a scholarship to study music over there." With pride in his voice, he boasted, "You won't believe this, but I'm touring with Stevie Wonder. I play the acoustic guitar. Sometimes I even get to do a solo, just for a minute when he introduces the band."

"I didn't know that," Breeze said, new questions filling her head.

"I wrote to you." Anger crept into his voice, "I wrote to you week after week and you never replied." The frustration in his voice hardened, "I thought maybe you had a new boyfriend." He shrugged his shoulders as if he didn't care, but the piercing pain in his eyes told a different story.

Flinging her arms outward, Breeze hotly accused, "I never got any letters!"

"I asked you to come to Europe with me. They had programs for high school seniors. I figured that your mother wouldn't go for it, but I wanted you to know about it, so you could decide."

"The last letter I got from you was after Christmas. It was your second semester. You wrote about your classes and Professor Quick." She could quote line by line every letter Lex had written for she had read them over and over to find a clue, a hint, an explanation as to why he had abruptly stopped writing her.

"Breeze, I swear to you that I wrote you. When you didn't respond I thought you changed your mind about us, so I stopped writing."

"I never changed my mind!" Breeze cried, struggling to hold back the tears. "You're lying!"

"I tried to call a couple of times, but you weren't home."

Noticing the look of disbelief in Breeze's face, he added, "I'm not lying to you. Please believe me, Breeze. I've been dying to see you. I came back just to see you. I'm supposed to be on the bus with the rest of the band on the way to Pittsburgh. We've got a concert tomorrow night. I shouldn't be here, but I had to see you. I couldn't understand what happened to us!"

"You should have stayed on the bus instead of coming here and expecting me to believe your lies," Breeze whispered between clinched teeth. The yellow and black tassel hanging from her graduation cap swung wildly from the angry movement of her head.

Lex had never seen Breeze so angry. Her jaws were firmly set and her eyes were funnels of fury. Cupping his hands under her chin, he forced her to look at him. "Have I ever lied to you?"

Breeze pulled her head away from his warm hands. "No, but if you wrote me, where are all your letters?"

Omar Blackwell threw a big graduation party for Breeze and her friends at a downtown hotel. It was a big bash. There was plenty of food, drink, and music blasted from large speakers. Everybody was having a good time, except Breeze.

Omar insisted that Breeze dance and mingle with her friends, but she wanted to go home. Late in the evening when Omar saw Breeze sitting alone, he sat down beside her. Concerned, he asked his solemn-faced daughter why she wasn't having a good time.

"I just don't feel good."

"You were fine earlier," Omar commented. "You should dance. Have fun! This is the first day of the rest of your life."

Breeze looked at her father and rolled her eyes heavenward. Omar was dressed in a black suit with an open-collared white shirt, and a red corsage pinned on the lapel.

"Baby girl, I can't believe you're all grown up now!" Omar said, putting his arms around Breeze's shoulders.

Breeze looked down at her feet, feeling the weight of the unknown future on her shoulders. "Sometimes I wish I was still a little girl." She leaned against her father's large frame.

"So do I," Omar admitted. "I missed so much of your growing up. if only your mother and I could have stayed together." Blotting the sweat from his brow with a handkerchief, he said, "She never understood my love for music. It never meant that I didn't love her."

Breeze looked into her father's eyes, mirrors of hers. "Have you ever told her that?"

"Years ago, but she couldn't understand the call of the sax."

"Is that what happened to Lex and me? He couldn't fight it?"

"I don't know, baby. I like Lex and I sensed he was trying to find his way. You both are very young, and I know how you feel about each other, but life is full of twists and turns and you never know what is going to happen next. Be strong, have faith in yourself, and know that I'll always be here for you."

Omar kissed her on the forehead. "Remember, we're going car shopping tomorrow. Have you decided what you want?"

"I don't know, Daddy." Breeze said, shrugging her shoulders. "Maybe something sporty."

"We'll find you something you like. We'll look tomorrow afternoon. You know I'm no good in the mornings."

"Okay!" Breeze said, softly smiling.

Omar gave Breeze a big, comforting hug. "Now go on and have a good time!" A tall youngster walked past them. "Hey, young fellow!" Omar called. "Do you know my daughter?"

Her classmate grinned. "Yes, everybody knows Breeze. She's the prettiest girl in school."

Omar smiled. "Well, I agree with that. Why don't you dance with my darling daughter?"

Russell extended his hand to Breeze and asked her to dance with him.

"Every time I see you sitting alone, I'm going to ask someone to dance with you," Omar warned.

"Oh, Daddy," Breeze murmured, but she danced with Russell, and as the evening progressed began to enjoy her graduation party.

Breeze was glad when the party was over so she could go home and go to bed. She was exhausted from non-stop dancing, but sleep escaped her because all she could think about was Lex. Her heart still felt the same, and she knew somehow that he wasn't lying to her today. But to believe that Lex hadn't lied would mean that her mother had been lying every time she asked if there was a letter in the mailbox for her. She tried to fall asleep, but a little voice nagged her to search for his letters, to see if she could find them hidden within the house.

Ma wouldn't do that. Ma wouldn't betray my trust, or would she? She hated Lex. She didn't want us to be together. Maybe she did. Maybe she hid the letters. Then find out, the voice taunted. *Where would she hide them? Where should I search?* Start at the top, the voice urged, the attic.

She couldn't ignore the voice—it grew louder as she tossed and turned, throbbing in her mind—so she decided to climb the stairs to the attic. She hated the attic, it was creepy and dark, and as a child when she ventured there, she had stepped on a rusty nail and had to be rushed to the hospital. Her mission then had been to find out what was in the forbidden place, but her mission now was to find the forbidden.

Breeze opened boxes, finding pictures, cards and keepsakes, but behind discarded furniture was the strongbox that her mother often kept important papers in. With trembling fingers, she opened the pewter-gray strongbox. When she touched the box, for reasons she could not fathom, she had the strongest and strangest feeling. She knew she had found what she was looking for. At the very bottom of the box was a stack of letters from Lex. She counted them: thirty-five letters.

As she walked down the stairs, one thought replayed in her mind: *Lex didn't lie to me, but Ma had...Lex didn't lie to me, but Ma had.*

Breeze returned to her room and read every letter with tears streaming down her face. She read the tender love letters over and over and found what she knew in her heart to be true:

Lex really loved her, he hadn't forgotten her, and he had planned for them to be together.

When Lillian got up in the middle of the night to go to the bathroom, she was surprised to see the stream of light under Breeze's door. She heard Breeze sobbing as she approached the door. Yawning, Lillian opened the door and saw Breeze drowning in a sea of tears, and the letters from Lex scattered everywhere. Lillian felt a stab of pain in her heart. This was the moment she had been dreading, the moment she hoped would never come. She wanted to burn the letters, but something had kept her from going that far. Now, as she faced her daughter who looked like a stranger, she wished she had.

"Baby, I didn't want you to be hurt," Lillian gently said.

Breeze's hair was like a rag doll's, scattered every which way on her head. Her eyes had watered and shimmered into a glassy stare. She felt so much anger at her mother that she thought she would collapse from the intensity. "How could you, Ma? How dare you think you can tell me who to love." The words poured forth from a well of resentment.

Sitting on the end of Breeze's bed, Lillian searched for the right words. "I was doing what a mother is supposed to do. I was protecting you."

"From what? You wanted to destroy our love. You destroyed my happiness."

"You only think you'd be happy. I know Omar is encouraging you, but he doesn't know what it's like. The wife of a musician is one of longing, a million good-byes, of waiting for him to come home, and not knowing if he will. And when he does return, you are strangers because he's been away for so long."

"Daddy's got nothing to do with this!" Breeze waved her hands angrily in the air. "Just because you and Daddy didn't work out doesn't give you the right to destroy my love," Breeze screamed, the pitch of her voice rising with her despair.

"Don't you understand, baby? *I don't want you to be hurt like that.*" Lillian reached out to comfort her daughter, but Breeze pushed Lillian's hand away.

"You had no right!" Shaking with pain and confusion, Breeze exploded, "Lex is not Daddy!"

Breeze's wails could be heard all over the house. Rayna and India rushed into the room, frightened by the loud and angry voices.

Hungover and bleary-eyed, Rayna was the first to ask, "What the hell is going on?"

"Ma hid Lex's letters from me. I knew she never liked Lex but I didn't think she would lie to me!" Breeze pointed a finger at Lillian. "All this time, Ma has been trying to break Lex and me up!"

"Mother, is that true?" India asked quietly, traces of sleep on her face.

"I don't want her to spend her life loving someone who's never around."

"Ma, that's for Breeze to decide," Rayna said. "You don't know what would have happened between them."

"I know plenty of women who married musicians, and we all ended up in the same boat. The men are never around. Their music comes first," Lillian choked, recalling her darkest feelings. "And you have to worry about the women who chase after them, and the ones they chase after. I don't want you to have to deal with that. You're too good for that, baby. My father tried to warn me, and I wouldn't listen, Breeze. I thought I was too smart for that. But what a fool I was. I learned the hard way, and I didn't want you to have to learn the same lesson," she said, her body trembling and her voice quaking.

"I won't stay here, Ma," Breeze announced defiantly. "I'm going to live with Daddy until I start school," she said as she proceeded to the closet, opened the door, and pulled out a suitcase. "If I go to school," she added spitefully.

Lillian clutched at her chest "Breeze, baby, this is our last summer together. I only want what's best for you."

Breeze spun around. "For me to be a lawyer, is that what's best for me?"

Lillian blinked back her tears to protest. "You'd make a wonderful lawyer. Even Judge Whittaker thinks so."

"I was going to be a lawyer to please you. When Rayna went off to study drama instead of medicine, I knew how disappointed you were, and I wasn't going to let you down. But you know what," she laughed, a hurt, hollow sound, "I really want to sing. Lex always said I was born to sing. Ma, I guess I am my father's daughter after all."

"I won't permit it." Lillian insisted, her words rushing out. "You can't get caught up in that kind of life. It's dangerous, it's wicked. People get hooked on drugs, and all kinds of terrible things happen. I've seen it with my own eyes. Women who were destroyed by music and drugs. I want you to have a decent, happy, respectable life." With her hands clutched together in a white-knuckled tightened fist, she released a long sigh. "Baby, I know I was wrong. But I did it because I love you."

"You can never justify wrong, Ma, isn't that what you taught us? You were wrong! I have to go live with Daddy because I don't know if I can ever forgive you much less face you again." Breeze wiped the tears from her face with the back of her hands. "I want to be who I am, and not what you want me to be."

India reached over and hugged Breeze close to her body. "Please, Breeze, don't do anything you'll be sorry for. Cool down, think about it," she whispered into Breeze's hair.

Breeze looked into India's mournful eyes, and realized how much would be left behind in the house she had been raised in, but when she glanced back at her mother, she knew what had to be done. Gently removing herself from India's embrace, Breeze whispered, "I'm calling Daddy and I'm going back with him."

"Chicago is so far away," Lillian said in a small voice. Breeze heard her mother, but still she made the call.

Rayna watched her sister hastily throw her clothes into suitcases, but Breeze ignored her tortured eyes, her pleading stare, and continued packing. Rayna grabbed Breeze by the shoulder. She wanted to tell her not to leave in the middle of the night and that they could work the problem out as a family, but her little sister looked at her with such intense emotions—the eyes of trust and innocence were replaced with hurt and sorrow—that Rayna was left speechless. Nothing she could say would dissuade Breeze from this decision, so instead she offered to drive Breeze to the hotel where Omar was staying.

After India silently carried the suitcases downstairs, she tightly hugged her bewildered sister. "I'll miss you, Breeze. It won't be the same around here without you," India whispered chokingly, tears rolling down both their faces.

Lillian stood silently at the top of the stairs and watched the daughter she cherished more than her life hug her adopted sister and walk out the door. She ran halfway down the stairs, but stopped short of pleading for Breeze to forgive her.

Breeze turned and even through her cloud of anger, she saw her mother's desperation portrayed in her tight features which now resembled a death mask. But Breeze's overwhelming devastation was stronger than her empathy, so she silently turned the knob to the front door.

"Please, baby girl?"

"No," Breeze whispered, and softly closed the door behind her.

Omar was waiting in the hotel lobby for Breeze when she arrived. He wondered what Lillian had done to upset Breeze, but assumed that it had something to do with Lex. He knew why Lillian didn't like Lex; he reminded her of him. Lillian had even tried to convince him to persuade Breeze to end her relationship with Lex, but Omar had flatly refused. "Let them live their own lives," he had told Lillian, knowing that he might as well be talking to the wind.

"Child, what's wrong?" Breeze fell into her father's arms, weeping. The pain on her face was raw: eyes of rage, mascara rimming her eyes like a raccoon, jaws clenched tight, and her mouth quivering like Jell-O. "Come on, let's get you upstairs."

In the hotel room, Breeze ranted and raved about her mother's betrayal. Omar listened patiently, amazed at the depth of his daughter's feelings. "She had no right, Daddy! She had no right!"

When Breeze was finished crying, she was beyond exhaustion, and fell immediately to sleep after Omar bundled her into bed.

The next morning, Lex rang Breeze's doorbell, hoping she answered the door. He was on his way to the airport, but he wanted to straighten things out between them. He rang the doorbell several times, but there was no answer. Lex was turning away when he heard the door open.

"Breeze is gone," Rayna softly said from behind the cracked door.

"What do you mean?" Lex asked.

"She found the letters, and had a big fight with Ma."

Suddenly the door swung open. "Get off my porch, Alexander Franklin!" Lillian shouted. "You made me lose my daughter. I curse you! I curse you!" She slammed the door so hard, the porch shook.

Stunned and confused, Lex was still standing on the porch when Rayna opened the door several minutes later. "She's at the hotel with our father," Rayna whispered.

"Thanks, Rayna," Lex said.

As Lex was leaving Breeze's house, she was on her way to Lex's house. Breeze pressed the doorbell, her mind whirling with questions that only Lex could answer.

Lex's mother answered the door and told a distraught Breeze that Lex was on his way to the airport.

"Breeze, are you all right?" Mrs. Franklin asked.

"Wait, Breeze. You look too upset to be walking around by yourself. I'll drive you back home," offered Mrs. Franklin. She had never seen Breeze with her hair hanging loosely on her shoulders. Her eyes were wild looking, and her clothes were a disheveled mess. This was not the young girl who had been in her house many times. This girl looked lost and abandoned, as if her world had collapsed.

Breeze turned away, but Mrs. Franklin stopped her. "I know it's hard, Breeze. Alexander loves you, child, really he does. But he's been wanting to be a musician for a long time—ever since he was a little boy. And now he has a big chance, so right now he needs to be free to live his dream. He's the guitar player for Stevie Wonder, and that's much more than he hoped for."

"What are you saying, Mrs. Franklin?" Breeze asked, trying to understand why her heart's desire was being denied.

"Sometimes it's hard to do two things that you love at the same time. Right now, it may be best for him to do what he's doing." As a couple of tears rolled down Breeze's cheek, Mrs. Franklin comforted, "He'll be back for you."

"I'm supposed to be in his life," Breeze protested. "We were going to pursue our dreams together, not apart!"

Gently, Mrs. Franklin said, "Honey, that may not be the best for both of you right now. I know my son loves you. And I love you like a daughter—I'm sorry it turned out this way. Just like it says in the marriage ceremony,

'What God has brought together, let no man put asunder.'
He'll be back for you."

"I'd better go," Breeze sighed lifelessly, not wanting to
hear anymore.

*Why doesn't anyone understand? Lex and I are supposed to
be together. You promised you would never leave me, Lex.*

*Why did you lie? Music means more to you than me? We
could have worked it out. Somehow, someway. If Ma hadn't
interfered. If you hadn't left…*

In a daze, Breeze walked the twenty blocks back to the
hotel. She went through the hotel's revolving door, and saw
Omar in the lobby, pacing the floor. He rushed over to her.
Puffing on a cigarette, he asked, "Where the devil have you
been?"

"I went to see Lex." Catching her breath in between
sobs, she said, "But he's gone."

"Darlin'," Omar said, "He was here." They moved
across the lobby to the lounge, and sat down on the sofa.

Lex had visited him, and they talked briefly. Omar
found himself in the most awkward position; he should
have been angry at Lex for causing his daughter such pain.
But he understood Lex's calling, it was the same calling that
he could not ignore.

"What did he say?"

"He was on his way to the airport, but he left you this
letter," Omar said, removing the letter from his jacket
pocket. He handed Breeze the letter knowing how hurt and
disappointed she was going to feel. He wished he could
shelter Breeze from the pain of love's despair. Omar prom-

ised himself that he would do everything in his power to ease her pain.

Sinking into the sofa, Breeze slowly opened the letter.

> Dear Sunshine,
> I hate to be the one to tell you, but I believe your mother has been destroying my letters. I suspected it when I was home that Christmas and I mentioned things that you didn't understand. I'm leaving this letter with your father, in hopes that you will receive it. I want you to know that I never stopped loving you. I can understand you being angry at me when you thought I stopped writing. I wish I could stay and spend the summer together like we did before—those were special times that I will never ever forget. I came home just to see you, but I've got to leave. I'm on tour for the rest of the summer.
> I came back to see if you would join me, but I realized yesterday that you wouldn't. Maybe this just isn't the right time for us to be together.
> Breeze, I love you with all my heart.
>
> Forever yours,
> Lex

CHAPTER FIVE

The Philadelphia church was packed with folks dressed in their Sunday best, but this was a Saturday, and they were waiting for a wedding ceremony to begin. It was scheduled to start at two o'clock, but at two-fifteen, the wedding's star attraction—the bride—had yet to make an appearance.

Downstairs, the wife-to-be was elegantly dressed in a beautiful, elaborately designed wedding gown. The gown was so richly detailed and uniquely designed, it could have been worn by a princess in a fairy tale. It was made of silk, satin, and lace, with thousands of tiny pearls hand-sewn along the bodice and bordering the hem. Any bride's eyes would have been wide with excitement to wear such an exquisite gown.

But Breeze's copper eyes were welled with tears. "You can't keep these people waiting forever," Lillian said impatiently. Walking away, she slammed the bathroom door and motioned for Omar to go inside. "Maybe you can talk some sense into her."

Wearing a peach silk dress cinched at the waist, Lillian maintained the beauty of her youth. Her smooth reddish-brown face was unlined, and the few pounds she'd gained over the years added depth to her small frame. Streaks of gray in her hair were the only sign of age.

Omar admired his ex-wife's firm body, giving her an appreciative smile. "You're looking lovely, Lillian."

Lillian loved the way Omar pronounced her name, Lil-li-an, properly, every syllable distinct. It made her feel special, like royalty, but she wouldn't dare let Omar know that the sound of her name in his mouth still moved her. "I bet you go around complimenting all the women."

"I don't find all women attractive." He gazed into her eyes, and said, "I was talking about you, Lillian. I've always found you attractive and I still do." A soft smile curled his lips with those last words.

"Me and how many other women?" Lillian protested, refusing to stare into the eyes that captured her heart so long ago.

"Why must you be so bitter? I was never the monster you made me out to be, and I'm not now." Omar was dressed in a white cut-away tuxedo, a peach bow tie under his collar and a corsage pinned on his lapel. His wavy black hair was slicked back, away from his receding hairline. His tall, broad frame towered over Lillian.

"Why is it that you can talk to Breeze, and she'll listen to you, but not me? I might as well be talking to…"

"You know why, Lillian. And that is probably why she is in there now crying her heart out. She's scared."

"Well, I still think it's for the best. Kyle comes from a prominent family; his father's an attorney. I think Kyle will make Breeze a fine husband. The kind of husband that will stay at home and take care of his family."

Eyes narrowed, Omar said, "I always took good care of you and the girls."

"From a distance. And that's not what family is about. I hope Breeze realizes that Kyle is the kind of man who will be there for her."

"But will she be happy, Lillian?"

Batting her eyes nervously, Lillian waved her hands in the air, dismissing the question. Glancing at the clock on the wall behind Omar, she said, "Jesus, it's two-thirty! Omar, please talk to Breeze. Tell her we have to get this wedding started!"

"I'll talk to her," Omar promised.

Lillian hated the fact that her meticulously coordinated plans for a perfect wedding were going awry. Breeze was being inconsiderate, she thought, and terribly rude to the two hundred people who were upstairs fanning themselves from June's insufferable heat. After all, she had only two months to plan the wedding, and was lucky to get the family church, the reception hall, the caterer, and the minister on such short notice. Lillian had handled the whole affair, except for the music and gown. Breeze's selection didn't match her tastes—the gown was too expensive and the music too contemporary—but she kept those opinions to herself. Everything seemed to run smoothly, as if the wedding was meant to be.

When Breeze announced that she was going to marry Kyle Patterson, Lillian was overwhelmed with relief: Breeze had finally gotten over Lex. For four years, Breeze never mentioned anyone and had never dated. Attracting men had not been a problem. Young men pursued her all the time, but when she wasn't in school, working, or studying, she spent time with Rayna and India or her friends from school.

"You just might like some of those men you turn away," Lillian had carefully suggested, even though the peace they made between them was as fragile as fine china.

Their relationship had never been the same after Breeze discovered the letters from Lex and had moved out of her mother's house to live with her father. Mother and daughter communicated from across a chasm as wide as the Pacific Ocean. It broke Lillian's heart that Breeze was so unforgiving. For six months, Breeze had even refused to speak to her. Lillian tried to communicate with her—sending her letters or calling her on the phone every day—but Breeze refused to meet her halfway. This side of Breeze's personality was an unwelcome revelation. Lillian never knew her sweet, sensitive child could be so stubborn and so entirely mean.

Lillian didn't see Breeze until India dragged her home for Christmas. India wanted things to be normal again; she had announced defiantly to a startled Lillian and a resigned Breeze that she wanted "us girls" together for the holidays. Disappointingly for Lillian, it was not a forgiving homecoming. It was a tense Christmas, the laughter and spontaneity, warmth and trust were like the ghost of Christmas past which haunted their holiday traditions.

Breeze's abrupt decision to go live with her father in Chicago hurt Lillian more than she thought possible. For two weeks Lillian was too sick to get out of bed. She didn't go to work. And she worried. She worried about Breeze morning, noon, and night. She worried that Breeze wouldn't go to college. She worried that Breeze would run off with a strange band to become a singer in a run-down, dangerous nightclub. But she was most worried about Breeze's state of mind. Lillian had watched a stranger walk out of her door. Dark emotions that she had never seen before swirled in Breeze's eyes.

How different are my children, Lillian thought. Angered, Rayna would have exploded, but after some time had passed, Rayna would have forgotten about the letters and the man. But Breeze had always been so sensitive and emotional. Forgiveness was possible, but it seemed memory would prevail.

Lillian felt deep remorse and guilt for causing Breeze so much pain. She prayed that Breeze would one day understand that a mother's intentions—to protect her daughter from pain—could be honorable, even though her actions were selfish. If she had had an inkling of the magnitude of Breeze's reaction, she never would have touched Lex's letters. It was the second biggest mistake of her life, because Lillian regretted hiding those letters as much as she regretted impulsively marrying Omar Blackwell.

At eighteen, living with her father on the Southside of Chicago, Breeze became reacquainted with her father's family. She traveled with Omar's band, singing in small clubs and hotels, and Oldies but Goodies revues. Breeze took lessons from an acclaimed pianist and discovered that she enjoyed the feel of the cool keys underneath her long fingers. She learned first hand from has-beens and wannabes what it took to make it in the music business. But the old timers' stories had taught her one thing: She wasn't ready for the cutthroat nature of the music business. Omar encouraged her to go to school, reasoning that with a scholarship from Howard University, Breeze had four years to decide what she wanted to do with her life.

As a student at Howard, she majored in pre-law and English literature, and learned with very little effort. After-school hours were filled with activities at various school clubs.

That is, until she met Kyle Patterson at the law library during her senior year. The mahogany-brown, lean young man blatantly stared at her. Breeze felt uncomfortable under the unrelenting gaze of the nerdy stranger sitting across the table from her, so she got up to leave. Nervously, Kyle jumped up to introduce himself, flashing a white smile while asking her out "to dinner or a movie or a walk in the park." She told him what she told every man who asked: "No."

The very next day, she saw him in the same section of the library. Again, he sat across from her and blatantly stared before asking her to attend a civil rights lecture with him. She declined.

For the rest of that week, Breeze avoided the library, but when she thought it was safe to go back in, Kyle was the first person she saw.

"You've been avoiding me," the second-year law student teasingly accused. Kyle was average height, thin, and behind the wire-rimmed round glasses was an attractive face. At first appearance, he looked like a boring intellectual. But over dinner, Breeze discovered that Kyle was charming, sensitive, intelligent, and funny.

He made her laugh, so she agreed to go out with him again. Soon they ended up spending a lot of time together and shared many common interests. They both enjoyed exploring the works of black artists, and spent a lot of time together perusing museums and art galleries, searching for works by unrecognized and well-known artists. It was a hobby they both relished, for both dreamed of owning a substantial black art collection.

Although Kyle made her laugh, his kisses didn't set her heart aflame. When they made love for the first time, Breeze felt the release of sexual tension, but without the sizzling sparkle of passion. He was the only man she had attempted to sleep with since Lex, and it didn't feel the same, no matter how much she tried to pretend that it did. Breeze discovered that there was a difference between the fiery flame of desire and the insipid heat of lonely need.

"How do you know if you're in love?" Breeze asked Rayna while visiting her sister in New York City. After graduating with a degree in acting from Carnegie Mellon University, Rayna moved to New York, determined to break into acting. She lived the waiting-to-be-discovered actor's life—auditioning, waiting for the phone to ring, and working as a waitress in between acting jobs. Rayna shared an apartment with India who was attending Columbia University.

"How the hell would I know? I've never been in love," Rayna said.

"Not with anybody?"

Rayna laughed harshly as she snubbed out her cigarette. "I've had a lot of men—more than I care to admit. I've never had an intense feeling for any of them. Basically, I think men are buzzards. All they want to do is screw you."

"Maybe that's because that's all you want from them," Breeze shrewdly replied.

Rayna looked intensely at her sister, thinking hard about her perceptive comment. "You may be right, Breeze. Maybe it's my way of protecting myself against men like Daddy. You withdraw while I flutter about like a screwed-up butterfly." Rayna stood up and moved into the narrow kitchen, just a few steps from the small combination living room and dining room, her armful of silver bangles jangling as she walked. "You know, Breeze, sometimes I wish Ma had never divorced Daddy."

Breeze's attention was jolted away from the game show on the television. "What! I can't believe you're saying that. You always acted like you didn't care one way or the other. But you missed Daddy, too."

"Yeah, I mean he was this bright light in our lives, and when he went away, the bright light turned dull like a forty-watt bulb," Rayna said.

"You know I hated that Ma divorced him. I always hoped and dreamed that they would get back together. When he spent the holidays with us, I would pray hard that he would never leave."

"Ma wouldn't allow it. She never let her guard down, not for one minute." Opening the refrigerator, she asked Breeze, "Want a beer?"

"Yeah," Breeze answered. "Sometimes I think she still cared. Some part of her did. According to Aunt Ruth, Ma was crazy about Daddy. I always wondered what happened to those feelings. Where did they go?"

"The music. The women."

"Do you really think Daddy was a womanizer? I never saw him that way," Breeze said, taking a bottle of beer from Rayna.

Cocking her head to the side, her expression was petulant. Harshly, Rayna said, "He was gone on the road too much, too long, Breeze."

"Maybe."

"You have blinders on when it comes to Daddy. You see what you want to see."

"Maybe you see more than you should," Breeze observed, sipping the beer.

"I just try to face reality. I don't sugarcoat it."

"Well, sometimes life looks better when you paint it a little…Is that why you don't trust men? Because of what happened with Ma and Daddy?"

"Maybe. And I haven't met anybody that I would be willing to let my guard down for. Nobody has just knocked me off my feet."

"Or maybe you stay away from the men who just might affect you like that."

"You know me pretty well, don't you, little Sis?"

"I think you put up a big tough front," Breeze said.

"Life is about pretending sometimes," Rayna leaned back against the sofa, resting her bare feet on the coffee table.

"Maybe that's what I'm doing, pretending with Kyle."

"Face it, Breeze…You're not going to have what you had with Lex. It's not going to be the same, so don't expect that kind of once-in-a-lifetime love again."

When Kyle asked Breeze to marry him, she said yes after agonizing over the decision for two weeks. She decided that she loved him, in a soft fuzzy way. It just wasn't the same degree of feeling. Her love for Lex was one hundred degrees of I-want-you, got-to-have-you love, but her feelings for Kyle were fifty-five degrees of I-need-to-be-loved love. It was a good feeling. It felt safe. Breeze concluded that the key to her happiness was the way Kyle felt about her.

Maybe one day, she had thought, *maybe my feelings will grow stronger.*

Years later, Breeze still felt betrayed by her mother and abandoned by her lover. She couldn't comprehend her twisted and contorted feelings. She couldn't clarify whether she was most devastated by her mother's actions or Lex's abandonment. It was incomprehensible what they both had done. As time went by, she resolved to hide the sorrow in the center of her heart, buried underneath all the good she had known, expected and wanted out of life. She didn't know how to release this bubble, which froze her deepest emotions, but she had to bury it to go on. Tragically, she buried it deep inside herself, so deeply nurtured that as the years went by, she couldn't find the strength to burst the fragile bubble in order to love Kyle.

At 2:45 PM on her wedding day, with tears flowing down her cheeks, Breeze told her fear to Omar that she was afraid her feelings for Kyle were not going to change.

"What if my feelings are lukewarm forever? I don't know if I can live with it and I don't think it's fair to Kyle."

Omar held his daughter in his arms. He dried trails of tears with the handkerchief that matched his white tuxedo. With his hands cupping her cheeks, he said, "Darlin', let go of what you had with Lex. Don't measure the rest of your life by two years. You have years of love and happiness to look forward to. Just don't look to the past for the answers to the future.

"Now, if you truly don't want to many this dude, I will go upstairs and take care of it. Don't worry about what your mother is going to say because if you really don't want to marry Kyle, then don't."

Omar paused, searching his daughter's eyes for an answer before continuing. "But, if you're going to get married, let's get upstairs before your mother has a heart attack. Baby girl, it's normal to have second thoughts—that's all a part of it." He stopped to peer into twin pools of turbulent confusion. "So what's it going to be?"

Breeze released a long sigh, and rested her head on her father's shoulders, squeezing her eyes shut. "Thank you, Daddy." She drew back the tears, pulling them inside to her secret place—a deep well in the center of her heart—and stood silently waiting for the well within to absorb the pain. When she felt as if she could say her vows without bursting into tears, she whispered, "I'm ready."

At three o'clock, beaming with pride, Omar Blackwell escorted his beautiful, trembling daughter down the aisle. Kyle's face was full of fear when he finally saw his bride. He had been so afraid that she had changed her mind.

Breeze and Kyle exchanged vows, both with fear in their hearts. He was afraid of her lukewarm love; she was afraid of the depth of his love. He knew that there was someone in her past, that there was a ghost in their relationship. They never mentioned it, but they both knew he was there, like a wisp of smoke, standing between them. But Kyle didn't care. His number-one goal to become Washington, D.C.'s attorney general came second to making the beautiful caramel-colored girl beside him happy. He wanted to erase the shadows from Breeze's eyes.

They smiled hesitantly at each other, washing away their fears. The minister pronounced them man and wife.

Arm in arm they walked down the aisle and took their designated spot to greet the well-wishers coming through the receiving line. Everyone was smiling, congratulating them on their marriage.

Suddenly Lex was standing before them, wishing them "the very best." Breeze was speechless. She felt like she was dreaming. Her mouth moved to say the right things, but she couldn't seem to put two words together to form a sentence. He was there, and then Lex was gone like a passing storm. Breeze felt Kyle watch her intensely. She had to force herself to come back to reality. She wasn't dreaming.

At the reception, Lex found her. Breeze knew he would. When she excused herself from the table to make her way to the bathroom, Lex was waiting at the door.

Knowing that he only had a moment to say what was on his mind, he spoke quickly. "I had to come. I had to say good-bye."

"You ruined my wedding!" Breeze cried.

"I didn't mean to. I just had to see for myself."

"See what, you selfish bastard?"

"I had to see you get married, and know without a doubt that you are out of my life. So I used the invitation you sent to my mother. You must have known she would tell me, Breeze. I care too much..." Lex reached forward to capture her hand.

"No," Breeze choked hoarsely, yanking her hand away. "Don't touch me...All you care about is what you want. All my mother cared about was what she wanted. No one seems to care what I want."

"Isn't this marriage what you wanted?" Lex asked, baffled.

"You're damn right it is. Besides, what I truly want can never be. Maybe it never was!" Breeze said, her voice quaking from the fragile bubble inside her heart.

Lex cleared his throat before choking out the inevitable question. "Do you love him?"

Breeze blinked back the tears which clouded her troubled brown eyes.

"Do you love him?" Reaching forward, he tilted Breeze's face toward his, forcing her to look up at him.

Breeze couldn't look into the eyes of the man who was the mirror of her soul and tell him that she loved another. Not when that love paled in comparison to her feelings for Lex, not when her love for Lex completely bore no resemblance to her feelings for Kyle. She couldn't lie, and yet, she could not tell him the truth.

Lex could read the answer in her face.

"What does it matter? Haven't you caused me enough pain?" Breeze murmured defensively.

"Seeing you get married," Lex interrupted, "I know now that it is really over. Our paths in life are far and wide apart from each other." He couldn't admit that he had chosen music over her, had let her go, and that he was paying a high price. Furiously, Breeze whispered between clenched teeth,

"How very philosophical. I hope 'our paths' never cross again, Alexander Franklin. Because if they do, it can only mean more heartache for me. So don't come back. Don't show up at the next important event in my life with any big revelations."

Breeze gathered up the fullness of her wedding gown and walked away, holding back the tears that threatened to fall.

Breeze's honeymoon in Hawaii was not what she expected. They were in paradise; the tropical trip was a wedding gift from Kyle's parents. But the confrontation with Lex weighed heavily on Breeze's mind. During the day, she tuned Lex out of her mind, but at night, thoughts of Lex would return. She didn't want to start their marriage off on the wrong foot so she pretended to enjoy Kyle's touch, sweetly succumbing to his urgent desires. But Kyle's tender caresses felt like snow gliding off leaves.

When they returned from their honeymoon, their relationship returned to the rhythm established prior to the wedding. Kyle had one more year of law school to complete, and having graduated with a bachelor's degree, Breeze worked for a judge part-time, still uncertain whether to pursue a law degree.

One hot evening, only three months wed, they were playing chess in their small one-bedroom apartment, fanning themselves from the suffocating heat. Kyle made a comment that startled Breeze.

"He was there...at the wedding," Kyle said, moving a bishop forward.

"Who?" Breeze asked distractedly, planning her next move to counter Kyle's aggressive strategy.

"The shadow. The man from your past who won't go away."

She looked at him and didn't know what to say.

Kyle understood more than Breeze realized. She tried to hide her misgivings, but Kyle saw through her camouflage. Sometimes when they made love, at the peak of their passion, Kyle felt that he had broken through her bubble and had freed her from the past. But in the morning light, the shadows in her eyes were still there, but it seemed, or so he hoped, that the shadow was slowly fading away.

Kyle was good to Breeze. His love for her was unselfish and undemanding, and she felt guilty that she wasn't able to return his feeling in the same way.

"It's rare for two people to love each other in the same way."

Breeze looked at him and saw the purest love shining in his face, not a bit of resentment or anger at her or the ghost. She resolved at that moment to accept the boundaries of their love.

Their marriage lasted eleven months and ended when Kyle was tragically killed by a white police officer who stopped Kyle for speeding. The policeman suspected that Kyle fit the description of a man who had robbed a bank earlier that day:black male, early twenties, slight build, 140 pounds, moustache, wearing jeans and a red T-shirt. The bank robber fled the scene in a black Chevy Camaro. Kyle was driving a black Chevy Camaro.

The white police officer claimed that Kyle had pulled a gun on him, but in the furious aftermath that followed, no gun was ever found. Kyle was merely reaching in the glove compartment for his wallet.

Kyle's father was a respected, influential attorney in Washington, D.C., and when the police officer maliciously killed his only son, Mr. Patterson, Sr., was determined to expose the insidious goings-on prevalent in the police force, to expunge bad cops, racist cops, crazy cops. They were guilty of abusing their authority and maligning the justice system. For many years, Mr Patterson had closed his eyes and ears to the cries of police brutality in the black community. He had political ambitions and didn't want to get involved in controversial issues that could jeopardize his future. But all that changed when he buried his son. Mr.

Patterson didn't care that he lost his appointment to judge because of his crusade against the police.

Instead, he became a spokesman and legal counsel for those unfairly subjected to police savagery. His wife, who was a social climber, tried to steer her husband away from his pain-inspired obsession, but her tearful pleas would not deter him from his newfound mission of justice for all.

The police officer who shot his son was suspended from the force, and was sentenced to jail for manslaughter—not murder—but that was not satisfactory to Mr. Patterson. He didn't want anyone to have to suffer from the bowels of racism, so he continued his crusade for an end to police brutality.

Mrs. Patterson couldn't face her losses, so she drank away the loss of her son and the loss of her social standing.

Breeze was overwhelmed with grief for the tragic loss of Kyle, and she was plagued with guilt that she was at fault for Kyle's untimely death.

If I hadn't married him, then he wouldn't have been there. It's my fault. I cheated him out of experiencing real love. If it weren't for me, he wouldn't be dead, Breeze thought.

The media coverage was unbearable: Every day there was a story about Kyle or his family's quest for justice. Lillian, Omar, Rayna, and India came to the funeral, their presence a balm to Breeze's weary spirit.

Omar held his daughter in his strong arms and consoled, "Keep moving, baby girl. Don't let the pain rest inside your soul. Don't be afraid of your dreams."

In her cloud of grief, she sensed that her father was telling her to become a singer. And somehow, she felt free to do it. Her inner voice was loud and clear: You want to sing, you want to sing. The morning after the funeral, she woke up feeling that Kyle was echoing her thoughts. She felt released, as if it was time to do what she was meant to do.

Two months after the funeral Breeze decided to move to New York to live with her sisters. Rayna and India were ecstatic that Breeze was coming to New York. Rayna was the lead actress in an off-Broadway play and India worked for an advertising agency during the day and attended graduate school at night.

Breeze decided that she was finally ready to pursue her music career. The uncertainty of life frightened her, yet gave her the impetus to pursue her dreams. She found the strength to deal with devastating disappointments of life—to bury the pain in her heart and keep on moving. She was now ready to face a music career.

CHAPTER SIX

It was strangely quiet. There was no throbbing music, no beating drums, no clanking piano, no twanging guitar, no blaring horn. Breeze wondered what had happened to the roaring applause and screaming fans. All she heard was the echo of high heels clicking on tile floors, the rustle of stiff polyester uniforms, and the whisper of white-stockinged legs brushing together.

As consciousness struck, confusion reigned in Breeze's mind.

Her nose was assaulted by a potpourri of scents. When Breeze opened her eyes, she thought she was in a garden. There were flowers everywhere: roses, daffodils, carnations, irises, jonquils, tulips, and lilies.

Breeze struggled to gain her bearings, looking around for a clue to explain where she was. When she saw the needle sticking out of her wrist with an IV bottle attached, she realized that she was in a hospital.

"It's about time you woke up," India said, lounging in chair beside the bed.

"I feel drugged," Breeze complained, her voice thick and garbled.

"You woke up for a few minutes when they first brought you up here, but they gave you something and you went out like that," India said, snapping her fingers.

"I feel like I've been sleeping for a week. What time is it?"

India looked at her diamond-encrusted Piaget watch. "It's three o'clock."

"In the afternoon?"

"Yes!"

"How long have I been sleeping? What happened to me?" Breeze asked groggily. She touched her forehead, the source of a dull, aching pain.

"You fainted on stage!"

"What?"

"You fainted from exhaustion, lack of sleep, not eating," India explained. "Your body couldn't take it anymore."

"I ruined the concert!"

"Breeze, you need to be worrying about your health." In an I-told-you-so tone, she added, "I've been trying to get you to slow down, but you never listen."

"Are they complaining?"

"Who? Your fans? Some are complaining, but most are concerned about you. Look at these flowers," India exclaimed, her hands sweeping the room. "This is only a fraction of what's arrived."

"I feel like I cheated them," Breeze moaned.

"Girl, get real. You fainted on your last song. They got their money's worth. Besides, your fans are very forgiving." Teasingly, she added, "They love you, they adore you, they…"

Breeze weakly laughed, "Stop." After a long sigh, she asked, "How long do I have to be in here?"

"Two days. They want to run some more tests on you."

"What kind of tests?" Breeze questioned, a bit worried.

"You'll have to ask your doctor."

Breeze attempted to sit up, but couldn't. She searched around for the button that raised and lowered the bed, but her movement was constrained by the IV attached to her arm.

She rubbed her wrist where the needle was inserted in a vein. "Damn, this thing hurts. What is this for anyway?"

"The doctor said you were dehydrated. They want to put fluids in you, and the IV is the fastest way to do it." India helped Breeze adjust the bed to a sitting position.

"Is that all?" Breeze asked suspiciously.

"That's what he told me."

"I want to talk to this doctor." Breeze fumbled around for the nurse call button. A few seconds after pressing the button, she heard a pleasant voice say, "I'll be right there."

Breeze was squirming around in the narrow hospital bed trying to get comfortable when a middle-aged black woman, short and stocky, came into the room. She had the air of a no-nonsense nurse underneath a friendly bedside manner.

Flashing an array of gleaming white teeth, the nurse smiled warmly, "Hey, Miss Blackwell. It's good to see you awake." The nurse adjusted the bed and fluffed the pillows. "That should be better. Are you comfortable?" she asked in a strong southern accent.

"Yes, ma'am. But I'd like to see the doctor. Is he here?"

"Dr. Fowler just left. He won't be back until later this evening. You need me to page him for you?"

"Yes. I want to know why I've got to be here for two more days." Gently raising her arm, Breeze continued, "And why do I have an IV?"

"Sugga, there's nothing to wormy about. The doctor just wants to keep you for observation to make sure you're okay. The IV is to get some nourishment in you. You're just so thin." The nurse shook her head back and forth, sucking in her lips. "Too thin if you ask me."

"I still want to talk to him. So would you please page him?"

"I certainly will. Now, is there anything else I can do for you?"

"I'm starving," Breeze said.

"I'll have some food sent up right away. What would you like?"

"A salad."

"If you want to get out of here, Miss, you're gonna have to get some food. A salad won't do much. If it were up to me, I'd bring you some of my greens, fried chicken, and candied yams. But I'm not allowed to feed the patients. I'll order a regular tray for you. I think they're serving spaghetti."

"That sounds good. But the fried chicken and greens sound even better. We've been on the road eating nothing but hotel and restaurant food. I could go for a good home-cooked meal."

"Me too," India said.

"I'll tell you what," the nurse said, hands resting on her broad hips, and head tilted to the side, "I'll fix you some chicken, greens, macaroni and cheese, yams, and corn-bread, but I'll bring it tomorrow. You should be feeling better by then."

"Okay, thanks a lot," Breeze said.

"I'll give it to your friend here, so nobody will know what we're doin'."

"I know it will be good," India said.

"I can cook now, that's for sure. But it'll take about thir-ty minutes for your food to get here, so I'll just bring you some juice," the nurse promised before leaving.

The nurse returned with apple juice, and placed it on the moveable tray in front of Breeze.

"Thank you, Mrs. Poole," Breeze said, reading her name tag.

"You're welcome, Sugga. Mind if I ask for your auto-graph for my son?"

"Not at all."

Mrs. Poole handed Breeze a sheet of paper. "What's his name?"

"Shadarious Poole."

"How do you spell it?"

Mrs. Poole called out the letters.

Breeze wrote, "To Shadarious: Wish you the very best. Stay in school."

Mrs. Poole took the autographed paper, carefully folded it, and put it in her breast pocket. "Thank you, Miss Blackwell. You sure have got a soulful voice."

For the first time since waking up, Breeze surveyed the room that did not look like a hospital room. She was in a private wing of Northside Hospital, in a suite that was as plush as the penthouse suite of the Ritz-Carlton Hotel. There was a wall unit with a large TV and VCR, a collection of video tapes, and a stereo system.

"I just better get well in all this luxury," Breeze remarked.

"Mother's on the cruise, so she probably doesn't know about this. Do you want me to call her?"

Shaking her head, a crease in her brow, Breeze said, "No, don't spoil her fun. I'm not that sick."

"Rayna can't come see you because of the play, but she's going to call around four," India said.

"Is she getting good reviews?" Breeze asked, knowing that the play might be the turning point in her acting career.

"Very good reviews. She's so excited, you can hear her heart beating over the phone," India said, chuckling.

"I'm happy for her. Rayna's been waiting for this for a long time," Breeze said. "I wish I could be there."

India opened her briefcase and searched inside for a folder. "I brought copies of reviews on Rayna's play, and there's an article about the concert last night."

"How bad is it?"

"Not bad. The critics were very sensitive," India said, handing Breeze the folder.

Breeze quickly scanned the reviews on Rayna's performance. She knew how much acting meant to Rayna. It was all she talked about after their parents had taken them to see *A Raisin in the Sun* when they were little girls, and through the years Rayna imitated every female actress that she admired, from Marilyn Monroe to Dorothy Dandridge.

"Remember how Rayna liked to do Mae West all the time? Ma would lose her patience when she'd try to talk to Rayna. You'd end up talking to Mae West or whomever she was imitating for the whole day," Breeze said.

India smiled, recalling Rayna's antics. "Mother said that she was obsessed."

Still laughing, Breeze added, "By the time Mother gave up fighting with Rayna and accepted that Rayna didn't want to be a doctor, I started with the singing. When she couldn't think of anything to say it was, 'That Blackwell blood is gonna be the end of me.' Uhm…she probably still curses my father to this day."

"Speaking of your father, he's flying in this evening to see you," India informed.

Genuine surprise reflected in Breeze's copper eyes. "He is? I thought he was in Europe."

"He said that his tour ended…"

Interrupting her, Breeze exclaimed, "India, what's that on your finger? You got engaged to Zeke and didn't tell me?"

"You've been asleep for twenty-four hours!" responded India, waving her engagement ring in Breeze's face. "I was wondering when you were going to notice."

"When did Zeke propose? I'm assuming it's Zeke." Ribbing her sister, Breeze teased, "Although you may have somebody I don't know about."

"Breeze, you know good and well it's Zeke. He proposed right before the concert," India beamed. Love danced on her face like glittering gold dust. The glow of love illuminated her island-girl beauty and twinkled in her midnight eyes.

"I knew when you met him, he was the one. You're both from the islands," Breeze said.

"Yes, he's from Jamaica, but he knows his family," India said ruefully. "Maybe it's my way of connecting with the past."

"It still bothers you, not knowing about your mother?" Breeze asked.

India nodded. "It still does. I'll try to find her one day. When I'm ready."

"So, when's the wedding?"

"Girl, we haven't figured that out yet," India said, looking at her left hand, proud of the two-carat pear-shaped diamond gleaming at her.

"You've got to have a huge wedding, India, wearing a gorgeous gown with an awesome train. I mean the works!"

"Who knows? We might elope," she teased, running her hands through her wavy black tresses.

"Not without me and Rayna," Breeze joked.

They laughed heartily.

"Zeke would kill us. He already thinks the three of us are crazy. He still calls us the three stooges."

India stood up and gathered her purse and briefcase. "I've got to get back to the hotel. I've been trying to get in touch with Keisha to cancel the auditions for the video."

"That's not until next week. I'll be out of here by then," Breeze protested.

"Look, Breeze, you have to get your rest. And you're not going to get better by working."

"I won't dance or move around. I'll just observe."

"Right," India said sarcastically. "You won't sit still for two minutes."

"Change it to Friday." Breeze opened her eyes wide and smiled beguilingly. "That will give me some time to rest."

Rolling her eyes heavenward, India said, "Sometimes you're a pain in the ass, Breeze." She paused at the door, "I'll see what I can do. Remember that Omar will be here about eight."

As Omar Blackwell eased through the door to Breeze's hospital room, she was so engrossed in the Lana Turner movie, *Imitation of Life,* that she didn't hear her father come in. Tears streamed down her face as she watched the final scene where the character Sarah Jane arrives at the funeral of the black mother whom she has denied all of her life. Sarah Jane opens the door as the hearse is preparing to leave and cries, "She was my mother! She was my mother!"

"Here's your father!" Omar chuckled. "Here's your father!"

"Oh, Daddy," Breeze cried between sniffles. "I didn't hear you come in."

Father and daughter warmly hugged as Omar planted a kiss on Breeze's forehead. Peering closely at her, he asked, "Darlin', how are you?" He cupped his hand under her chin.

She smiled reassuringly, "I'm just fine. The doctors say I'm going to be all right. I just have to take better care of myself."

"Will you listen to your doctors since you won't listen to your family?"

"Yes," Breeze sheepishly answered.

"If you had a husband, I betcha you'd take better care of yourself. Look at you: all skin and bones."

"The way they're feeding me, I'm going to be fat."

"You need to be eating!" Omar scolded. He took a seat in the chair beside the bed. He removed his hat, revealing a slightly balding head, and sat it on his lap. Omar was now in his late forties, large-framed, broad-shouldered with cheeks round and full from years of blowing on his saxophone.

"How 'bout a boyfriend? The tabloids claim you and Michael Jackson have been dating."

"Daddy, I can't believe you read those things. You know I don't know him that well. Besides, Michael is rather eccentric."

"That Mitch Davidson wasn't 'eccentric,' to use your word, and you let him get away."

"I didn't like him!" Breeze exclaimed defensively, her arms flailing in the air.

"He got bucks!"

"So do I," Breeze shot back.

"I keep forgetting my baby girl is rich, rich, rich."

'Well, anyway, Mitch may be a millionaire, but we just didn't click. And what about you, Daddy?"

"What do you mean?"

"Why haven't you married in all these years?"

"Once was enough. Besides, I'm married to my music."

"What about a special lady?"

"I haven't felt that way for a woman in a very long time. I mean a long time."

After lecturing Breeze about her love life, Omar filled her in on his European tour. He was proud to report that the Europeans remembered him. He was given the "star treatment" that he never received in the United States.

"They appreciate good jazz in Europe," Omar bragged. "Even the kids. Darlin', it's strange to look out on a sea of white faces who think that you're the greatest." Chuckling heartily, he said, "But then I am the greatest. Yup, I had a grand old time in Europe."

Breeze smiled to herself as she was flooded with childhood memories of the years Omar came home from his gigs. Excited and animated no matter the hour, he would always have a story to tell, each one better, more interesting, and funnier than the other.

Breeze remembered staying awake, waiting to hear her father's footsteps at the door. She would pretend to be asleep when Lillian came in to check on them, but as soon as Lillian turned off the lights and closed the door, Breeze's eyes would stare into the darkness, listening acutely for any sign of her father's imminent return.

"Rayna! Rayna!" she would whisper across the room.

But Rayna was usually fast asleep. By the time she was eight Rayna had given up on her father's nighttime visits. Rayna wanted to see her father just as much as Breeze did, maybe more so, but spared herself the feeling of abandonment when Omar didn't come. Rayna decided that it wasn't worth waiting up, staring into the darkness, imagining crazy things about the bizarre people on the curtains that might come alive in the darkness when no one was looking, or the noises she heard in the closet and under the bed. But Rayna would awaken as soon as Omar entered the room.

If the sudden lights didn't wake Rayna, Omar's presence did. The smell of Omar—the strong, stale musky odor of cigarettes and the sometimes sickening smell of alcohol on his breath—would permeate the room.

Breeze never had to be awakened. As soon as she heard Omar's jangling keys twisting in the front door lock, she jumped out of the bed and peeked out the bedroom door. When she spotted Omar coming down the long hall towards her room, Breeze would quickly close the door and jump into bed. Breeze's heart would pound in her chest, her eyes twitching as she forced them to remain closed.

Standing over her bed, Omar would say, "I saw you, Breeze. I saw you peeking out the door."

"Oh, Daddy," she would giggle, wrapping her little arms around his chest and breathing in all that stale smoke with joy.

It had been a long time since she saw that on-top-of-this-world glow on her father's face. When Omar had stopped performing after his heart attack five years ago, it seemed like something inside of him had died. But now, he was alive and vibrant, reunited once more with his music.

She interrupted Omar in the middle of a colorful, spiced-up story. "Daddy, why don't you play on my next album?"

"What?" He looked thoughtfully into his daughter's matching copper eyes, the color he had inherited from his grandmother and passed on to Breeze. She had inherited many things from his family—her soft brown coloring, her musical aptitude, and her gentleness of spirit, so much like his mother who was one-quarter American Indian.

"My next album is going to take a walk on the jazz side. I want to do classic songs like Billie Holiday's 'Strange Fruit' and Sarah Vaughn's 'Misty,' and 'Black Coffee.' "

"Now you're cooking!" Omar laughed.

"Who better to play the sax than you?" Breeze insisted.

"Now you're cooking with grease!" Omar exclaimed, slapping his knee.

CHAPTER SEVEN

Edmund Mitchelson walked quickly down the hall to Breeze's hospital room. It was very early, the time of day when the sun yawns and stretches as it prepares to come out of hiding. Edmund was an extremely busy man, every second in his life had to count.

Edmund was fully awake and alert, but the hospital was still on the night shift: The hallways were empty, nurses' station lightly manned, and patients were still in their drug-induced state of sleep. Any minute the atmosphere would change with the arrival of the first shift. The hospital would come alive, bustling with action: orderlies wheeling patients down the halls, nurses prepping for surgery, food servers bringing breakfast, and nurses administering patients' medicine.

Edmund wanted to see Breeze before the pandemonium began.

Noiselessly, he entered the room. He was instantly struck by Breeze's beauty, illuminated by rays of the morning sun peeking through the blinds. Breeze was all shades of brown: caramel skin, copper-brown eyes, and chestnut-colored hair. Her skin looked so irresistibly soft and smooth, he had to restrain himself from touching her cheeks.

He stood there and watched her for five minutes, amazed at how delectable she looked, struck by emotions he hadn't felt in a long time. Emotions not experienced since falling in love with his first wife at the age of twenty-four. Everyone had accused him of marrying Lorna Gordon for her money and her father's connections in the music business. Ironically, he had truly loved her, but success, jealousy, affairs, and rumors claimed their love. He left Lorna after four years of marriage and established Harmony Records, Incorporated, to prove himself to the industry.

Perhaps, he thought, *the whispers are true: Am I in love with Breeze?* He had heard the chorus of speculators, summarily dismissing them as gossipmongers. Besides, he was wary of singers. His second wife had been a singer who only loved what he could do for her career, and consequently had left him for another man. It was an episode in his life that he did not want to repeat, an experience that left him resistant to relationships. Edmund steeled his heart against women and maintained a reputation as a ladies' man. No one meant very much to him. Until Breeze. He could remember their first meeting as if it were yesterday…

Edmund knew that Breeze was extraordinarily talented from the moment he laid eyes on her. She had been singing in an off-Broadway musical, *Your Arms Are Too Short To Box With God.* She had pure, undeniable, singing power.

Unbeknownst to Edmund, Breeze was not the regular performer, but the temporary understudy. The director and cast were in a frenzy trying to find a replacement for their laryngitis-stricken understudy when Rayna convinced them to recruit her sister. "She can really sing. I mean really sing," Rayna bragged.

Playing the lead role, made famous by Patti Labelle, meant that Breeze sang a variety of vocally-challenging songs. If theaudience's jubilant response was an indictor, she had indeed met the challenge of the role.

Edmund was astonished when he heard this young woman sing. *I've got to meet her,* he thought. *With those golden lungs, I've got to sign her. She could break sales records with that voice.* A sweet, sleek soprano voice, she hit high notes, holding them so long the audience found themselves subconsciously breathing for her. She sang with thunder in her voice, and Edmund was fascinated, his eyes solely on Breeze for the entire show.

Afterwards, Edmund went backstage to meet the gifted performer. The heavy stage makeup did not hide Breeze's effervescent beauty. Handing Breeze the playbill, Edmund asked for an autograph. A first for Breeze, she scrawled her name with elation and I-can't-believe-this-is-happening-to-me euphoria.

"Now will you sign a contract?" Edmund had asked, his eyes intense, his tone direct.

A New-Yorkized Breeze glanced up in a sidelong fashion to ask, "What's your game?"

Breeze had been the victim of three scams, and now treaded the quest-for-stardom waters carefully, wary of false promises, name-dropping, and get-over, screw-you schemes.

Edmund introduced himself, and although Breeze immediately recognized the name, she didn't believe he was who he claimed to be.

Eyes narrowed suspiciously, she questioned, "How do I know you're who you say you are?" noticing the expensive cut of his suit, possibly custom-tailored.

Breeze had seen pictures of Edmund Mitchelson, but she wasn't sure whether this fortyish, ebony-skinned, ruggedly attractive, gangsterly-dressed man was the president of Harmony Records. There was an air of confidence in his commanding presence and power in his dark, penetrating eyes that suggested he was for real.

Edmund reached inside the left pocket of his suit jacket and handed her his business card.

Still skeptical, she asked, "Mr. Mitchelson, just what kind of contract are you talking about?"

"A recording contract for an album. You've got an incredible voice. Jazz, gospel, and soul all rolled together. I haven't heard such vocal range and styling in a long time."

"And you're going to make me a star," Breeze cynically remarked.

"Your voice is going to make you a star," bantered Edmund bemusedly, enjoying her skepticism.

With both hands on her hips, she leaned back and spoke bluntly. "Do you know how many people say that bullshit?" Breeze was about to walk away when the director, who happened to be an old friend of Edmund's, walked by. Vincent shook hands with Edmund and exchanged conversation about the show, their lives and mutual friends. Breeze listened with her heart pounding in her ears.

"He really is Edmund Mitchelson of Harmony Records?" she asked Vincent, restraining herself from jumping and hugging the world.

"I've been knowing this cat for a long time. We go way back." Vincent slapped Edmund on the back. "Got to go, man. Tell your friends about the show. It's hot every night."

"Now, can I get you to consider a contract?" asked Edmund, smugly smiling.

Breeze gave him a coquettish smile. "How about lunch tomorrow?"

Edmund stepped back and stared at this bold woman. Most wannabe stars would leap at the chance to sign their name on the dotted line. He had been followed and harassed by so many women with stars in their eyes that Breeze's cool response was intriguing.

"Name the time and place."

Grinning wickedly, Breeze said, "Le Cirque. I've always wanted to eat there."

Touching her shoulder, Edmund predicted, "Breeze, tomorrow will be the first of many dreams to come true for you."

It didn't matter to Breeze that it snowed, hailed, sleeted, and rained on the day of the meeting with Edmund. She was going to get there no matter what the weather conditions; she was on the road to her future.

With Rayna and India in tow for moral support, Breeze arrived ten minutes early for her luncheon meeting. After she introduced Edmund to her sisters, they exchanged conversation about the latest trends in the music industry. Rap was on the rise, and video was the best way to promote a song and an artist. India and Rayna couldn't help noticing the rich and famous who were eating lunch and conducting business at the tables around them. Breeze wished she had a camera to take pictures of dining in such a celebrity-filled restaurant. But this moment would go into her permanent memory bank.

After lunch, Edmund pulled out the record contract, and he talked about his plans for launching Breeze into stardom. Breeze listened silently, taking in every word, hypnotized. Edmund was going to hire top producers and find the best material to showcase Breeze's voice. The young women were in awe. They knew Edmund had the power and clout to do everything he promised. Breeze felt deep in her heart that this man meant everything he said. After two years of trying to break into the business, it was about to happen—she was on the brink of realizing her career ambition.

Breeze read the contract carefully. There were many things that she did not understand, but the basics—royalty percentages, advances, promotions—were pretty clear. She passed the papers over to India and Rayna for a quick review before signing them.

"Don't you want to have a lawyer look that over?" Edmund asked.

Pinning him with an assessing gaze, Breeze replied, "My instinct tells me that I can trust you."

From that day on, Edmund Mitchelson became more than just a nameless face in the audience. He became an integral part of Breeze's life. With the magical power of a genie, Edmund changed her life forever. A few weeks later,

Breeze moved out of the apartment she shared with her sisters into a luxury apartment paid for by Harmony Records, Incorporated.

Breeze worked with song writers and musicians and helped produce her debut album in six months. She co-produced two songs on the album from some of her own material. The first single released, "I Believe in Love," her own composition, bolted up the charts like a nuclear missile.

It was true that Edmund Mitchelson discovered Breeze and masterminded her phenomenal success. He was involved in all aspects of making Breeze a star, from contracting the hottest producers and selecting the songs to approving the album cover. Harmony insiders found Edmund's detailed involvement odd. His staff usually handled the production and management of artists.

Edmund was the mastermind, but it was Breeze's ingenious marketing suggestion that made her success a feat for the *Guinness Book of World Records:* Her debut album was released without a picture or name. It was simply entitled, *Introducing B.B.* The debut song, "I Believe in Love," was hauntingly beautiful, her resonant voice deep and stirring:

Some people say that love isn't real
Jaded and hurt by the disappointment they feel
When love unravels and hurls you into a pit of despair
You convince yourself that you don't care

Can't see it, can't touch it, don't want it,
So love isn't real

But love is life's deepest riches
Full of treasures beyond your fondest wishes
Worth more than rubies, diamonds, and pearls
Love brings happiness to the world

I believe, I believe in love
I can feel it, I can breath it, I want it
Love is life, life is love. Love is.

Some people say love is an illusion
The cause of all confusion
It can twist your mind and tumble your emotions
Like the wind and the waves of a stormy ocean

Can't see it, can't touch it, don't want it,
So love isn't real

But love is the reason we exist
The power of love too strong to resist
So don't fight what was meant to be
Because love controls your destiny

I believe, I believe in love
I can feel it, I can breath it, I want it
I believe in love 'cause it's real
Love is life, life is love. Love is.

It was the mystery of her identity that had the public's attention and the media buzzing.

No one at Harmony Records believed that releasing an album without a picture of the artist would work. They predicted that the album would bomb, no matter how good the material, or how much they influenced radio stations to play it. They were all surprised that Edmund went along with Breeze's ridiculous suggestion.

Little did anyone realize that this marketing ingenuity was the recipe for megasuccess. The tabloids went wild with stories centered on B.B.'s real identity. Television and radio stations even conducted opinion polls and special contests to find the mystery "face behind the voice."

There were jokes about B.B., there were B.B. sightings, and countless women who claimed to be "the real B.B."

Fans wondered: What did the initials B.B. stand for? And, is B.B. a black or white singer?

It wasn't merely the mystery of B.B.'s true identity that caused the single to claim the number-one spot for weeks and sell two million copies. The quality of her songs, style of music, and her powerful voice overwhelmed the music industry used to slickly-marketed, media-packaged, studio-dubbed singers.

The first time Breeze heard her song, "I Believe in Love," played on the radio she was shopping in Bloomingdale's. She wanted to tell the world, "It's me! It's me! I'm singing on the radio!"

The first two singles from the *Introducing B.B.* album raced up *Billboard's* Rhythm & Blues and Pop charts as if they were on the way to an emergency. The public, inflamed by the media's daily speculation, demanded to know the face behind the voice. Harmony Records was afraid the public would turn against Breeze if she waited too long to reveal herself, and so a press conference was called to introduce Breeze.

Edmund Mitchelson and Jillian Bayer, vice president of marketing at Harmony Records, stood before the media. Edmund said, "Ladies and gentlemen, we thank you for coming. The last few months have been exciting and completely unexpected for Harmony Records. Not too long ago, I discovered a singer performing in an off-Broadway show. After the show, I went backstage and offered her a contract."

Smiling broadly and proudly, Edmund continued, "The rest is a glorious success story. I would now like to present B.B. Miss Breeze Blackwell!"

Out walked four women identically dressed in dark sunglasses, hooded scarves, and black spaghetti-strapped skintight dresses. They walked up to the four strategically placed microphones and began to harmonize the lyrics of "I Believe in Love." The media went wild, shouting "Which one? Which one?" in frustration.

The four singers harmonized the second verse until one by one, they trailed off, leaving Breeze's distinctive voice solo. Breeze stepped in front, took off her dark sunglasses and scarf, and introduced herself. "Hello, everybody. I'm Breeze Blackwell." Her radiant smile and friendly manner immediately endeared her to the press.

Breeze's picture and comments at the press conference appeared in every major newspaper across the country. No longer the mystery singer, Breeze became the most photographed celebrity for the next few months. She was on the cover of every major magazine, *People, Ebony, Essence, Rolling Stone, Jet,* the list was endless. She was famous, a singing sensation, an international star. She went from being unknown to well known. She was fully exposed.

While gazing down at Breeze sleeping in her hospital bed, Edmund realized that it had taken almost three years for him to admit that his interest in Breeze was far more than business.

When Breeze opened her luminous copper eyes, Edmund knew the rumors were true. He decided that he was going to do everything in his power to make the woman he had turned into a superstar his. He smiled at her warmly.

In due time, he thought, *you will be my woman. Mine.*

"Good morning, Breeze. It's Edmund."

Breeze rubbed her eyes with her fingers, unsure of what she was seeing. "I was dreaming, but there was so much light, it didn't seem like a dream."

"I'm real, baby."

"Hi, Edmund," Breeze said with a sleepy smile.

Edmund bent over and planted a kiss on Breeze's cheek. "How's my star doing today?"

"I'm fine…I can't believe you came all this way to see me."

"I had to make sure you were okay. India told me you were all right, but I had to see for myself."

"Do I pass the test?"

"Yeah, you'll pass."

India entered Breeze's room with a bouquet of wild orchids. Breeze looked up from the book she was reading, and smiled, "Lex."

"Who else sends these strange flowers?"

Breeze admired the colorful array of orchids, feeling a surge of emotion from deep inside, and retrieved the card. It read, "Breeze, hope that soon you can lie on the beach, run in the grass, and walk in the rain." It was simply signed, "Lex."

Breeze quietly placed the flowers on the nightstand.

"Edmund has been here. I can smell his cologne," observed India.

"Look what he gave me!" Breeze showed India a diamond-studded pin in the shape of a musical note.

"It's beautiful!" India admired the custom-designed piece. "You better let me take it with me so it won't get stolen."

"I can't believe that he bought it for me."

"Breeze, I told you that man likes you. You can say that he's just concerned about his investment, but I tell you, Edmund has more on his mind than business when he's looking at you."

Breeze shook her head. "Now you sound like Ma."

India sat back in the lounging chair. "Do you remember that night in New York when you first came home to tell me about Edmund? I was still in graduate school, and Rayna was starting to get parts."

Memories of the past filled her head and lit up Breeze's face. "Mother was worried to death that I would actually get a break. She was still hoping that I would give up and go on to law school." Breeze smiled, her eyes trance-like, lost in the past. "I remember that night. It was the night before the magic began."

Breeze and Rayna had bounced into India's bedroom, waking her from a deep sleep with a sudden flood of lights and their boisterous screams: "Breeze is going to be a star. She's got a record deal!" Rayna announced.

"I'm going to be a real singer," Breeze said headily. "It's finally going to happen!" she sang, before flopping on the end of India's bed.

Sleepily, India groaned, "What are you all talking about?" She had been in the middle of a dream, a dream that she wanted to continue. She sat up slowly, wiping sleep from her eyes, and pulled the blankets up to her neck.

"Breeze is going to sign a recording contract tomorrow. She could have tonight, but she wanted to wait until tomorrow. Why? I don't know, except that she's crazy, if you ask me."

Sliding back under the covers, India cried, "You woke me up for that?" She pulled the blankets over her head.

"This ain't no joke, India, we're serious," Rayna protested. "Very serious."

"As serious as Grandma's sweet potato pie." Breeze tugged on the blanket. "I met Edmund Mitchelson. He came by to see me after the show," Breeze boasted.

Underneath the blankets, India muffled, "The Edmund Mitchelson? From Harmony Records?"

"That's the one!" Rayna said.

India threw the blankets off her head and started screaming, "Oh yeah! Oh yeah!"

"When he told me who he was I didn't believe him. I was kind of rude at first," Breeze explained. "But when Vincent knew who he was, I was dumbfounded. I felt like a fool, but I just knew he was a phony. I was going to ask him to show me his driver's license…"

"Breeze, you didn't?!" Fully awake, India's eyes were wide in surprise.

"If Vincent hadn't come by, I would have made an ass of myself."

"OOOh," shrieked India "You met Edmund Mitchelson!"

"Yeah, girl, and he wants me to meet him for lunch tomorrow at Le Cirque."

"Ohhh!" cried India "Le Cirque! Maybe you'll see Diana Ross or Billy Dee Williams."

"Breeze picked the place."

"Go 'head, Breeze!" winked India.

"Tomorrow I meet my dreams," Breeze said excitedly. "And I want you guys to come!"

"Le Cirque? There's no way I'd refuse," remarked Rayna. "I'll just be a little late for rehearsal."

"I'm supposed to meet with Professor Wilson tomorrow," India said, "but I'll reschedule. There's no way I'm not going to Le Cirque!"

"Girls! We got to celebrate!" Rayna pronounced.

"Yes!" Breeze said, waving her arms in the air.

"Asti Spumanti," they screamed, "here we come!"

Breeze, Rayna, and India stayed up until three in the morning, talking, laughing, drinking the bubbly, and dreaming aloud. They drank two bottles of Asti, toasting to their envisioned success.

"I'm going to start my own advertising agency," claimed India

"I'm going to be the first black woman to win an Oscar for best actress," Rayna predicted.

"And I'm going to be a great singer. My name will be remembered alongside Billie Holiday, Sarah Vaughn, and Ella Fitzgerald," Breeze said.

They fell asleep with visions of the future burning brightly in their minds.

"We used to be so silly back then," Breeze recalled, chuckling.

"Those were some fun times," India said. "Back to the present—did Edmund tell you he wants Lex to produce a song on your next album?"

"No!" Breeze said, her thick eyebrows crinkled together. "He didn't mention it."

"Lex's songs are hot. His hits are getting bigger and bigger."

"I always knew he would make it. He had that 'got to make it' look in his eyes when we were kids. It's so wild—he was the first to tell me that I could sing. And now, after all these years, we may finally get to work together."

Breeze looked over at the orchids, a twinge of sadness tracing the edge of her smile.

India knew Breeze was thinking about her lost love. "I wonder if Lex thinks about you as much as you think about him."

"Maybe it's just wishful thinking, but I think he does."

"And you're never going to find out?"

"What am I supposed to do? Call him up and say, do you still think about me? Do you wonder what could have happened between us? I've got too much pride to do that, India, so I'll just keep my crazy thoughts to myself."

"How will you ever know?"

"That's the hard part. After all these years, I can't imagine him calling and saying, 'Let's finish what we started when we were teenagers.' " Breeze pulled her knees up to her chest. "Somehow I don't think so."

"But that's what you're waiting on," India said.

"No, the right man just hasn't come along," Breeze responded defensively, her eyeballs enlarged in righteous indignation.

"Edmund is crazy about you," India exclaimed.

"He's crazy about the money I make him."

"Girl, don't fool yourself."

"Even if you are right, I don't feel the same way about him," Breeze said. She was quiet a moment before she remorsefully said, "Remember what happened before, when I married Kyle?"

"Breeze, stop blaming yourself for what happened!" India gently scolded. "That cop killed Kyle, not you. A trigger-happy, racist cop."

"I know. But, I shouldn't have married him. Maybe he wouldn't have been there!" Breeze poured water from a small plastic pitcher into a glass. "He loved me more than I loved him. After all these years, I don't know if I ever loved him. I just thought I did."

"You're going to have to chance it again. I mean, I love Zeke and he loves me, but I don't know who loves who more. We just love each other."

"You know what I mean," Breeze continued. "I have a hard time falling in love, and I think it's because Lex and I just stopped. There was no ending. There was no conclusion to our relationship. Somehow it's blocked other loves from coming into my life."

"Don't waste your life waiting for Lex to come back into your life," India advised, affectionately patting her sister's arm.

CHAPTER EIGHT

Breeze woke up at six AM. with a burst of energy. She was tired of lying around in bed watching television and reading books and magazines. Five days of following the doctor's orders of complete bed rest was making her restless. It was time to get back to living her life.

She hopped out of bed, walked over to the window, and opened the curtains. Sunlight poured into the room, announcing a new day, rejuvenating her spirit. She decided to exercise in order to stay in shape for the next tour. Pulling off her silk nightgown, she put on green gym shorts and a T-shirt with the words "Just Breezin' " scrawled across the front.

Breeze walked down the spiral staircase of her spacious, contemporary New Jersey home, through the wide two story. She opened the door that led to the bottom level of her tri-level, custom-designed home, an area containing an entertainment room, exercise room, and a recording studio. The exercise room was equipped with a treadmill, rower, a Stairmaster, stationary bike, skier, and Cybex fitness equipment. She warmed up on the ballet *barre*, stretching her legs and arms before working out on the exercise machines.

An hour later, she read the newspaper and chatted with Thelma, who was preparing breakfast: fruit, toast, and eggs.

Thelma, a large, dark-skinned woman in her mid-fifties, usually came three times a week to cook for Breeze. She was a friendly woman and talked incessantly about her ten children and six grandchildren. After eating breakfast, Breeze returned to her bedroom to get dressed for the day.

While in the shower, she began to hum the song that had been lulling in her mind, a soft melody that had stayed with her throughout her hospital stay. She wanted to capture the muse before it got away, so she went down to her recording studio.

Breeze sat at the piano and tried to play the right keys on the piano that complimented the rhythm of her feeling. Humming thoughtfully, she sang aloud the words that were flowing in her mind, "The love that never was, will it ever be?"

Standing by the door, arms crossed, India interrupted, "You're supposed to be resting."

Breeze did not glance up, but continued to lovingly run her fingers over the black and white keys. "Girl, I'm tired of that bed. If I stay in it any longer it's going to swallow me up."

"Well," India said, giving Breeze a cursory examination, "You do look better."

"I feel all right. I'll take it easy, but I'm not staying in the bed all day. It's a good thing that I got sick on the last show of the tour and didn't have to cancel out."

"That truly would have been a nightmare," concurred India "I'm glad you're feeling better because we've got to get a video out on 'The Affair.' It's getting a lot of air play even though it hasn't been officially released."

India entered the room and stood next to the piano. "Edmund wants to know how you feel about Debbie Allen producing it. She can schedule you in and have it done in two weeks."

Breeze had to think about it; she normally produced her own videos.

India explained, "I thought it would be one less thing for you to worry about. She's got some really good ideas and I think you'll like it."

"I know she's a good director, and very creative...I'll meet with her, and we can talk about it."

"What were you playing?" asked India.

"The beginnings of a new song. Some melody that's been in my head since I was in the hospital."

Breeze and India were interrupted by the maid, a petite Hispanic woman. Isabella said, "Excuse me, Breeze. Your mother is here."

"She is?" Surprised, Breeze turned to India "Did you know she was coming?"

India shrugged her shoulders. "She didn't tell me. I talked to her when she got back from the cruise two days ago and she sounded tired."

"Mother never just jumps up to visit. You have to practically drag her out of the house. I hope nothing is wrong," Breeze remarked as they walked upstairs to greet their mother.

They found Lillian Blackwell in the living room admiring Breeze's extensive art collection. Original paintings from African-American artists lined the walls throughout Breeze's house: Jacob Lawrence, Romare Bearden, William

Tolliver, Henry Tanner, Hale Woodruff; and sculptures by Elizabeth Catlett.

Lillian appeared radiant and tanned in a fuchsia pajama-styled silk pantsuit. Breeze and India exchanged surprised looks; the outfit was too sophisticated, too contemporary for Lillian.

"Every time I pull into your driveway I can't believe that this is my baby's house," Lillian said as she ran over to hug Breeze and India. "It's a mansion."

"Aren't you supposed to be in bed?" Lillian scolded.

"I'm tired of that bed, Mother." Appraising her mother from head to toe, Breeze said, "You look wonderful. You sounded so tired on the phone, I can't believe that you hopped on another plane."

"I had to see you, Breeze, especially since I didn't make it to the hospital." Lillian put her arm around Breeze's waist and hugged her again. "If I had known you were sick I would have cut the cruise short. I'm very hurt that no one called me." Her eyes on India, she said reproachfully, "India, you should have called me immediately."

"She didn't want me to," India said.

"It wasn't serious, and I didn't want to spoil your vacation. We had to beg you to go as it was," Breeze explained.

"I'm your mother, and I hope you know I would have come back to see about you if I had known you were sick," Lillian said, rubbing Breeze on the back.

"I know, Mother. But it doesn't matter now. I'm fine."

Lillian ran her hand across Breeze's cheeks. "Well, I'm glad you're doing better. I just wish you would call me Ma again. I haven't heard that since…"

Breeze gushed to avoid the subject, "You must have had a really good time. There's something different about you," assessing her mother, trying to determine what was different.

"Breeze's right, I was thinking the exact same thing," India said. Snapping her fingers, she said, "That's it. You changed your hair."

Lillian self-consciously patted her hair. "No, it's just grown out from that awful haircut. I paid that woman one hundred dollars and she mined my hair. She was a butcher, not a beautician. I'll never go back to her."

"And you lost weight," Breeze said.

"Ten pounds," Lillian bragged, twirling around to show off her figure.

"Well, let's get your bags," India said, moving to the door.

"Not so fast, girls," Lillian said in a distracted, anxious tone. She held her hands up to stop them from walking past her. "I have something to tell you."

"What?" Breeze and India spoke simultaneously, worried looks painted on their faces.

"Sit down first."

As India and Breeze sat on the settee in the two-story foyer, Lillian stood before them nervously wringing her hands. She didn't say anything for several minutes.

Finally India asked, "Mother, is something wrong?"

"No, no. There's nothing wrong. It's just hard for me to tell you."

"Is it something about Daddy?" Breeze inquired.

"No! I haven't talked to that man in years. I'm still angry with him for stealing you away from me, Breeze."

Breeze stood up, hands on her hips. "I don't want to hear that again. Every time Daddy's mentioned, you want to go into that mess from the past. if that is what you want to talk about, I'll just go back to bed."

"Sit down, Breeze. I don't want to talk about the past." Lillian spoke seriously and chose her words carefully before continuing. "You know for a long time I devoted my life to raising you girls. Between you girls and the church I've been very busy. Too busy for myself. You know, they put me in charge of activities. I do all the weddings, and I try to help folks with their hardships and visit with the sick. You know, Mrs. Pebbles is in the hospital and she's doing poorly and her ungrateful kids won't even go to see her..."

Lillian's eyes fluttered and flickered. She threw her arms up in the air and blurted out," I met a man on the cruise. We had a wonderful time." She paused a moment before saying, "He proposed to me the last night of the cruise."

Breeze and India shrieked, "What!" and jumped up from the settee.

"I don't believe it! I'm happy for you, Mother. But I don't believe it," Breeze exclaimed. She was shocked, and she wasn't sure whether to be excited or worried. It had been years since Lillian dated.

"Yes! That is wonderful! Who is he?" India asked, excited, but concerned about this unexpected revelation.

Less anxious, Lillian said, "I didn't expect this to happen. I wasn't prepared for it to happen so fast that I didn't get to prepare you all."

"Who is he? Tell us all about him," Breeze said. She had always assumed that Lillian would end up marrying Mr. Wells from church. She knew that Lillian liked Mr. Wells, and they dated on the pretense of church business, but Breeze, India, and Rayna sensed that something was going on between them. A new man, a man her mother had only known for ten days, was a big surprise.

"I know it happened so very fast. But I feel like I've known him for a long time," Lillian happily explained. "He was on the cruise with some friends, old army buddies. I met him the first night at dinner, and we took all the tours together and had loads of fun. I can't remember the last time I had so much fun. He lives in New Jersey and is divorced. He was a perfect gentlemen and treated me like such a lady. I hated for the cruise to end and certainly didn't expect him to propose."

"Propose?" shrieked Breeze and India concurrently.

"Where is he?" Breeze asked, eyeing the front door. "We want to meet this man."

"That's why we're here," said Lillian, smiling with a youthful glow. "I wanted him to meet my family." She walked toward the door, her proper walk a little lighter, bouncier than before.

"I have never seen Mother so, so happy," Breeze said, throwing her arms in the air.

Sweeping her silky black hair off her face, India exclaimed, "I don't know what to think. Mother engaged?"

"She hasn't dated in such a long time, I hope she knows what she's doing," Breeze worriedly remarked.

"Yeah, I hope he's not twenty-five or some kind of gigolo," expressed India.

"Oh my God," Breeze gushed, as she walked out the front door and down the steps. Her mother's fiancé was standing in front of a cab.

The man who would be her stepfather looked exactly like her father. Breeze wouldn't look at India to keep herself from laughing. He had the same wavy hair, pale brown skin, long nose, and wide face as Omar Blackwell. He was taller and bigger, a husky sort of man with a high-pitched laugh that belied his size.

Lillian stood next to Albert, dwarfed by the giant of a man. Bashfully, Lillian made the introductions: "Daughters, this is Albert Anderson." She looked up at Albert who smiled reassuringly and took a deep breath. "My fiancé."

Albert nodded his head and in a vibrating voice said, "Ladies, it's a pleasure meeting you."

Thank goodness he's not a young stud, thought Breeze. *He's well-dressed and seems like a gentleman. On second thought, maybe he's an old stud. And, how do you lecture your mother on safe sex? He looks just like Daddy. I can't believe it.*

I just hope he makes her happy. Wonder what he does for a living? Probably retired, India thought.

"Breeze, I'm a big fan of yours. My kids buy all your music," Albert said.

"Thank you, Albert. How many kids do you have?"

"Three boys and two girls. My youngest still lives at home with her mother," Albert explained.

"You're divorced?" questioned Breeze, scrutinizing the giant stranger.

"For ten years," Albert replied, returning Breeze's assessing stare.

"Come on inside," Breeze welcomed. "Let's go out by the pool and get better acquainted."

Sitting at a table by the pool, they drank iced tea as Lillian and Albert told Breeze and India all about their cruise. Lillian was full of smiles and laughs, glowing with happiness, telling stories about the Caribbean islands they toured.

"I thought you would have a good time on a cruise," India remarked.

"I sure did. I sure did," Lillian admitted.

"Now we have two reasons to celebrate," Breeze said.

"What's that?" Lillian asked, pleased that Breeze and India didn't protest her pending marriage.

"India's engaged!" Breeze announced.

"Oh, baby, you are? Congratulations!" Lillian got up from her chair and gave India a big, warm hug. "Are you and Zeke going to have a big wedding?"

"We haven't decided yet."

"Let me put together a fabulous wedding for you," Lillian offered.

"I don't know," India said, taking a handful of nachos from the bowl in the center of the table. "Zeke doesn't want all that attention."

"Oh, weddings are for the bride," Lillian explained.

I've been trying to convince her to do it up," laughed Breeze.

"I'm thinking about it," India admitted.

"What about you, Ma?" Breeze inquired. "Are you going to have a big church wedding?" She glanced over at Albert, noticing how intently he watched Lillian.

"Goodness no," Lillian answered. "I'm too old for a big, lavish wedding. I want a simple, elegant wedding. Something appropriate for a woman my age."

"So, when is the big day?" India asked.

"Soon," interjected Albert, peering into Lillian's eyes. "Life is too short to wait."

Rayna's performance in *The Piano Lesson* by August Wilson won rave reviews for her spectacular dramatic performance. The crowd greeted her curtain call with a standing ovation. She loved every moment of the crowd chanting "Bravo! Bravo! Bravo!" and she glowed like a flashing neon light. It had been such a long time since she heard an audience's applause. She hungered to hear the echo of hands being struck together, the ripple of spontaneous thunder in the theater. It felt like heaven.

She spotted Breeze, India, Lillian, and her mother's fiancé in the front row and blew an exaggerated kiss in their direction.

Rayna hadn't worked as an actress in a year. She called the past twelve months "The Year of Disappointment," because not one of the roles she auditioned for did she get. She even tried out for parts that she felt were beneath her, but the sting of rejection was still the same. Every time she hoped that a particular role was going to be her talisman, absolutely nothing would happen.

As the curtains were drawn, Rayna thought, *This is it, this is going to be my lucky break.*

Breeze, India, and Lillian watched proudly as Rayna signed autographs. They waited for Rayna to finish talking to her fans, some dressed in jeans and some in furs. They knew Rayna needed to hear every compliment "You were wonderful!…You are a star!…What else have you been in?

I can't believe I've never seen you before."

When the theater was about empty, Breeze, India, and Lillian squeezed into Rayna's small dressing room, which was flooded with flowers of every type. They hugged and carried on as if it was Rayna's first theater performance.

Her arms wrapped around Breeze's waist, Rayna said, "I'm sorry I couldn't make it to the hospital, B.B. You know I thought about you everyday."

Giving her sister a stem look, Breeze responded, "I'll forgive you *this time.* But it wasn't anything serious, thank goodness. And, I know you had this show to do. I'm just glad that your career has taken off."

"Amen," Lillian said, with an edge of I-told-you-so in her voice.

Rayna, her head tilted back, reacted defensively. "I am determined, Ma. Very determined. Otherwise I would have given up long ago."

Lillian moved beside Rayna. Leaning her head on Rayna's shoulders, she affectionately patted Rayna's ribs. "You need to gain some weight. Are you eating right?"

"Such a worrier. Believe me, Ma. I'm all right."

There was a soft knock on the door.

"Oh, that's probably Albert," Lillian said beaming, clapping her hands together. She opened the door and ushered Albert in.

"Come in and meet my oldest daughter." Proudly, she added, "The Broadway actress."

Albert entered the room, and after closing the door behind him, stood directly in front of it. There wasn't anywhere else to stand in the cramped room which wasn't much bigger than a closet.

"Rayna, honey. This is Albert Anderson," Lillian said, her arm wrapped inside Albert's bowed arm. "We met on the cruise, and we're going to be getting married."

Rayna shook Albert's outstretched hand. "It's good to meet you, Albert." Staring boldly into his face and with a devilish grin she said, "You look just like somebody I know." She looked at Breeze and India and suppressed the urge to laugh.

"I hope it's somebody you like," Albert remarked. "You put on a great show. I don't go to the theater much, but I really enjoyed the show."

"Thank you, Albert," Rayna replied distractedly as she spotted India's ring. "Girl, what a rock!" exclaimed Rayna, pulling India's left hand to get a closer look at the engagement ring.

"I know," India said. "Isn't it gorgeous?"

"Zeke did good, if I must say so myself. Why don't you and Ma have a double wedding?" Rayna suggested.

"No offense, Mother, but I want my very own wedding day," said India.

"That's right. We're going to have two very different weddings. There's no way to combine them," explained Lillian.

Breeze said, "We came to take you to dinner, Sis. Wherever you want to go. How about Japanese?"

"I'm starving. I'm always hungry after a performance. There's this great Japanese restaurant on Forty-seventh."

"Sounds good to me," India said.

"Give me ten minutes to get out of this makeup and change clothes."

"We'll meet you up front," India said, before leaving with Lillian and Albert.

Taking off her stage clothes from behind the hand-painted screen featuring an abstract reproduction of dramatic masks, Rayna asked Breeze to find her belt in the dressing table drawer. "The black one," Rayna specified, while pulling on a pair of black pleated pants.

Breeze rummaged through two drawers, pausing when she noticed one of the drawers was full of liquor bottles.

A deep crease in her brow, Breeze asked, "Rayna, what's all this liquor for?" Her voice was accusatory and concerned.

"We're always partying around here. You know how theater people are. People give you liquor and you collect them," Rayna quickly explained, poking her head out from behind the screen to see what Breeze was doing.

Breeze pulled out two bottles of whiskey from the top drawer. "Most of them are empty," she said, tossing the empty bottles into the overflowing basket on the side of the dressing table.

Rayna's head disappeared behind the screen as she cried in annoyance, "Damn, Breeze, you're getting to be just as bad as Ma. You know I'm a slob. I've never kept a clean dressing room in my whole career. There's nothing wrong with a party or two. What do you want from me?"

Breeze had a funny feeling that sometimes Rayna was the only one at those parties. She squeezed behind the screen, just as Rayna pulled a bright, colorful sweater over her head.

Rayna glared at her. "Don't harass me, Breeze."

Her eyes narrowed suspiciously, Breeze sternly said, "Look, I know you've been going through some rough times, but don't lose your dreams to the bottle."

Rayna stopped what she was doing and returned her sister's probing stare. She was about to tell Breeze that she was jumping to the wrong conclusions, but her sister knew her too well.

Bowing her head, Rayna sheepishly said, "I hear you."

"I mean it, Rayna. You drink a lot and I know it. But you need to stop because when your dreams are ready for you, you might not be ready if the bottle takes over."

"Don't get too deep, okay?" said Rayna, looping the gold-studded belt through the belt loops. "Besides, I haven't been drinking much since I started working."

Breeze gave Rayna a penetrating look, not entirely convinced that her sister's confession was the truth.

"Breeze, get out of here now." Shooing her with dismissive hands, Rayna noted, "there's hardly enough room for me back here."

Breeze squeezed around the rusty screen and sat down at the dressing table.

"I want to talk to you anyway," Rayna said, as she stepped around the screen, fully dressed in a pair of black, pleated pants and a multi-colored sweater. "What do you think of Ma's engagement? Don't whitewash the whole thing, be honest. Let me know the real deal."

"I don't know," Breeze began. "I want her to be happy, but this happened so fast. And, we don't know much about him. I'm almost tempted to have him investigated."

"Breeze!" Rayna chided, looking into the mirror, fixing her makeup.

"Well!" Breeze exclaimed, throwing her hands in the air. "We don't know much about the man. What if he's a con man?"

"If they don't rush the wedding, we'll have time to check him out," Rayna said, looking at Breeze through the mirror.

"That makes sense."

"I just can't believe that Ma is getting married again. She always said that she never would do it again."

"That's because she knew there was no way she would remarry Daddy, so she found second best," Breeze replied. "A man who looks just like him."

Breeze and Rayna cracked up in laughter.

"They look so much alike it's uncanny. The same facial structure, long nose, everything. He looks so much like Daddy I wonder if Grandma had twins and gave one away," Breeze uttered.

"All these years she fussed and complained about what an awful man Daddy was, but deep down inside she still loved him. She never stopped wanting him," Rayna said.

"Isn't that wild? You never know what a person is really thinking and feeling," Breeze concluded. "Not even your own mother."

"I wonder how Daddy feels about her. Maybe he still loves her," Rayna pondered.

"I think Daddy is kind of lonely. When he had his heart attack, this woman used to come see him every day, but I always got the feeling that she got on his nerves," said Breeze. "I don't think he has anybody special. Just his music."

"Ma just couldn't handle Daddy being a musician. She was too jealous." Rayna said. "Now she's got a man who looks just like Daddy, and she doesn't have to compete with the music. How does he act around her anyway?" Rayna inquired.

"He seems to love her. I just hope he's sincere." Walking toward the door, she added, "But, I wonder if he knows that he's the spitting image of our father."

CHAPTER NINE

Breeze and Edmund were the only customers in the exclusive French restaurant. Louis Louis was usually very busy. Customers made dinner reservations weeks in advance to dine in the elegantly decorated dining room, with its high ceilings, provincial designs, crystal chandeliers, and Louis XVI furnishings that evoked romantic France. It was not unusual for the restaurant to seat more than two hundred diners in one evening, but this particular night was different. Louis Louis was reserved for two.

Breeze didn't know what to think when she was escorted into the empty restaurant and discovered only Edmund inside. From the moment Edmund's limousine had picked her up, the distinct feeling that this evening was more than just a "business celebration" shadowed her every thought. A dozen white roses had been delivered to her house every hour since noon, but not one had had a card. She didn't know who was sending the flowers until she got into the limousine and discovered a box of white roses. This time there was a card. It read "Surprise!"

She had noticed a change in Edmund's behavior since her hospital stay and was intrigued by his sudden interest. She ignored India's teasing about Edmund's "schoolboy crush," but as she rode in her Cinderella-like carriage, Breeze realized that her relationship with Edmund was about to change. She could no longer ignore it: Edmund was bringing it front-and-center.

Breeze cared a great deal for Edmund, and wondered if she could fall in love with him. There were times, when they first started working together, that she could have easily fallen in love with him, but she kept those feelings under control. Since he never gave her any indication that he was interested in her romantically, she knew it would have been risky to let her feelings go down the dangerous road to love.

When they worked together on the first album, Breeze had been in absolute awe of him. Edmund was Mr. Harmony, the star maker, and had launched the careers of many singers. Breeze couldn't help but be affected by his bigger than life persona. Edmund had turned her life around and made her dreams come true. There were many moments that she had felt love for him, but she wondered how much of those feelings stemmed from gratitude. Since he never made a move toward her, she concluded that there were boundaries to their relationship. It was to be a business relationship, and she dared not cross the line.

But now, as she looked across the table at Edmund, she sensed that his feelings had deepened beyond their business. How deep, she didn't know.

The waiter poured champagne into the fragile glasses, then Edmund raised his glass and toasted: "To Breeze, the woman I'm going to learn more about."

"Ah," she laughed uneasily at Edmund's romantic declaration, while lifting her glass to meet his. "I had a feeling that this was not just a business dinner." They sipped their champagne while trading wary stares.

Edmund the man was quite different from Edmund the businessman. He was warm and witty and had lots of interesting and funny stories to tell about the music business. There were many new things about him that she learned: He was born in a small town near Detroit and went to college on a football scholarship. At one time Edmund even had dreams of making it into the National Football League, but met stiff, talented competition from many with that same dream of athletic superstardom. He didn't make the first draft.

They enjoyed a delicious dinner of *escargots en croute, bisque de humard au cognac, les escalopes de veau chasseur,* and *la mouse au chocolat.* Breeze saw the unmistakable gleam of desire dancing in Edmund's eyes, spotting for the first time what India had long ago proclaimed as Edmund's obvious romantic interest.

Breeze couldn't resist teasing him in this new light about his reputation as a ladies man. Edmund, his hands turned up, shrugged and casually explained that it was "just the nature of the entertainment business."

Edmund spoke of his first marriage. She detected a tone of remorse in his voice. But when he spoke of the second marriage, there was no mistaking the anger and pain.

"She was a bitch and she betrayed me," Edmund expressed bitterly.

"Those are strong words, Edmund," Breeze gently observed.

"Strong, but accurate," began Edmund, after signaling to the waiter to remove his dinner plate. "She was very pretty and very young. I saw her singing in a hotel lounge and was somehow entranced. I mean, she didn't have a great voice. She sounded good singing certain kinds of songs, low key songs, but not much of a range. Every evening after I conducted my business for the day, I would go to the lounge and watch her perform. The audience was mostly men and, boy, did they love to watch her sing! She was a very pretty girl.

"By the third day, I introduced myself to her, and we started going out. She didn't have any family, had been on her own since she was fourteen, but she had big dreams of becoming a singer. She wanted to be the next Diana Ross. She used to say 'Be my Berry Gordy and I'll be your Diana Ross.'

"I tried to tell her that she needed some vocal training and it would take some time. But she was impatient. And by that time, I was madly in love with her, had moved her into my house, and would do anything to make her happy. So, whatever she wanted I did my best to accommodate her.

"She wanted to get married so we went to Las Vegas. We hadn't known each other very long, but I was hooked. A little after we married, I started getting material for her album and hired a producer. He wasn't a well-known producer, but I liked his style, and I thought he would be able to write songs to suit her voice. She worked hard on the album and took singing lessons every day. But one day, I found her in bed with the record producer."

"Oh, Edmund, I know that was painful," Breeze soothed.

"She wasn't even sorry. Not in the least. She claimed to be in love with this man, and I was too old for her. I finally saw her to be what some of my friends had seen all along. She was manipulative and determined to get what she wanted no matter who she hurt. I threw her out of the house and out of my life. Months later she had the nerve to come back begging for forgiveness, but what she really wanted was for me to help her career. The album didn't do very well, and she was nowhere close to being the next Diana Ross."

Edmund stopped talking and drank from the glass of water freshly poured by the waiter.

Breeze had noticed the pain in his voice as he told the story of his unhappy marriage. She didn't interrupt him, and when he paused to quench his thirst, she remained silent, waiting for him to finish the story. When the look of today replaced the pain of yesterday on his face, she realized that he was finished talking about the past.

With a rueful smile, Edmund said, "I swore I would never get involved with a singer, but the word 'never' always comes back to haunt you."

"Never say *never,*" Breeze chuckled.

"You were married once. What happened?"

Breeze's face clouded with past memories. "My husband was murdered by a white policeman a week before our first anniversary," she explained with suppressed emotion. Edmund detected the hesitation in her response and the sadness in her voice.

"What happened?" Edmund asked, totally surprised by this revelation.

"A racist cop murdered him in cold blood," Breeze said bitterly. "He claimed that Kyle had a gun, but he didn't. And the cop tried to justify what he did by claiming that he thought Kyle was the man who had robbed a bank earlier that day."

"The 'all black folks look alike' excuse," Edmund said cynically. Rubbing his beard thoughtfully, he asked, "Did anything happen to the cop?"

"Oh yes. Kyle's father is an attorney and he went on the warpath. The cop was suspended from the police force and convicted of manslaughter. He was sentenced to jail for eight years."

"Good. Usually they just get a slap on the wrist."

"Kyle's father changed after that. He was real ambitious and political, but after Kyle's death, he found his conscience and became a strong advocate against police brutality."

"And how did it affect you?"

"It's strange, but it was after his death that I found the courage to become a singer."

They were silent a moment, absorbing the new information they had discovered about each other, developing a deeper understanding and insight.

"Something your mother was against," Edmund said.

"She was dead set against it from day one. I didn't even realize that I could sing until I was fifteen." She paused and then said, "She didn't want me to have anything to do with the music business because of my father."

With a troubled expression she tried to hide, she continued, "He was always on the road somewhere. 'I got a gig,' Daddy used to say. 'I got a gig to go to.' I hated him being gone all the time, but that's the way it always was. It ate away at my mother. When she couldn't take it anymore, she left him. I was a little girl, and I hated that my father wasn't ever coming home anymore."

"Yeah, I know your father's reputation. His talent and love of music must have been hard to compete with. Omar Blackwell can play some sax. My old man used to listen to him. He's a real jazz man."

"Yes, father and daughter would work well together," Breeze hinted. When Edmund didn't react, Breeze said, "I want him to play on my next album."

"Ah," Edmund nodded his head and laughed. "That's what you're getting at. I think you two would sound great together. I should have thought of that."

The waiter cleared their plates from the table.

"After Kyle was killed, I was an emotional wreck, so I left D.C. I kept putting off going to law school because I really wanted to sing, but I was afraid to admit it. So, I moved to New York—Rayna and India were here. It didn't take long before I was making the rounds, singing in clubs, and sending in demo tapes."

Edmund sensed that there was more to the story of Breeze's marriage. While talking her voice had changed, and her tone was sad, almost remorseful. He had a feeling that Kyle was the reason Breeze treated men with a long-handled spoon. Returning to the sensitive subject, he asked, "Were you in love with your husband?"

Breeze looked down at her finished plate for several seconds before she met Edmund's probing gaze. "I loved Kyle," she said softly. "I wish he hadn't been killed."

"Have there been others? I mean, have you been in love with anyone else?" Edmund prodded, searching her clouded copper eyes for the answer.

"Yes," she replied, not meeting Edmund's eyes, looking past what she could physically see in the restaurant to a time in her life that she could not forget. "I was very young and uhm...my mother didn't appreciate him. He was a musician like my father." She paused before adding, "She made sure I didn't see him."

Edmund reached across the table to grasp her restless fingers. "I should apologize for prying, but I want to know. What happened?"

"When he went to college, Mother hid his letters from me..."

"And when you found out?" Edmund prompted gently.

"By that time, it was too late."

"And...what?" he asked, his hands tilted her head back in his direction. "Look at me...Have you been in love since?"

Breeze returned to the present and stared back at the handsome man sitting across from her. Shaking her head, she answered sadly, "Not the real thing."

A wistful smile ruffled his mouth. "Like the song said, 'Ain't nothing like the real thing.' "

Breeze stood before the crowd, her hands grasped nervously around the podium. In the hotel lobby of the Marriott Marquis in Atlanta, Georgia, she was photographed and filmed wearing a black double-breasted jacket and matching cuffed pants. Her hair was swept off her face, twisted into an elegant French knot. Loose curls hung around her temples.

Breeze cleared her throat She was the guest speaker at a black-tie dinner to raise funds for the New Birth Theater Company. The audience of theater advocates, politicians, business people, and dignitaries were not there to hear Breeze Blackwell sing; instead they were anxious to know how much Breeze intended to donate.

"When I performed here in Atlanta a few months ago, I heard on the news that the New Birth Theater Company was in financial trouble. They were in jeopardy of losing corporate funding, and donations from other sponsors were questionable. The newscaster painted a bleak picture. My staff looked into the situation. When I learned the history of the New Birth Theater Company, the quality of the productions, the openness to new talent, and that plays that premiered here often went on to New York, I was very impressed. I felt compelled to do something.

"I'm a strong advocate of the arts. I believe that creativity and artistic talent should be treasured and nurtured. That is why I would like to offer $100,000 towards keeping the New Birth Theater Company open to the community."

Jamal Josten, Artistic Co-Director and Founder of the New Birth Theater Company strode across the stage with a dance to his step, immensely relieved that he didn't have to close down the theater. He accepted the check and thanked Breeze for her "very generous donation."

Breeze was motionless as the makeup artist for *Essence* magazine finished applying purple lipstick to her lips. Her face was a palette of unusual colors: orange, blue, red, purple, and yellow. Looking in the mirror, she smiled bemusedly at the woman with the funky hairstyle, crazy clothes, and psychedelic makeup that stared back at her.

She laughed at herself.

"The photos will come out nicely. I promise you," the makeup artist said reassuringly.

"But who's the person in the picture?"

"Your fans will see a different side of you."

"If they recognize me," Breeze chuckled.

"Perfecto! Perfecto!" Cleo said, clapping his hands. He was a short, thin, light-skinned man. An expensive 35 mm camera hung around his neck. "You look great! Let's get started. I've got some great ideas for some wonderful shots. You have such an artistic home. It's fabulous."

Cleo was frail looking, but he bubbled with energy. "I don't want to take shots of you lounging by the pool. No! No! No! Or eating in the kitchen. No! No! No! Or working in the studio! No! No! No! That's too passé, dove. Your home is a work of art, your photos must be a work of art.

"Miss Blackwell, I've been dying to see your art. I mean I would have killed for this assignment." He looked at Breeze, repeatedly blinking his small, squinty eyes, one contact lens-colored blue and the other colored purple.

Rising up from the chair, Breeze said, "Call me Breeze. Now, where do you want to get started?"

"I want you to stand next to that fabulous Romare Bearden painting!"

A scowl crossed Breeze's face.

"You don't get it do you?"

"Not really."

"See, you're an artist. You love art. Your house is a work of art and you've got a serious collection of art, spotlighting different Black artists. So I had you made up to look like a work of art. That's the concept, dove. And I want to take pictures of you in various poses. A work of art among her collection of art. *Tres chic!*" Cleo enthusiastically explained.

"Oh…," Breeze said. She liked the idea. It was an unusual concept. It might be more fun than the usual boring photo sessions. "I like it, I can't wait to see what I look like as a piece of art," she smiled indulgently.

CHAPTER TEN

Breeze and Edmund stepped out of the limousine and were immediately surrounded by reporters, photographers, camera people, and screaming fans. They were swept into a melee of hyperactivity as award-nominees and guests arrived at the Shrine Auditorium in Los Angles for the American Music Awards.

Breeze looked elegant and sophisticated in an ankle-length gown designed especially for her. The halter-back gown, shimmering with glittery rhinestones, featured a high side slit that showed off her curvaceous legs. Diamonds shimmered around her neck and dangled from her ears. Undoubtedly, she would make the best-dressed list. Breeze greeted the crowd with her neon smile, and waved at the swarm of onlookers.

"How do you feel, Breeze?" asked a smiling interviewer in a sequin gown.

"I feel wonderful!"

"I feel lucky! She's gonna win big tonight," Edmund boasted, attired in a grey double-breasted tuxedo.

"How does it feel to be nominated for best video, best pop song, and favorite female R&B singer? Do you think you're going to win?"

Breeze laughed huskily. "I don't come to these awards expecting to win, so it's very exciting when I do. I'm always happy to know how much my fans admire and appreciate my music."

"The competition for the best video is hot! You're up against Madonna, Janet Jackson, and Paula Abdul. Any predictions?"

"No, I don't predict," Breeze answered. "I like to wait to see what happens."

Edmund, standing in the background, interjected, "I came to help her carry out her awards. All of them."

This was the second year that Breeze had been nominated for an American Music Award. The previous year she had won three American Music Awards, two Grammys, four Soul Train Music Awards, two MTV Awards, and a People's Choice Award. It was an exceptional and exciting year for someone new to the world of stardom.

Last year, cameras zoomed in and broadcast Breeze's did-I-really-win reaction: Breeze screamed out in glee and jumped out of her seat. When Breeze saw how zany and silly she looked, she was embarrassed, but fans found her genuine excitement all the more endearing.

This year Breeze resolved to be sophisticated and cool. Not that she wasn't thrilled and wrought with anticipation—she was even more excited this year. When her name was called among the list of nominees, she felt the insides of her stomach ooze to the floor. And when she was announced the winner it felt her heart had jumped out of her chest and fallen onto the floor with her stomach. She had to look down to make sure her heart and stomach really weren't there in front of her. She had only seconds to gather her composure—her stomach and heart in their proper places—and walk up to the stage to claim her award.

Following the televised award show, Breeze and Edmund mingled with the music industry's finest: singers, musicians, songwriters, producers, and other limelight celebrities. She offered congratulations to other American Music Award winners, posed with entertainers for the press, and granted interviews.

After three years in the spotlight, Breeze still felt as if the reality of her success was light years beyond her fantasies.

For a brief moment, Breeze stood alone. She observed the famous and rich people mingling around her as if she wasn't a part of it. *This is real,* she thought. *This is what happens when you make it in the music business. And, you've made it.* Breeze felt as if she were in the clouds of another universe.

"You're not dreaming. This is reality," spoke a deep, husky voice from the past. A voice she only heard in the whispers of her dreams.

She spun around and saw Alexander Franklin. "Lex!" She was startled out of her euphoria. She stared at Lex as if he were an apparition.

"Give me a hug, baby." As Lex and Breeze embraced, he whispered softly in her ear, "Sunshine."

"You still can't believe it?" Lex teased, a broad smile warmed his very attractive face.

"No," Breeze replied, her arms spread wide. "Nothing could have prepared me for this!"

"I told you that you were born to sing, Sunshine. I knew it all along."

Lex had planted the seed, the realization that she had a gifted voice. This seed had transformed dreams, this seed bore the fruit of a talented, award-winning singer.

"Lex, congratulations on your awards." He'd won two awards for producing and songwriting. Tagged "the hit-maker," he was making a distinct mark on the music industry.

"Thank you, Breeze," Lex said, enjoying the sound of her name in his mouth. He paused, his eyes travelled from her face to her feet. "I'm glad to see you've recovered. You look even more beautiful than I remember."

"The doctors made me rest so much that I felt like screaming."

Lex had changed from the picture she had planted in her mind. The teenager had become a man, an undeniably handsome man with confidence, even a bit of cockiness in his demeanor. Breeze sensed a seen-it-all, done-it-all air surrounding him, a wariness in his deep, dark brown eyes. His hair was combed back, rippled with waves, and he sported a smooth beard.

They stared at each other, thirsty for the sight of the other.

He still has the same affect on me, thought Breeze.

I still want her, thought Lex.

"I still think of you," Lex admitted simply.

After all the years of hoping to hear Lex say those very words, Breeze didn't know what to say. It was amazing how you could be in the same business and never meet.

Her eyebrows rose in surprise. Self-consciously, she fiddled with the spiral diamond earrings. She searched his eyes for honesty.

Lex moved closer to Breeze, his hand lightly touching her naked arm. He stared into her liquid-gold eyes before confessing, "Breeze, I've never forgotten what we had."

"That was a long time ago…"

"There's so much I want to say to you, but this is not the place." He bent his head to capture Breeze's avoiding gaze. "Let's go to dinner."

"I don't know," Breeze said in a hesitant voice.

Breeze started to say something from the myriad of thoughts and feelings whirling inside her, but was interrupted when Chanelle Diamond sauntered over and attached herself to Lex.

Chanelle Diamond was a tall, thin, leggy, pecan-skinned woman with a seductive voice and ordinary face. Chanelle wasn't pretty, nor was she ugly, but she oozed sensuality. She put her arms around Lex's waist and gave Breeze a he's-with-me stare.

Breeze groaned inwardly at their interrupter, realizing fully the implications of this particular female's presence.

Chanelle broke into the music business singing with The Jewels, an all-girl group. They were a popular group and claimed several hits on the R&B charts. When they took on a new name, Chanelle Diamond and The Jewels, with their second album, they crossed over musical audiences, increasing their popularity. Chanelle Diamond and The Jewels scored two hits, and were the opening act for several concerts. Dissension developed in the group when it became apparent that Chanelle Diamond wanted most of the attention and publicity.

Chanelle left the group after signing a one album contract with a major label. But the album was a flop; her fans didn't like her flamboyant new image, and her songs sounded like imitations of other artists' music weakly disguised with new lyrics. Her album collected dust in record stores and was eventually returned to distributors. Chanelle was now a woman with a mission: to regain her pop singer status.

Dressed in a plunging, shimmering gold gown, Chanelle weakly smiled at Breeze, barely concealing her fangs. "Congratulations. I thought you would win," she said.

Breeze responded, "Thank you," refusing to acknowledge Chanelle's insincerity.

"I heard you went to school with Lex," came the opening play.

"Yes, I did."

"Did you ever play together?" Chanelle inquired with a bored tone.

A vivid memory of Miss Abbot's wedding reception flashed concurrently in Lex's and Breeze's minds.

"Not really. She sang for me once when my regular singer didn't show," Lex explained.

"Oh really," was Chanelle's dry response. Running her fingers possessively across Lex's cheek, Chanelle said, "Lex's sound is so hot I want him to produce my next album."

"I'll see you soon, Lex," Breeze said. "Have got to go, Chanelle. Oh, keep trying, dear." Breeze smiled at Lex and walked away.

Edmund hosted an after party to honor Breeze and other Harmony Records artists. It was a victory party, a celebration of success. Harmony Records was already a powerful force in the music industry, but signing Breeze and her unheralded success made it possible for Harmony Records to reach its ten-year goals in five.

Harmony Records' plans to venture into the movie-making business were becoming an immediate possibility. Sales from Breeze's two albums exceeded sales from all Harmony Records artists for the preceding five years. Edmund was talking with movie producers and screen-writers, searching for an exciting screenplay that would break box office records. The future was shaping up exactly the way he wanted it to, and much faster than he had expected.

Edmund and Breeze stood on the balcony overlooking the pool area. They could see the garden, the gazebo, and guest house in the distance. Edmund's vintage California home—built into a hillside—was full of wide French doors. Its spacious design—eighteen-foot ceilings and fifty-feet long rooms—evoked a feeling of openness.

"You are a beautiful woman, Breeze," Edmund said with desire lighting his eyes.

The compliment startled Breeze, not because of what he said, but how he said it. "Thank you, Edmund," said Breeze, suddenly uncomfortable. "You look good yourself." She tugged playfully at the skinny red bow tie under his shirt collar.

"I don't just mean physically. I think you are a beautiful person. You are very special."

Blushing, Breeze's gaze shifted back to the view below. "Well, thank you."

A waiter whisked by and refilled Breeze's tall, slender glass with champagne. Feeling deliriously happy and a little reckless, Breeze decided to extend her three drink limit.

Breeze sipped the champagne, savoring the taste. "You throw a great party, Mr. Mitchelson." Her glass raised in mock toast. "Everyone is having a great time."

She looked below at the crowd of celebrators. They were dancing, swimming, and cavorting in dark places stealing kisses and more. Ripples of laughter filtered above as everyone celebrated the evening's success with champagne, food, and music.

Edmund's eyes roamed Breeze's body, noticing the soft curves beneath her body-caressing gown. "Did I thank you for winning tonight?"

Grinning merrily, Breeze replied, "Did I thank you for carrying the awards?"

"Did I thank you for making me richer?"

"Did I thank you for discovering me?"

"Did I thank you for staying with Harmony?"

They burst out laughing. "Have we thanked each other enough?" Breeze asked. Facing Edmund, her back was against the balcony. A soft breeze blew her hair around her face.

"I enjoyed having dinner with you," Edmund said.

"So did I."

"I'd like to go out with you again."

Breeze arched her eyebrows in silent response. She drank the rest of the champagne in a quick gulp, and gave him a provocative, taunting look. "I know we're not talking business."

A soft, sensual smile etched the lines of his mouth.

"You're right, I just want to get to know you. I want to spend time with you." Edmund gave her a deep, intense gaze, wondering if Breeze knew just how serious he was.

She leaned lightly into him and said, "I'll go out with you." Suddenly, her head was spinning around like a child's toy top.

Noticing Breeze's trembling fingers, when the waiter came by to pour more champagne into Breeze's glass, Edmund placed his hand over the rim. "Just how many glasses of champagne have you had?"

"Don't know. Maybe five," Breeze said, setting her glass on the balcony ledge.

"You were drinking at the Awards," observed Edmund.

"I had a few. It was that last drink." She massaged her head, "I drank it too fast." She looked up dizzily at Edmund, leaning on him for support. "I feel awful."

"Come with me, Breeze. You need to lie down."

The next morning Breeze woke up with an incredible throbbing sensation in her head, and massaging her temples with her hands seemed to intensify the pain. She hated feeling this way.

She raised up slowly and looked around the elegantly decorated bedroom. The walls, curtains, and bedroom accessories were coordinated in the same textured pattern of vivid purples and bright yellows. Across from the queen-size brass bed was a mahogany dresser and a matching armoire etched with delicate carvings.

Breeze heard a light tapping at the door. "Come in," she said. Edmund entered the room with a tray piled high with food. "Good morning, Breeze. How are you feeling?" he said cheerfully while placing the tray in front of her.

"Awful," Breeze answered, running her hands across her face and through her tangled hair. "I'm starving. Whenever I drink, the next day I'm ravenous."

"You're either starving or can't stand the sight of food," Edmund said sympathetically.

Breeze took a sip from the tall, cold glass of milk.

Out of his jacket pocket, Edmund produced a bottle of Motrin, and with a smug smile, handed it to Breeze.

"Oh, thank you, Edmund. I feel like my head is going to fall off." She opened the bottle and took out two capsules. She swallowed them and washed the pain relievers down with water. She glanced over at Edmund, who was sitting on the edge of the bed.

"Edmund, I feel so embarrassed. I can't believe I drank so much."

"Don't feel bad. I enjoyed looking after you."

She looked away sheepishly, noticing her black gown lying neatly across the chaise lounge. She frowned at the pink satin gown that she was wearing and tried to remember when she had changed clothes. She threw Edmund a suspicious glare, observing his cheery good mood. *I know I didn't drink that much,* Breeze thought confusedly.

"Well...what happened?"

"Has anyone ever told you how young you look when you're asleep?" A sly smile creased the folds at the edge of Edmund's twinkling eyes.

"What did we do?" Breeze glanced at the covers to see if Edmund had actually slept in the bed with her. The bed was undisturbed on the other side.

"You went to bed and I...spent the rest of the evening entertaining my guests."

"Edmund!" Breeze admonished. "I thought maybe...we had...you know...

"Slept together," Edmund chuckled. "Breeze darling, I would never take advantage of you, no matter how tempting the sight of your body is. If it happens, we both will be very alert and willing partners."

Breeze smiled weakly, relieved that nothing had happened. Avoiding his gaze, Breeze nibbled at the food on the tray.

"I have to go, but you can go back to sleep or do whatever you feel like. I've got a plane to catch."

"I think I'll go back to sleep for a while. Hopefully my headache will be gone when I wake up."

"Do you need anything?"

Breeze winced when she tried to move her head. "Oh, that makes my head hurt worse."

Edmund gently touched Breeze's face, lifting it towards him. "I want you to feel better," he said, leaning down, and lightly kissing Breeze on the lips. Without another word, Edmund turned away and left.

CHAPTER ELEVEN

Breeze was frightened. Butterflies were holding a convention in her stomach, and her head felt as light as the air she was floating in. She closed her eyes and clutched her stomach, hoping her fear would go away so she could enjoy the thrill. In spite of her fear, she didn't want the ride to end. Not yet.

She was five thousand feet in the air, floating freely in a hot air balloon, and below, the people, houses, and buildings looked like a miniature village. Breeze would only take quick peeks outside the balloon before the realization of being at the mercy of unpredictable Mother Nature would send chills up her spine. She covered her eyes with her hands.

"Oh my God!" she cried, when the balloon took a sudden dip. "We're so far up!"

"Are you okay?" Lex asked with a bemused smile tugging at the corners of his mouth.

"Yes and no," Breeze sighed, wondering how and why she let Lex talk her into taking a ride in a hot air balloon. Her initial reaction was, "Are you crazy?" But something had dared her to be bold.

I wonder just how bold I'm really beginning to feel, she thought, *looking at Lex in his blue jeans and open-necked shirt. Am I bold enough to undress him?*

It was their second date since seeing each other at the American Music Awards. With Breeze living in New Jersey and Lex living in Los Angeles, it was difficult to find a mutually convenient time and place. They finally agreed to meet for dinner when Breeze flew to Los Angeles, and Lex cancelled a business meeting.

Breeze had arrived at the restaurant a half hour late because she couldn't decide what to wear. She didn't want to be conspicuously sexy, nor did she want to be too sedate—she wanted to be elegant, yet sensuous. Breeze felt as she had on their very first date ten years ago when she scattered her clothes all over her bedroom.

After changing several times, she decided on a simple but scintillating strapless purple dress with a jeweled waist that barely touched the tops of her knees; accessorized by a sparkling diamond necklace with matching earrings and elbow-length purple gloves. She wore light makeup: crimson red lipstick, a layer of mascara and a touch of blush.

Lex felt the stirrings of familiar emotions, feelings he had tucked away, but not forgotten, when the maitre d' escorted Breeze to the table. She still had the touch of innocence and sweetness that she had at fifteen; but at twenty-six, she was a fully-developed, undeniably successful woman. *You look good to me, baby,* thought Lex.

Lex stood up to greet Breeze. As the waiter pulled out the chair for Breeze, Lex said, "Hello, Sunshine."

Breeze's full lips moved fluidly to form a beaming smile. She thought of the first time Lex had called her Sunshine, and noticed how sophisticated Lex appeared ten years later. The awkwardness of the teenage boy was replaced by the worldliness of significant accomplishment. She sat down, intrigued by the friend-stranger sitting across from her in an Italian-tailored black suit.

He's a black prince, that's what he is, Breeze thought. Lex smiled back, his teeth shining like white pearls. All the things Breeze had planned to say to him rushed out of her mind like a speeding train.

"I'm glad you could make it." Lex's eyes took in every detail of her body, every nuance of her face.

"So am I," she said in a silky voice. "So am I." Slowly, she removed the long purple gloves.

"Let's pretend," Lex began. "Let's pretend that this is our very first date. That we are a man and a woman who are out for the first time. What happened ten years ago didn't happen because we didn't know each other."

Breeze leaned forward, her tempting breasts in full view. "Why?" she asked. Shadows of uneasiness left her face: This was not going to be an evening of past recriminations. She wasn't ready for dredging up the past. The well inside her heart was buried deep, too deep for tears.

"We have to see what happens between us today without interference from the past if we go beyond today, then we'll know it's because of what we feel today, because in the end, what's going to really count is how we feel today," Lex explained. Leaning forward, his dark eyes were serious, his mouth, tight and grim.

Throughout the day, thoughts of Breeze had lingered in his mind. Their first date after so many years. He wondered what the evening would be like, whether Breeze still cared. He did not want to rehash the past, so he decided to take a more positive approach.

"And if it goes beyond today?" Her velvet-smooth voice held a challenge; seduction gleamed in her eyes.

"It'll explain a lot of things."

Breeze tilted her head back and peered curiously at Lex. She wondered what he meant by that comment.

Lex continued, "When the time comes, we'll deal with the shadows of the past. That will be the only way we'll get to the future."

"By finding out if there is something here today?"

The question hung between them in midair.

They eyed each other, searching for a sign, a subtle hint, that they were both still in love. Their lives had changed, years had dashed by, but their love somehow remained. Both already knew the answer, but wouldn't dare admit it to each other. First, they had to admit it to themselves.

Breeze and Lex didn't kiss on their first date. They talked, laughed, and enjoyed being in each other's presence. Three weeks had passed before they saw each other again.

In Breeze's panic-stricken eyes, Lex saw that the fear of falling was overpowering the thrill of floating in the clouds. Breeze took a deep breath and tried to relax, but her marble-like form betrayed her fragile control.

Lex caressed her face, feeling the softness of her cheeks, and asked, "What can I do to make you feel better?"

"Hold me," she whispered into his ear.

He put his arms around her shoulders, and she leaned against his body. With Lex's comforting closeness, Breeze closed her eyes and succumbed to the sensation. She felt the exhilarating lightness of floating in the air. Slowly, she began to relax.

For the first time in ten years, Lex kissed her. He kissed her softy and tenderly, warm and deep. He ran his fingers across her lips, and kissed her again, reclaiming her lips, devouring their softness, as if they belonged to him.

The kiss was a spark of desire, setting off a slow burn of anticipation.

"This is fun, right?"

"I'd rather be on the ground!" she said honestly.

Lex started telling her jokes and silly stories. She laughed, intrigued to discover new things about him.

"There are so many things about you that I don't know," Breeze whispered. "It is as if we really are meeting and getting to know each other for the first time."

"We are," Lex replied by gently kissing her cheek, his hand running through her wind-blown hair. "Ten years ago, we were just coming into ourselves. We were just learning about life."

Chanelle Diamond picked up the telephone and dialed Lex's phone number. She let it ring continuously, impatiently drumming her gold-painted fingernails against the handset. *Still no answer,* she thought angrily, *after twenty rings.* She slammed the phone down, knocking the phone on the floor. "Damn," she grumbled, putting the phone back together and placing it on the table.

Chanelle was frustrated and furious—her life was in shambles. She was frustrated because several record companies had rejected her demo tapes for a second album, and no one—agents, producers, managers—returned her calls. Only a year ago, when she was with The Jewels, record companies and producers were eager to help her launch a solo career.

Chanelle's solo album was a flop. The critics' reviews were merciless: "You should have stayed with The Jewels." "Find your own style." When the first two singles didn't get much airplay on radio stations, she had a third single remixed by a popular rap group. But when it was finally released, radio stations wouldn't even play it. Nobody was buying her album.

She missed all the excitement: the tours, the fans, the autographs, the interviews, the paparazzi. She was quickly fading out of the limelight, and Chanelle wasn't ready to give up her fame. She expected The Jewels to fade away without her, but they drew more fans when they replaced Chanelle with another singer. Renamed, The Golden Jewels, her former group was one of the hottest girl groups.

Chanelle wanted to make another album, or at the very least, record a single. She wanted Lex to produce the album. With his musical genius, she hoped to regain her popularity. If Lex agreed to produce at least a couple of songs, she speculated, then maybe a record company would offer a contract. But Lex claimed to be too busy with other projects. Lately, she realized furiously, he had even been too busy to see her. Something had changed between them. The signs were there.

Lex was preoccupied and distant. He didn't call much, and they rarely saw each other. She knew that Lex didn't want a serious relationship; he had made that clear on their first date.

"I'm married to my music, baby," he forewarned. But Chanelle had planned to change his mind.

She picked up the phone again and pressed the redial button. The phone rang and rang and rang.

Ever since the American Music Awards, thought Chanelle, *Lex has been impossible to reach by phone. It's that Breeze Blackwell bitch. I know it,* she fumed.

Lex's phone had rung more than fifty times before he answered it He heard the insistent ringing while unlocking the front door. When Lex answered the phone and heard Chanelle's squeaky voice, he regretted that he had forgotten to activate his answering service. She told him that she was coming over and hung up before Lex could respond.

Chanelle slipped into a sheer black dress; the chiffon material was transparently thin. She jumped into her red Corvette and hit the freeway going over 75 miles per hour.

A scowl covered Lex's face when he opened the door, annoyed at Chanelle's transparent game. She greeted him with a kiss, but her wide smile faded when she met his serious gaze. "Chanelle," he tersely said, "I told you I was busy. I'm working." He shut the door behind her, and turned down the hall.

Chanelle trailed after him past the laundry mom, through the kitchen and down the stairs to the entertainment level. This level was fully equipped with recreational activities: a game room with pool table, video games, and pinball machines; a viewing room with a ceiling-to-floor projection screen, televisions, VCRs, video cameras, and a collection of movies; and a listening room equipped with state-of-the-art stereo equipment. The studio was outside, on the other side of the pool, tucked behind a cluster of trees.

"I miss you, Lex." Chanelle flopped down on the large, plush, turquoise leather sofa. She pulled off her sandals and leaned back against its cushy softness. The room was in Santa Fe colors—pinkish-peach, greenish-blue, and rustic brown—the trendy colors of chic Californians.

"Chanelle, I keep telling you I'm busy. I've got several projects to finish by next week," he said distractedly over his shoulder. Lex stood at the bar and mixed two drinks: a scotch and water for himself and a gin and tonic for Chanelle.

"When are you going to be free to help me?" Chanelle asked in a pleading tone.

Lex sat down on the sofa near Chanelle and handed her the drink. She took a sip from the glass and cracked, "How nice of you to remember."

Ignoring her loaded comment, his lips twisted into a cynical smile. "I've got other projects lined up after I finish what I'm working on now." He retrieved the remote control from inside the Aztec crafted vase on the sofa table and pressed a few buttons. Two panels on the wall opened up to reveal a large television screen. Images from CNN appeared on the screen.

Lex had been avoiding Chanelle, hoping that she would get the message and just let the relationship end. But he realized Chanelle was not the kind of woman to be ignored. Knowing that her career was on the decline, Lex didn't relish ending their relationship. He didn't want to add to her disappointments, but he knew he had to be true to his heart.

Rubbing the back of his neck with his hands, he cleared his throat, "Chanelle, we need to talk."

"Oh, baby, let me massage you. You look tense," she suggestively offered. She inched closer to Lex and placed her hands on the base of his neck and began to gently knead the tight muscles. "You know I give good massages," she whispered into his ear.

"I don't need a massage," Lex said irritably. He pushed her hands off his neck and abruptly stood up. He walked back over to the bar. Frowning, his eyes stern under drawn brows, he said impatiently, "I'm serious, Chanelle."

Chanelle recognized, but ignored the gloomy expression on Lex's face. She knew what the scowling, contemplative look meant, and didn't want to hear it.

"Baby, I know what you need," Chanelle purred.

Seductively, she glided across the room, like a hawk claiming its prey. She wrapped her arms around his waist and began rubbing her scantily-clothed body against Lex. Her hands reached for the zipper on his pants.

Lex grabbed her hands. "Stop, Chanelle!" he commanded, glaring at her angrily.

"What's wrong, Lex?" she whined, her body still pressed against his. She gave him her most sad-eyed, petulant look. "You used to like…"

"I'm going to be straight with you." He eased away from Chanelle and pointed for her to sit down on one of the bar stools. Chanelle wiggled onto the stool, and provocatively parted her legs hoping that Lex would notice that she wasn't wearing panties.

"I don't think we should see each other anymore," Lex said. His voice was direct, his face stern.

"Why?" Chanelle asked in a shocked whisper. She hadn't expected him to end the relationship. Not so abruptly.

"Because it's not right for me," Lex explained.

"I don't want it to be over. I can't take this, Lex. Everything is going wrong." She put her hand on her forehead and closed her eyes for a minute before continuing. "Record companies keep turning me down. I owe a recording company 'production money.' I thought at least I had you to count on," Chanelle sobbed dramatically.

"I don't have anything to do with those record companies that you've been dealing with." Gently, he continued, "I'm very sorry that things aren't going your way. But it's not fair to you for me to continue the relationship when I feel the way I do. I've got too many things pulling at me."

"That's why our relationship has suffered. Maybe, if we lived together, then it can be like it was in the beginning."

"I have never lived with a woman, Chanelle. And I'm not going to start now," Lex explained, staring at Chanelle with an expression that indicated that her living together idea was out of the question.

Chanelle wanted to push the idea, but Lex's harsh face and tone made her change her mind. "Lex, please don't do this. I can't take all this rejection." She covered her face with her hands.

"I'm sorry, Chanelle. I don't want to hurt your feelings, but I don't like for things to linger if it doesn't feel right."

"If we just spent more time together, Lex, it would be different. It would be better."

"Chanelle," Lex said as he grabbed her shoulders. "Stop this fantasy of yours. We had a good thing, but now it's over."

"I don't want it to be over," Chanelle cried, tears shimmering in her eyes. She was hurt and angry.

"Chanelle, please. Pull yourself together!" He handed her a cocktail napkin.

She cried quietly for a few minutes, and then dried her tears. She excused herself and went into the bathroom, returning a few minutes later without the tears.

"I'm sorry, Chanelle, but you know this was never serious." Lex stood behind the bar, flicking the television channels with a handheld remote.

"I was hoping…" her voice trailed off. She went over to the sofa and picked up her purse. "Okay, but at least do me this one favor. If I can get somebody to sign me, will you help produce?"

"Maybe. I'm not making any promises, but I'll think about it"

In the executive conference room of Harmony Records, Breeze Blackwell, Lex Franklin, Edmund Mitchelson, and Jillian Bayer ended their brief meeting in full accord—Lex and Breeze were going to work together on her next album. Edmund had been anxious to have Lex work with some of his artists. Lex's sound was innovative. It was the new jack sound of the nineties: a mixture of hip-hop, rap, and rhythm and blues, all rolled together.

As they discussed the final details of the contract, Breeze thought back to the time when Lex had secretly taped her singing and revealed her talent to her. And now, irony of ironies, they were going to be making music together.

"I hear you're about to venture into the movies," Lex commented.

"Yes, I'm working on it as we speak," Edmund replied.

"If you're looking for a script, a good friend of mine is a writer, and he's got a screenplay that he's been shopping. If you're interested, I'll have him send it to you."

"I'm always interested in finding good talent. After all, finding Breeze was my miracle," Edmund said as he reached over to grasp Breeze's hands.

"Yes, Edmund, you were very lucky to find me," Breeze teased, avoiding Lex's probing gaze.

Frowning, Lex observed the interchange and began to wonder if there was more to Breeze and Edmund's relationship.

"Is the script any good? I've read hundreds of terrible scripts," asked Jillian Bayer, in charge of Harmony Record's newly-formed movie division.

"I haven't read it, but Malcolm's a good writer. Some producer was interested in it, but he couldn't get anybody to finance it"

Interested, Jillian nodded her head. "Have him send it to me. I'd like to read it," she said.

Edmund's secretary announced Edmund and Jillian's conference call over the intercom. Lex shook hands with Edmund and Jillian, sealing the deal. They left Breeze and Lex to discuss the music and song compositions.

"It's funny how things work out, isn't it?" Lex said, sitting across the wide rosewood conference room table. Fabric paintings hung on the wall blending with the pleated shades and plush carpeting in muted greys, pinks, and blues. "We are going to be working together!"

Laughing, Breeze said, "Funny and oh so strange." She paused thoughtfully before saying, "I wonder why it's happening like this?"

"What do you mean?"

"It's strange how our lives have come back together again."

Lex understood exactly what Breeze meant, but he wouldn't reveal his thoughts.

And Breeze dared not divulge her deepest thoughts. It was as if the years apart had been planned, because their lives were supposed to connect years later like pieces of a puzzle that fit perfectly together.

"We have to go out and celebrate," Lex suggested.

"Are we celebrating that we'll be working together professionally?" Breeze inquired, seated comfortably in the high back leather chair, tapping a pencil softly against the table edge. "Or are we celebrating that our lives have crossed again?"

"A little bit of both. But even if we weren't working together, I'm glad that we are getting to know each other again." He gathered the signed contract papers and put them in his briefcase.

"Me too, Lex. Uhh, just don't take me on a hot air balloon ride again, okay? Let's keep our feet on the ground." Breeze's soft chuckle sounded like music to Lex's ear.

A moment of silence passed before Lex broke the quiet. "Remember when you got married?"

She looked at him slowly, a soft crease between her brows, "What made you bring that up?"

"I was the best man for a friend's wedding on Saturday, and you know the part where they say 'Is there any reason why these people shouldn't be united in holy matrimony? Speak now or forever hold your peace'?"

"Yes?"

"I had gone to your wedding to stop you from getting married," Lex confessed in a rush of words.

She stared at him for a long minute, digesting what he said, while flashing back to an unhappy period in her life. "But you told me that…"

"I know what I said was very different from what I wanted to say," Lex smiled rigidly. "I wonder how different things would have been had I spoken from my heart and not from my mind."

They thought about what might have been had they taken control of their destinies at that very moment, that split second that would have changed the direction of their lives. The scenarios they conjured up in their minds were different, yet they were the same—they were together.

"There are so many questions between us, and not enough answers," Breeze said.

"That's because it's up to us to find the answers and write the ending. Our ending, not someone else's."

"And how do we do that, Lex? Go back in time?"

Lex walked around the conference room table and stood behind Breeze's chair. He spun the chair around so she would face him. "if it could be done, I'd go back in time. Even if it meant living on the brink of my dream." He pulled Breeze out of the chair. His dark brown eyes traveled over her face and searched her eyes. He grabbed her face with his hands and crushed his lips against hers. The touch of his lips on hers sent a shock wave through her body. Parting her lips, she raised herself to meet his kiss, responding to his warm and sweet lips. Blood pounded in her brain, leapt from her heart, and made her knees tremble.

"I want you to go away with me. I want us to spend time together without any distractions. No intrusions. We can finally put the past to rest and find out if we have a future."

"Go away?" Breeze questioned, recovering from the kiss that sent spirals of desire through her. She leaned back against the table and looked up at Lex, mixed emotions on her face.

"Yes! Go to the islands for two weeks. Just you and me, baby."

"Two weeks!" she exclaimed.

"That's a long time to be alone with someone," Lex said, putting his arms around her waist, drawing her next to him.

Encircled in his arms, Breeze had no desire to back out of his embrace. His masculine smell, mingled with a hint of cologne was overpowering. She was conscious of where his warm flesh touched hers.

"I can't clear my calendar. I've got too many things scheduled," she protested.

"If you say you will, I will. Just let me know when, and I'll let you know where."

CHAPTER TWELVE

Lex woke suddenly. He had been dreaming, a dream that wanted to pull him in deep, but he fought his dream's magnetic power and willed himself to awaken from the dream's frightening clutches.

In the dream, Breeze was only a short distance away—waiting for him to come to her. But he couldn't seem to reach her for every time he moved to press his fingertips on her face, she instantly dissolved and reappeared further away. The space between them widened with every advancement he attempted. He gazed into her fearful copper eyes and cringed; he desperately wanted to rescue her, to capture this manifestation of love. She was so close, just a touch away, a breath away.

Lex thrashed restlessly around the bed, as sweat poured from his brow; his eyes flashed open, momentarily confused by the unfamiliar surroundings—the ceiling fan spinning above, the green-flowery bedspread and the strange abstract painting of three old women hanging on the wall across from the bed. His mind returned to the present, and he remembered that he was far away from Los Angeles, on a quaint little Caribbean island where the pace of life was like a slow, Sunday rain. His eyes focused on the small alarm clock—it was only six AM Time seemed to move at its own, unhurried pace, as if tomorrow didn't matter.

Will Breeze come today? he wondered. *Maybe she'll show. I hope so.*

He'd been waiting for three days.

Lex had flown to Aruba three days earlier to meet Breeze so that they could spend time together, away from life's idiosyncrasies, to test their love, to justify their intense attraction. To finally answer the painful questions that had been haunting them both.

Lex arrived a day early and rented a secluded beach house where the beauty of the island was unblemished by tourism and urbanization. He phoned Breeze and half-teasingly, half-seriously told her that he was impatiently waiting for her to get there.

They planned to be together for two weeks, which meant canceling recording sessions, rehearsals, meetings, and interviews. Clearing their schedules was difficult because their reasoning couldn't be explained to others and didn't stand up under close scrutiny even to themselves. It was spontaneous. It was something people did when in love.

❧

India knew where Breeze was really going and why. "You don't fool me, Breeze. You can tell everybody else that you're going off to some island to study native dance for some new dance moves, but, girl, you're not going to palm that story off on me! You're going to see Lex."

Breeze glared at her sister and continued packing her clothes. She didn't know why she had tried to hide the truth. India knew that this day would come. She had seen it coming ever since Breeze and Lex had gone out to dinner after the American Music Awards.

India persisted, "Why else would you have a suitcase full of sexy lingerie?"

Breeze tried to frown; instead a girlish giggle burst forth. She had forgotten to close that suitcase. "You're too damn nosy!"

"I'm glad you're doing it!" India blurted out while plopping down on the bed, her arms flung wide.

"Aren't you going to ask what I think?" India asked, folding some of the clothes scattered across the four poster bed.

"I suppose I can't stop you," Breeze laughed as she peered at her adopted sister through heavy lashes. "Well, what do you think? I'm crazy, huh?"

"You've got to find out if there is anything between you two. That's the only way you're going to have peace of mind; otherwise, honey, you will be restless for life."

Breeze's attention was diverted from the collection of Louis Vuitton suitcases scattered around her bedroom as she slammed one shut. "I don't know, India," Breeze said. "It's crazy to still be affected by this man, after all these years. We were kids, but what we felt was more than puppy love."

"I know it was special, Breeze. Remember, I was there," India leaned against the pillows, her eyes aglow with fond memories of their teenage years. "I don't know anybody who's experienced a love like that I can understand why it would stay with you, why it's had such a hold on you."

"It won't let me go, India, no matter how hard I try to let it be!" Breeze spat out the words resentfully.

"You didn't let it go because Mother destroyed it. It left a mark, and you won't be free until you two face each other and sort it out." India reached out to still Breeze's agitated movements. "It may work, honey, and then it may not. But girl, you'll find out for sure."

Breeze appreciated her sister's sensitivity. She hugged India, and silently thanked God for bringing this special person into the family. She was so glad that someone understood her feelings. "Rayna would say I was crazy."

Shrugging her shoulders, India commented, "You know how hardcore Rayna is."

Her packing complete, Breeze sat on the edge of the bed, a troubled expression on her face. "I feel bad for Edmund. I can't say we have a relationship yet, but I know he expected it to be."

"Breeze, it can't be until you resolve the past."

She felt a wave of anxiety run through her body, felt it physically, a kind of shock wave with the force of an explosion. "I know. But I feel like I'm about to go down a dark tunnel without any lights or anything to guide me except a voice that keeps saying, 'Keep going.'"

"I guess you have to follow that voice until you know what's at the other end of the tunnel."

The glaring sun stood high in the middle of the sky when Breeze descended from the small, chartered plane. She had to shield her eyes from the sun. Her dark sunglasses weren't strong enough to deflect the sun's vibrant rays.

Every day when she called to tell Lex that she was going to be detained, she fully expected him to say he was returning to Los Angeles. But he had promised to spend fourteen days with her, and he was willing to wait it out. She felt a subconscious fear, a half-hope, that he would say he was leaving. Then she wouldn't have to face the truth: Now was the time to find out if the love that never was, could ever be.

Lex awaited her arrival at Aruba's airport. In three days his mocha-brown skin glistened like cooked brown sugar. The image of a seductive islander was further enhanced by shorts, sleeveless T-shirt, sandals, sunglasses, and a sharp straw hat.

Removing his sunglasses as she approached, he smiled in relief while watching her climb down the plane's stairs.

She is worth waiting for, Lex thought. *She's awesome.*

Dressed in a floral lace, white jumpsuit, and gold-speckled white sandals, Breeze was a vision of supreme loveliness. He wanted to slowly strip off her jumpsuit, to look at her luscious maple-colored body. He wanted to roll in, to feel the heat of her body. *Can't wait to get you next to me, baby. Soon. Very soon.*

"Baby, I'm so glad to see you."

Those words and his devastatingly sexy smile did something to Breeze's breathing. Lex pulled her close to him, and they searched each other's eyes. Lex's gaze finally settled on her full, bee-stung lips. She watched his mouth move closer, her eyelids slowly lowering with the first light and exploring touch of his lips against hers. Then his exploration changed, assuming a crushing insistence.

Breeze was sorry she had ever kept him waiting.

"What do you want to do?" Lex asked in a loaded tone.

Already wilting from the heat of the sun, Breeze said, "Go swimming!"

Lex beamed an indulgent smile down at her upturned sunny face. "The house is just steps away from the water. Let's jump in the ocean as soon as we get there."

Lex carried Breeze's suitcases to the car. She got inside on the passenger's side while Lex put her suitcases in the trunk. When they stopped to get some gas, Lex disappeared for a few minutes and returned with a present for Breeze.

"A hat!" she gleefully cried.

Lex had ducked into the open market, and quickly negotiated with a street vendor. "Since you didn't bring one, and you are definitely going to need a hat to protect yourself from the blazing hot sun."

Breeze tilted the floppy straw hat toward the front of her face and turned the rearview mirror towards her.

"Don't hide your pretty face."

Lex removed the hat, and his eyes boldly raked over her, dropping from her eyes to her mouth to her shoulders to her breasts. Something intense flared through his entrancement, and he smothered her lips with a burning kiss.

A laughing young man, who was waiting to use the gas pump, interrupted the kiss. "Go home, mon, if you must have her now," he teased in an island accent.

Lex moved away from Breeze, turned on the car, reposi-tioned the rearview mirror, and pulled off, tapping the horn lightly at the islander.

As Lex drove along Aruba's magnificent coast line, Breeze felt as if she had been transported to another place, another time. There were miles and miles of brilliant, unspoiled sugar sand beaches and an ocean water bluer than the finest piece of turquoise. She could see the sail-boats on the horizon moving gently with the refreshing ocean breeze and the swift movement of jet skis ripping through the bubbling blue water.

"There'll be enough time to see everything," Lex prom-ised, watching Breeze take in all the sights. It was the most beautiful place she had ever seen. The sky was a powder blue, sprinkled with billowy soft clouds. She rolled down the car window so she could feel the island wind and smell the ocean air.

"Fourteen days," Breeze said. "Oh, well…eleven days."

"This will be the happiest time of our lives. I promise you that I can feel it," Lex said, squeezing her hand reas-suringly.

After four days of indecision and anxiety, Breeze began to relax. She hadn't been certain that this rendezvous with Lex was the wisest path to follow. After her flight was air-borne, Breeze had been a ball of confusion, doubt plagued her every moment in the air. When the plane landed, she would have given anything to be home once more, but when Breeze saw Lex's joyous expression she knew beyond a shadow of a doubt: She had made the right decision.

The beautiful beach house was a fortress of seclusion, a personification of a private paradise. There was a spectacular view of the sparkling blue ocean and baby powder soft coral beach for miles around.

Breeze surrendered to the serenity of the island. It seemed that all her worries and concerns disappeared as soon as she passed through the door. The tall palm trees surrounding the house kept it cool; the leafy trees seemed to block out the realities of their lives.

Everything they wanted or needed was there: a well-stocked refrigerator, wine cellar, swimming pool, sauna, Jacuzzi, and exercise equipment.

"So, what do you think?" Lex asked, after bringing in Breeze's suitcases.

Breeze looked around the huge room filled with lush tropical plants and white wicker furniture, felt the soft breeze generated by the ceiling fans twirling in the air above and murmured, "I like it. It's so comfortable and peaceful," while waltzing down three steps into the sunken living room.

"I sent the staff away. A valet will check with us daily to see if we need anything, but we'll be alone. Just me and you, baby, twenty-four, seven." Lex paused, a frown creasing his forehead. "Does that frighten you?"

"A little…," Breeze confessed, a playful smile etched on her mouth."…And it intrigues me."

"Do you want the pool or the ocean?"

"Are you kidding? I'll take the ocean!"

In the bedroom, she quickly changed into a metallic gold bikini—the top barely covered her brown nipples, and the thong-cut bottom was deliciously revealing.

When Breeze sauntered out to the deck, Lex was waiting for her dressed in swimming trunks. Breeze remembered that Lex had a well-tuned athlete's body, but over the years, she anticipated he would have gained weight. Standing against the deck with the turquoise ocean and its patterned reflections of the sun in the background, he proved her presumption incorrect: tall, brown, taut and muscular. She couldn't resist the urge to reach out and stroke his chest full of curly black hair. Lex inhaled deeply, enjoying the feel of her fingers playing with the hair on his chest.

God, she is delectable, he groaned to himself. His arms encircled her, bringing her close to him, tantalizing his senses with her honey-colored skin: smooth, sweet temptation. His lips covered hers urgently.

Pulling away from his embrace, Breeze smiled wickedly, "You need to cool off," and stepped back from him.

"Something wrong?" he asked.

"No...no, everything is...yeah...everything is fine. Didn't your Mama tell you that you shouldn't be so easy?" Breeze baited, hands on hips, neck swiveling from side to side.

"Yeah, baby, but she didn't tell me I was going to have to drown for accepting an invitation," Lex's hands motioned towards her suit, "that was stamped guaranteed satisfaction." Breeze dissolved into peals of laughter. "It's a good thing we're not going into the ocean, because you'd sure heat it up," she quipped as she descended the stairs.

"Hey…you don't play fair…I thought you wanted the ocean…"

"You need to cool off fast, lover boy…

"Well, I'm just a boy where you're concerned."

Breeze jumped into the pool, swimming quickly out of reach.

The afternoon continued to be carefree and light-hearted: swimming, bantering, and playing in the water—the air charged with sexual tension.

Neither was prepared for their venture into passion. When they paused for a long, cool drink, Lex unceremoniously leaned over to kiss her succulent lips and moved ever so slowly down the softness of her neck. They didn't know whether it was the heat of the sun, or the burning coals of their suppressed desire that left their bodies burning. Inside the cool house, Lex picked Breeze up and carried her into the bedroom, lowering her in front of the bed. She removed her bikini bottom as he took off his trunks. They toppled onto the bed, skin touching skin, enveloped in ecstasy.

Lex placed both hands on Breeze's face. He kissed her deeply, twirling his tongue inside her mouth. He slowly moved from her lips to her chin, and then to her neck and shoulders, running his tongue against her skin—back and forth, back and forth, and then lightly kissed her wet skin. He placed his fingers around the shoulder straps of her bikini top and, as Breeze leaned back, he pulled the straps down and took it off. He kissed her breast and suckled her nipples furiously.

His hands went between Breeze's thighs and felt the moistness of her desire. He couldn't resist tasting her. He loved the taste of her, the touch of her, the softness of her skin. As he entered her, Breeze called out his name over and over. Never had she felt so good, never had he felt so much pleasure. They had waited too long for this moment to let it end quickly. Lex plunged inside her, deeper and deeper, filling her up, taking her to la-la land, to a place she had never been. And, when they finally came together, they were in each other's power.

Before she fell asleep, she heard Lex whisper her name as if she were a part of his dream. Sleepily, she raised herself up onto an elbow and gently touched his face—just to make sure he was not a mirage. Breeze sighed as she settled back down into the covers, a tranquility she had never felt before showed in her sweet smile.

An exploration of Aruba became an exploration of each other, their feelings, their memories, their life experiences.

Standing on the sailboat deck, Breeze could feel the ocean's undercurrent as the waves tumbled back and forth, carrying the sailboat away from the shore. The ocean was active, the water in never ceasing motion. But the wind was calm, listlessly moving the air. It was hot underneath the cloudy sky, in spite of the sun's hide and seek game.

"Are you sure you know how to operate this thing?" Breeze teased, standing next to Lex as he steered the boat further away from the island.

"Of course, baby!" Lex said, eyeing Breeze's legs behind his sunglasses. "Fasten your life jacket."

Miles away from shore, Lex turned off the motor and released the anchor. He joined Breeze at the side of the boat, looking at the row of hotels lined along the shoreline, the sunbathers perched on the beach and the water-lovers splashing in the ocean. Breeze bobbed her head to the reggae music playing on the radio.

"Happy?" Lex breathed into her ear. The nod of her head, her smile was the reply.

His mouth nibbled at her ear, his tongue strolled down her neck, and fingers trailed down her shirt to stroke her breasts. He pulled her down to the floor of the boat, kissing her lips, feeling her breasts, caressing her thighs.

"Lex, we can't do this out here," Breeze protested, fighting the desire coursing through her body. "Somebody will see us."

"No, they won't," Lex said, unzipping Breeze's shorts.

"What if we crash into somebody?" Her rational mind didn't want to enjoy the delicious sensations she was feeling. "Trust me, baby," Lex assured, his mouth pressing against her breasts, his fingers probing her innermost parts. Reason gave way to passion underneath the silky blue sky.

A few hours later, Lex turned the boat around, and headed back to the island.

"There has never been another woman like you, Breeze. I know you might not want to talk about this, but if we are going to go on from here, you have to forgive me for letting you go. Can you?"

"I don't know, Lex. I've been angry and resentful about it for so long, it's become a part of me."

"Do you really believe that I went off to school and forgot you? If you read my letters, you know that I didn't. I was confused. I was torn by my love for music and you, but I never forgot you."

Breeze sighed heavily, and wiped away droplets of sweat from her face. "My mother shouldn't have interfered!"

"She shouldn't have, but that was ten years ago. Now we are the ones in control. We're in control of this!" he murmured emphatically. "And the only way to really be together is to let go of the past."

"I know. Sometimes I think that maybe it was best this way. We may have gotten into each other's way, held each other back career-wise. You knew you wanted to be a musician since day one, but I didn't know that I wanted to sing until later. If we had been together back then we might never have made it. Our careers might have been unfulfilled dreams."

Lex reached forward to cup her face between his hands. "Can you forgive me for not coming back and fighting for you?"

Suddenly, tears started to flow down Breeze's cheeks.

Lex said, "Baby…baby…I didn't mean to make you cry."

"No…no…It's all right…I haven't cried about it for a long time," Breeze whispered against his chest. "I thought the tears were all gone." He bent over and kissed away each teardrop that fell from her eyes.

Lex cradled Breeze in his arms as she cried, his loving comfort melting away the pain that had been buried inside her heart for so long.

Beneath the star-laden midnight sky, Breeze and Lex shared a late-night picnic on the beach. The meal was simple: cheese, bread, wine, and grapes. Lex put a piece of cheese into his mouth and fed Breeze from the bunch of grapes.

"Tell me about Kyle," Lex said quietly, sitting across from her, pressing his bare feet against hers.

Suddenly, Breeze felt the coolness of the night playing against the back of her neck. Sitting with her knees up against her chest and her feet buried in the sand, she was wrapped in the warm comfort of a multi-colored shawl, cocooning herself. She stared out at the ocean and was amazed at how the sky seemed to touch the ocean off in the distance. Memories of her brief marriage were buried in the cobwebs of her mind.

She was so quiet and still that Lex regretted the question. "I'm sorry…You don't have to talk about it, Sunshine."

Breeze lifted her head and met his eyes filled with concern. "It's a memory I'm not comfortable with. It's a memory that I feel guilty and sad about."

"I know it seems petty because of what happened, but I was always jealous of him. The time he had with you, the nights…"

"What I did to him was unfair. I didn't love Kyle the way he loved me. In the end, he knew and accepted it. I married him to get over you." She looked at Lex, not quite able to make out his expression in the darkness, but she sensed a shifting in his emotions.

Breeze continued, "That was wrong and unfair. And that he was killed bothers me deeply. I've always felt like it was my fault," she explained in a strained voice that seemed to come from a long way off. She shivered as the ocean rumbled to stir the night.

"Don't blame yourself for what that racist cop did. I heard the story. Mama told me all about it," Lex consoled, rubbing her bare feet with his, the sand oozing between their toes.

"It's an ugly, ugly story. What happened changed so many people's lives. His father didn't become a judge, his mother became an alcoholic." She paused to fight the eerie sadness that threatened to engulf her. "I wonder, if I hadn't selfishly married him, maybe he wouldn't have been there, maybe that cop…"

"Breeze, don't do that to yourself. Life has too many what ifs and if-nots that are unexplainable. You have to leave some things alone. Please don't believe that you are the cause of the unexplainable, because you're not."

They stretched out on top of the blanket, contemplating the waxing moon, a shimmering crescent in the night sky, surrounded by the winking stars. They lay in silence, snuggled under the shawl, enjoying the comforting presence of each other, listening to the restless waves rushing towards a thirsty shore. The sound became the melodic rhythm of a soothing lullaby.

CHAPTER THIRTEEN

"It's still raining out there," Breeze said, peering out the kitchen window at the heavy raindrops pounding against the glass. She turned toward Lex, who was standing in the doorway. "I don't want to go back out in that mess."

"Neither do I," Lex agreed, his arms folded casually across his chest, a lazy grin on his face. "We could watch a movie, or we could go to bed early…"

Putting her arms around his neck, Breeze said, "Is that all you think of?"

"Sometimes," he admitted, giving Breeze a sly smile. "Or we can play cards."

A bright smile lightened her gloomy face. "Yes, I'd love to beat you at five hundred. Remember how I used to always beat you?"

"That's because I used to let you. I didn't want to hurt your feelings."

"Maybe at first, but I used to beat you when you weren't being nice. You get the cards, and I'll go find a pad and pencil."

Downstairs in the living room, they sat on the floor, a box of playing cards between them. Lex shuffled the brand new deck and dealt eleven cards apiece before placing the remaining ones and a face-up card on the floor.

Looking at the array of cards in her hand, Breeze predicted, "This is gonna be my night," before reaching over and plucking a card from the top of the deck.

"Not without a fight."

Breeze won the first game. As they played several games, they talked about their careers, how differently things had turned out, and their future aspirations.

"Lex, how'd you get into producing? All you ever used to talk about was playing the guitar, about being the next…"

"Jimi Hendrix," Lex finished. "It's funny how things happen in this business. That's what I started out doing. But when I started writing music and producing songs for people, that seemed to be my real talent. Plus, it's where the money is. After being on the road for years and playing with different bands, I started getting tired of it. After I produced a few songs that hit big, I was in demand. Eventually I stopped going on the road, and writing music and producing is all I've been doing."

"Do you miss it?" Breeze asked, laying out a spread of aces.

Lex gave her a frustrated glare. "Not like I used to. Now I'm in a different side of the music business. And I like it better. As a matter of fact, I may get my own record label," he bragged, laying out two spreads, the remaining cards in his hand.

"Lex!" Breeze cried, holding a handful of high cards which meant that she had lost that round.

"My own record label. Chameleon Records."

"That sounds wonderful, Lex," Breeze said, writing down their scores. "When will you know?"

"In a couple of months. I'm pretty sure it's going to happen."

"You always were confident. Or should I say cocky."

"Well, you got to think positive if you want anything to happen."

"I'm mighty confident that I've beaten you three games out of five," Breeze boasted.

"Let's make it best out of seven."

"Such a sore loser," Breeze teased, shuffling the cards for another game.

A few minutes before midnight, Lex quietly reentered their bedroom and gently sat down on the king-size bed. He stared at Breeze for a long time and thought about how much time they had lost. He thought of all the women that had been in his life. Those relationships were based on sexual need and companionship; no one inspired him to feel the way Breeze did. The women in his past flashed in his mind, their names, bodies and faces, but the presence of their being was as elusive as smoke rings in the air.

But Breeze was a lingering perfume—a phantom—her presence a recurring dream that sweetly plagued him no matter how far he travelled, how many women, or how intense his ambition. She was ever-present, trapped in the corners of his very being, and inescapable.

He touched Breeze's face, rubbing the back of his hand against the smoothness of her sun-kissed skin. She had fallen asleep in the sun and woke up feeling dizzy and nauseous. She awoke with his touch, her copper eyes opening in the darkness.

"Water," she whispered, her voice dry like a withered leaf. Lex poured water into a glass from the carafe on the nightstand and handed it to Breeze. She drank the water and handed the glass back to Lex.

Breeze moaned, "Now my head hurts." Her hand moved across her forehead.

"I wish I could kiss it away," Lex nodded sympathetically.

Breeze closed her eyes, waiting for the throbbing pain to subside. "Thank you."

"For what?"

"For asking me to come here. For wanting me to come back into your life again."

"There's no need to say thank you for that. After being with you again, I had to find out if there was more between us. There wasn't an option." Passionately, he added, "I would do anything for you."

Tears rolled down Breeze's face. "We've been cheated."

"I know. We may have been cheated out of the past, but, baby, we don't have to be cheated out of the present or the future." Lex swallowed and struggled to gain control of his emotions. "There is no doubt in my mind that I want you in my life. I can't imagine life without you. We can't let anyone interfere with our lives again."

Lex held Breeze and they whispered of their past quietly until dawn.

"That was so much fun!" Breeze cried, stumbling though the front door. "We should have stayed longer."

"They were getting ready to close," Lex said. He was wearing a casual tan suit, with a white cotton shirt, tan socks and tan loafers. He followed Breeze, dancing her way to the bedroom.

They had spent the evening at one of the island's exclusive hotels that featured fine restaurants, several discos and bars, and a large casino. They ate, danced, and gambled.

Breeze pulled Lex into her embrace, replaying dance moves from earlier that evening. Lex shifted his feet, his eyes twinkling at Breeze's glowing happiness. "It was fun dancing with you," she said.

Breeze slipped out of the orange and white chiffon halter dress, and gold metallic sandals. Her hair was brushed back into a long ponytail, clasped together with a large gold bow. Traces of orange lipstick, cinnamon blush, and gold eye shadow lingered on her face. "I had to come out of these," she explained, pulling a pair of white pantyhose out of her purse. "That club was hot and crowded and funky."

Lex laughed with Breeze.

"Look what else I have." She dumped a bunch of casino chips out of her purse. "I was killing them in blackjack."

"Breeze, you're supposed to cash them in."

"I know," she said impishly. "It seemed more exciting to have these chips."

"You just want an excuse to go back to the casino," Lex chided.

Breeze threw her head back giggling, and said, "Maybe." She pulled a short black nightgown out of the drawer and slipped it over her head.

"When'd you learn to gamble like that?"

"I sat next to this black woman who was a professional gambler, I guess. She told me what to do, when to fold, when to hit, what to bet, everything."

"Oh," Lex said, "I wish somebody had been at the crap table helping me keep my money, instead of losing."

"Maybe you'll win it back tomorrow."

Lex shook his head ruefully. "The sign of a gambler."

Yawning, Breeze said, "I'm hungry, Lex. Would you fix me a sandwich?"

"I'll be right back."

When Lex returned ten minutes later with a tray of late-night snacks—two chicken sandwiches, potato salad, and fruit—he found Breeze sprawled across the bed, fast asleep.

Breeze and Lex woke up feeling exactly the same. It was bright and sunny outside, but they both felt as if rain had whitewashed their souls. It was their last day together.

In twenty-four hours, they would return to their separate worlds. Life would be normal again. But how could anything in their lives be normal again after two weeks in paradise, after three-hundred thirty-six hours of absolute happiness?

Breeze's head lay in the crook of Lex's arm. She breathed a deep, sad sigh. Her feet were wrapped around his as she whispered, "Back to reality. In twenty-four hours, it will be all over."

"Baby, I hate to see it end too. I don't know what I expected, but I didn't expect this. We went beyond what we had when we were teenagers," Lex said.

Breeze said, "Yeah, I thought those feelings just didn't die because we didn't end it."

Lex ran his fingers gently across her lips and kissed Breeze lightly on the fullness of her mouth. "It can't end now," he simply stated, searching Breeze's eyes for a sign that she felt the same. Breeze's eyes were mirrors of his.

They were quiet as they thought about the unknown— the future.

"What happens after the perfect interlude?" Breeze asked.

"The perfect interlude," Lex repeated, agreeing with Breeze's description of their adventure in paradise. These last two weeks could just be a passionate interlude, a blissful time of their lives.

"Lex, where do we go from here?" Breeze asked, the pace of her heartbeat quickening against his chest. Or the last weeks could be a prelude to something more, a prelude to their connecting in ways that go straight to the heart.

Lex, leaning on his right elbow, with his head resting on his hand, admired the woman beside him. She was the only one who could make him feel like this—like the sun after the rain. She was the only woman who had meant more to him than music.

"Breeze, I've been thinking about this ever since you got off the plane," Lex began. "I know beyond a shadow of a doubt that I don't want to be without you. I don't want us to lead separate lives."

"No, we can't go back to the way it was before," agreed Breeze, wondering if Lex was going to ask her to marry him. However exciting the prospect was, she wasn't sure whether she wanted to get married right now. It was too soon, and there was still so much about each other that they needed to learn.

"I want you to be my wife…"

Breeze closed her eyes, wrestling with the emotions she felt: joy, excitement, fear, love. She heard the words she longed to hear, but questioned whether they were moving too fast.

Lex went on, "Sunshine, I don't want to disappoint you, but I think we should live together first because everything has happened so fast. I don't want to be reacting to island magic."

Breeze giggled. "Is that what this is? The island has cast some kind of mystical, magical spell over us, so now we can't separate reality from magic?"

"I know you feel it. Ever since I've been here I've felt like I've been transported to another world, another place, another time…"

"Lex, I know what you mean…I feel things I've never felt before. It's like there's a maturity to our feelings."

"Do you feel comfortable with us living together?" Lex paused and swallowed nervously. "I don't want to hurt or disappoint you. I don't want you to think that I don't want to marry you because, Sunshine, if you want to get married right away, I will."

"Lex, I know we have to get to know each other better in the real world. I don't want to rush into marriage either. The answer is yes. Yes, I'll live with you."

Smiling slyly, she moved closer to him, rubbing her body against his. "Right now," she planted kisses on his neck and shoulder and said, "I want you to work some of that island magic."

CHAPTER FOURTEEN

When Breeze sauntered off the plane at Kennedy Airport, she was surprised to see India and Rayna waiting for her.

"Rayna! India!" she shrieked. They hugged and kissed each other excitedly. "I didn't expect to see either one of you," Breeze declared.

"Since you finally hooked up with Lex, I had to hear all the details firsthand," Rayna explained, sporting a new haircut, a sleek ear-length bob with a full fringe of bangs. Three pairs of gold hoops in succeeding sizes dangled from her earlobes.

India said, "She didn't trust me to tell her. Girlfriend was convinced I would leave out something important."

"Like, did it feel as good as it did the first time?" asked Rayna.

Breeze shot back, "Girlfriend," in mock vernacular, "it felt even better."

"Ah, you needed it, didn't you, baby sister?" Rayna teased.

"Yes," Breeze admitted, shaking her head at Rayna's outrageous attitude.

"I just want to know if you had a good time. I don't need to know the details," India said.

"Who are you kidding, India?" Rayna asked, leaning back with her hands on her hips. "The details are the good part." Squinting as she examined Breeze, Rayna said, "Girl, you got dark! You must have stayed in the sun."

Breeze's caramel-colored skin had turned a deep, cinnamon brown. She extended her arm, proudly displaying the beauty of the sun's kiss. "That sun is so strong that you get tanned just walking out of the airport," explained Breeze. "It was a blast! I had the best time of my life." It showed in her face. She radiated sweet contentment.

"I can't believe you didn't call. Not once...," said India.

"Once I got off the plane and saw Lex, I completely forgot about the rest of the world. I felt like I was sixteen again!"

"You look happy, Breeze," Rayna said. "I could tell the moment those doors swung open and you strutted out that you were happy."

"I am. All those nagging questions and doubts that have been hanging over my head for years are gone. Our love is no longer a mystery. It is, not was."

"Where is the Negro?" Rayna inquired. "I thought he might fly in with you."

"He had to get back to L.A."

"Well...what happens next?" India asked, her jet-black hair hung loosely down her back.

"India, you look just like one of those island girls I left behind," Breeze said.

"I am an island girl, remember?" India said ruefully.

"Oh, that's Breeze Blackwell," a shrill voice screamed. Seconds later, a group of fans surrounded Breeze, Rayna, and India. "Can I get an autograph? Can I get an autograph?" the voices demanded.

Breeze politely signed autographs, chatting warmly with the group of teenagers.

They got into the limousine just as a new group of screaming fans approached. The limousine driver pulled away from the curb, leaving the fans screaming, "There's Breeze! There's Breeze!"

"Now what happens? Do you ride off into the sunset and live happily ever after?" asked Rayna.

Breeze paused before announcing, a wide grin curving her lips. "We're going to live together," Breeze said, "before we get...married."

"Surprise, surprise," Rayna teased.

Sitting across from Breeze and Rayna, India asked, "Why not just get married?"

"No...not yet. We have to get to know each other in the real world first," Breeze sighed wistfully. "The last two weeks were like paradise, but there's so much about each other that we don't know. We love each other, but can we live together? Can a real relationship work?"

"That makes sense," agreed Rayna.

Fully understanding her sister's feelings, India inquired, "Where are you two going to live?"

"That was our first disagreement. I wanted him to move out here with me, but he's got so many projects in L.A., and the studio is in his house, so it only makes sense for me to move in with him. Eventually we'll look for a house together, and since it will take time to find one, I'll just move into his."

Arms folded across her chest, India said, "Well, that disagreement was easily worked out."

"I found out how stubborn Lex can be."

"He's stubborn and you're headstrong. What a combination," Rayna said.

"So, what's been going on with the album?"

"The new single, 'The Affair' is about to hit number one. I'll give it another week," India informed.

"That's wild!" Breeze said, smiling wildly.

"My baby sister is making history. Every single a number one hit. You got it going on, girlfriend!" Rayna affectionately patted Breeze's legs.

"I should have a party to celebrate," Breeze said. She stretched out her legs. "No, maybe I should wait until I'm moved in with Lex."

Updating Breeze on other issues, India said, "Coca-Cola is after you again to do commercials. When Pepsi found out about it they started calling, and the best part is that they want to sponsor your tour."

"What does Edmund say?"

"He thinks you should go with one of them. It'll save Harmony money. Coke will probably sponsor your tour if you sign with them."

"I'll talk it over with Edmund and Jillian."

"Are you going to sell the house?" Rayna queried, looking into a compact mirror, applying ruby red lipstick to her heart-shaped lips.

"No, this is where we'll stay when we come to New York. I'll just move some of my things out there...India, how do you feel about working in L.A.?"

A smug smile framed India's lips. "You won't believe this but Zeke wants to move to L.A. after we get married, and I've finally decided on a wedding date."

"When?" Breeze and Rayna asked simultaneously.

"Saturday, August fifteenth!"

"She wants us to be bridesmaids," Rayna added. "Mother's helping me plan it. She's so excited!"

"I know she is. Ma has done at least a hundred weddings," Rayna commented, returning her makeup case to her purse.

"Your wedding is my gift. Whatever you want, cost is no object."

"Oh, Breeze, you're too much."

"Mother won't mind. She's always wanted to do an expensive, extravagant wedding."

"She's already picked out this outrageous gown. It's too tough, girl!"

Thinking about Lillian brought a slight frown to Breeze's face. "What is she going to say when I tell her about Lex?"

"It'll trip her out," Rayna predicted, "but she'll get over it."

"What about Edmund?" India asked.

Rayna raised her eyebrows in surprise. "Breeze, you been getting it on with Edmund? He's a good looking man. What took you so long?"

"We were just getting started when Lex came back into my life."

Rayna waved her hand across her face and snapped her fingers. "And Lex knocked him out of the box."

Breeze didn't realize how tired she was until she got home. Fun in the sun and little sleep was exhausting. Her mind was in a tailspin thinking about all the things she needed to do. She had phone calls to return and mail to read, but once she saw her soft, comfortable bed, Breeze couldn't resist climbing into it for a short nap.

When Breeze woke up hours later, she couldn't believe that she had slept through the evening. She picked up the phone to call Lex, but newly found courage made her dial her mother's number instead.

Lillian answered the phone after three rings.

"Hi, Mother. How are you?"

"I'm fine, baby. How was your trip?" Lillian's voice was cheerful.

"It was fabulous. I had a wonderful time."

"I was just going over India's list. I don't know how to trim this thing. She's got so many folks that she wants to invite," Lillian grumbled.

"Don't trim her list. Why rain on her parade? Let India invite as many people as she wants."

"Half of the people on this list must be Zeke's friends. I don't know these names."

"It doesn't matter. Whatever makes them happy."

"At this rate, we'll be sending out a thousand invitations, for Pete's sake," Lillian complained.

"I called to tell you something."

Concern rang in Lillian's voice. "You aren't sick, are you?"

"No, Mother, I'm fine."

"Is something wrong?"

With an edge to her voice, Breeze replied, "No, it's something good."

"I bet I know: Your latest song, 'The Affair,' went number one."

Breeze smiled. "I'm glad you pay attention to those things. But I really called to tell you that I'm moving to L.A."

"You are?" The inflection in Lillian's voice revealed uncomfortable surprise. She had a funny feeling there was more news.

"I'm going to live with Lex," Breeze announced in a rush of stilted words.

There was a long silence which loomed between them.

"Did you hear me?"

"Yes, Breeze, I heard you. You're going to live with Alexander Franklin," Lillian said nervously, her eyes batting wildly.

"I was with Lex when I went to Aruba."

"The same Alexander Franklin."

"Of course."

Silence crackled on the telephone line.

"You never got over him," Lillian flatly stated.

"No, Mother...I've always loved him."

Long, uncomfortable moments passed as both contemplated the unacknowledged breach that now threatened to become a chasm.

"I was wrong, Breeze. So very wrong," Lillian choked on her words.

"You hurt me more than you know."

Coughing back the tears, Lillian continued, "You two must really have something special to still want each other after all these years."

"Very special."

Lillian could hear the love in Breeze's voice. "Does he love you as much as you love him?"

"Yes!"

"Breeze, honey...will you ever forgive me?" Lillian painfully asked.

"I'm not angry about it anymore. I've got what I need now. I've got Lex."

"But, baby girl, we have to make our peace. In spite of the pain I've caused, you've been a wonderful daughter. I mean you bought me this house, a car, and you've sent me on trips. But I've never heard you say you understood or forgave me for what happened."

"I want you to have these things. I love giving you things. What kind of a person would I be if I didn't share my success with my family?"

"Will you ever forgive me? I mean really forgive me?" Lillian asked.

Breeze hesitated before answering because buried in the well was still a great deal of anger. Hopefully, with Lex back in her life, it would melt. The pain would be healed by a revisitation of love. "I know it's wrong for me to be unforgiving, but it's hard to forget the past. I felt betrayed. Betrayed by someone who I believed would never let me down. As time goes by, it will hurt less and less. Love tends to fill in the gaps. Now I finally have that love in my life."

The flight to L.A. was rocky. It was storming fiercely.

Angry thunder, mad lightening, and wicked winds played seesaw with the private plane, bouncing it around as if it were a weightless feather. Every time Breeze or India attempted to stand up, the plane would take a sudden dive, throwing them back into their seats. Securely fastened in, they prayed that the plane would land safely.

Breaking the long silence, India suddenly woke Breeze to ask, "Breeze, would you do me a favor, no matter how crazy and wild it seems?"

Breeze had been lightly napping, but the seriousness in India's voice got her full attention. She looked into India's anxious eyes, and soothed, "You know I would."

"I don't know anything about my real mother. All I have are those old pictures that I once showed you. I've always wanted to know what she looks like now, what kind of person she is, whether I have brothers and sisters, aunts and uncles." India paused, her voice heavy with loss. "What happened to her? *If* she's alive, I want to know why she didn't come back for me!"

Breeze saw the anguish in India's dark eyes when she talked about her real mother, a smoldering pain, laced with burning flashes of anger. "India, I've seen you looking at those pictures. I see the pain in your eyes. Honey, if I can help, please just say the word," Breeze said gently.

"Would you help me find my mother?"

"India, I'll do anything to help you. I love you," Breeze said reassuringly.

India released a sigh of relief, the tension slowly easing from her face. "I want to know what happened to her!" she exclaimed, clutching the arm of her seat. "I'm about to get married and start a new life, and I want to know more about myself. I feel American but I'm really an island girl. I don't know anything about Trinidad, about my heritage. I've got to know, Breeze. I've got to find out."

"I understand," Breeze soothed. *We both have been haunted by lost loves,* Breeze thought.

Engulfed by her thoughts, India peered out the window, but did not see the eerie dark clouds and sudden flashes of lightning. Moments of silence passed before India quietly said, "So Zeke and I are going there for our honeymoon."

"That's a great idea! I'll get a private detective to find her. India, it might be a simple matter of giving all the pictures and papers you have and seeing what he comes up with!"

"Yes…yeah…I don't know…I'm scared, Breeze. I just hope she's not dead!" declared India with bitterness and confusion coloring her voice.

"Why do you think she's dead?"

"Because she never came back for me!" India said, pounding her fist on the armrest.

"I'm sorry, India. There's no way of knowing."

"I hope she's alive. I hope she's alive because I want to know why she forgot me," India whispered as a lone tear weaved down her smooth, dark skin. "I need some answers, Sis."

Breeze woke up with a smile of contentment on her face. She thought about her first night of living with Lex, how wonderful and relaxing the evening had been. He had made dinner for her, and they talked about all the things that needed to be done to finalize her cross-country move.

She was a little disappointed that he had to leave so early to catch a plane. But, she concluded, early flights, late studio sessions, and business trips were going to be the norm living with a busy record producer.

Breeze hopped out of bed and went to the bathroom to wash her face. She donned neon green biker shorts and a long T-shirt before proceeding to the small exercise room right outside the bathroom. It didn't have the equipment she was used to, but the rowing machine, bike, and Stair Master would suffice.

She got on the bike and pedaled slowly, familiarizing herself with its electronic functions, when she heard the doorbell ring. Downstairs at the door, Breeze was flabbergasted to see Chanelle Diamond shoving the door into her chest.

Before Breeze could react to her unexpected, unwanted visitor, Chanelle very rudely asked, "What the hell are you doing here?" She whisked through the foyer into the living room as if she owned the place.

Indignant, Breeze responded, "I think the question is what are you doing here?"

"I came to see Lex!" She was dressed in a long rayon-blend shirt with matching palazzo pants. The black and white polka-dot ensemble had a twist-front bra, openly revealed underneath the unbuttoned shirt.

"He's not here."

"When will he be back?"

"He won't be home until tonight."

Angry shock registered on Chanelle's face. Removing her dark sunglasses, she gave Breeze a sinister look. "What do you mean home?" she demanded.

Breeze smugly smiled. "I live here."

A wicked snarl crossed Chanelle's lips. "You're lying. Lex don't play that," she growled, hands defiantly on her hips.

"You better get your facts straight before you call somebody a liar."

"If it is true, then you won't be living with him for long!" Chanelle said, pacing around the living room. "Because, honey, I've got some news for you. It'll shock you." She paused for effect, standing in front of the marble fireplace, directly across from Breeze who stood in the doorway. "I'm pregnant with Lex's baby," she proudly announced, staring into Breeze's face, gauging her reaction.

Breeze felt as if a ton of bricks had been dropped on her stomach. Her face remained impassive, not revealing the angry turmoil inside her mind and heart. "I'm not going anywhere even if you're having Lex's baby, that is *if* you're having Lex's baby."

"It wasn't that long ago that me and Lex had something going on." Cockily, she added, her sunglasses flinging in the air with the agitated motion of her hands, "And I know Lex wouldn't wan this baby to…"

"Look, if you are carrying Lex's child, then it will be between you and him how you work this out." Breeze walked across the room, closer to where Chanelle stood. "But let me tell you something, Chanelle. That changes nothing between us because I'm not going anywhere!"

"You just think you know what he's going to do. But you don't know him that well." Chanelle walked quickly across the room, around the corner, and down the hall to the front door.

"I know enough. I know you have nothing to do with what goes on here!"

Chanelle's mouth hung open as Breeze slammed the door in her face.

It was after midnight when Lex sprinted up the stairs, softly whistling the new song he was working on for Breeze's next album. All day his thoughts kept straying to his new life, the fact that Breeze was in his house, sharing his bed, a part of his life.

Lex quietly crept into the bedroom so as not to disturb Breeze. After removing his suit jacket and hanging it on the valet, he walked over to the bed and leaned down to kiss Breeze.

Before his lips reached Breeze's face, she leapt up angrily and screamed, "Don't kiss me!"

Lex jerked back, bewildered by Breeze's strange behavior. "What's the matter with you?" Lex turned on the bedside lamp. He needed to see if Breeze's angry voice matched her face.

Breeze's nightgown was twirled around her body from her restless sleep, and it shifted to reveal one caramel breast hanging out of the gown. Lex eyed it hungrily, but the furious glint in Breeze's eyes was like a flashing red light.

"Chanelle says she's pregnant!"

"What!"

"She came over here looking for you this morning, and told me she was pregnant after I told her I lived here."

"That bitch!" Lex uttered angrily.

"Excuse me," Breeze said indignantly.

"I'm sorry, Breeze, I didn't mean to curse at you. But Chanelle has been a real pain in the ass. I told her before the trip to Aruba that our relationship was over. She knew at the Awards show that things weren't the same between us. We were never serious anyway." He walked across the room and sat on the black camelback sofa near the armoire. The contemporary bedroom was decorated in black and white, offset with red accessories.

"Apparently you didn't make yourself clear!" Breeze pulled off the covers and bounced out of the bed.

"She doesn't want to understand. The main reason Chanelle is after me is so that I can produce a track for her. She's been bugging me for months," Lex explained.

"Did you turn her down?" Breeze asked in a I-hope-you-did tone.

"I've told her several times that I was too busy." Easing out of his shoes, he said irritatedly, "I told her I had other commitments."

"Well, maybe she thinks you'll make time."

"I don't have time and I don't want to produce her. She's a marginal singer, and she wants me to save her career. I don't have time for that kind of bullshit. I don't know where she came up with this pregnancy ploy."

Sitting on the edge of the bed, Breeze said, "You better hope it's a ploy. But I take it that it is possible for her to be pregnant with your child."

Remorsefully, he said in a quiet voice, "I was involved with her Breeze, but we haven't been together in a couple of months."

"I'll tell you what, Lex. I don't want to deal with her. I told her that I'm not going anywhere even if she is carrying your child."

"You did?" He had removed his pants and shirt and left them lying on the sofa.

"That's what I told her." She stormed over and stood directly in front of Lex, her eyes brimming with righteous anger. "But what I want to know from you is, what do you plan to do about it?"

"I don't believe she's carrying my child, and before I do anything about it, I want proof. I want to see some tests that prove she's really pregnant."

"Oh, I see you've been through this before." It was a disappointing realization. She whirled around and returned to sit on the bed.

"Look, Breeze, I know the games that women play. If she is pregnant, then I want proof that she's carrying my child. I don't believe Chanelle is pregnant. She is too concerned about her career, and I know that having a baby is the last thing on her mind."

Breeze swallowed and heaved a long sigh before asking, "But if she is pregnant with your baby, what then?"

Sitting beside her, he humbly said, "That doesn't change anything between you and me. I will take care of my child. I will not let a child of mine grow up without me, but I'm not going to let some crazy woman play me. I know what you're thinking, but I don't believe she is pregnant."

He tried to touch her face, but she jerked her head away from him. "If she is it doesn't matter. I love you, Breeze. I want only you."

Breeze climbed back into the bed. "I don't know what to think, Lex. It hurts to think of you with anyone else."

"That was before you. Now that you are back in my life, I don't want another woman."

Breeze rolled over, her back to Lex. "Good night, Lex."

"Breeze, I'm sorry about Chanelle. I'm sorry she came over here like that. I told her in plain English before we went to Aruba that our relationship was over. So please, don't let her come between us. We have to be more connected and stronger if we are going to be together in this crazy business. People will do anything to get what they want, and they don't care if they hurt me or if they hurt you."

"Lex, I just hope that you don't have any more pregnant ex-girlfriends," Breeze whispered bitterly.

Lex leaned over to kiss Breeze, but she moved closer to the edge of the bed. "Good night, Lex."

Edmund's door was answered by a young woman of Spanish descent whom Breeze followed to the back of the house where the pool was located. Wearing tortoiseshell sunglasses, she quietly watched Edmund swim lap after lap around his large, kidney-shaped pool.

"Breeze," Edmund smiled as he stepped out of the pool, beads of water glistening on his short-cropped hair and ebony skin.

"Hi, Edmund," she said, and handed him a towel.

Edmund dried himself with a thick, freshly-washed towel, and padded over to the lounge chairs.

"Would you like something to drink?" Edmund asked as he lifted the pitcher of lemonade.

She nodded her head, so Edmund poured two glasses of ice cold lemonade and handed a glass to Breeze.

"You sure got tanned on your vacation!"

Breeze chuckled. "Everyone keeps telling me that. I must look different."

"You do. The color looks good on you. You look like a chocolate drop, ready to be devoured."

Breeze smiled in appreciation of the compliment, but hesitated to respond. She took a seat on the patio furniture across from Edmund. An umbrella covered them, shielding them from the midday sun.

"So," Edmund said while placing his glass of lemonade on the white outdoor table, "what brings you here?"

Breeze removed her sunglasses. "Our relationship has changed so much that I don't know where we are…" She paused, searching for the right words.

"You came to tell me about you and Lex."

"How'd you know?"

"I made it my business to know."

"Why?"

He looked straight into her troubled expression. "You know why, Breeze," Edmund replied without apology.

Breeze looked away.

"When you disappeared for two weeks, that was the tip-off. You have never gone away that long and not told anybody where you're going and why.

"I wasn't fooled. I knew something was going on between you two when we met to sign the contracts. Lex couldn't keep his eyes off you, and you tried hard not to stare back. India told me a long time ago that you were haunted by your first love. It didn't take me long to figure it all out."

"I wanted you to hear it from me instead of the tabloids." She drank some of the lemonade, enjoying the tangy taste. "And I wanted to tell you in person that Lex and I were living together."

"Well, that I didn't know," he said disappointedly, sinking back into the padded lounge chair.

"We have to get to know each other better before…"

"You plan to marry him, Breeze?"

"Yes!"

Studying Breeze's face, Edmund saw the glow in her eyes, and the proud, expectant smile. "Will Lex make you happy?" Edmund probed.

"Yes!"

"That's what matters to me. I had three years to admit my feelings for you, but didn't. I hesitated because I promised myself I wouldn't get involved with a singer." Wryly Edmund concluded, "I waited too long."

"India used to tease me about you, but I never took her seriously. You never gave me a clue."

"That's because I didn't admit it to myself. And when I realized what I felt for you, I acted too late."

"I just don't want us to be awkward and uncomfortable with each other."

"No, Breeze," Edmund shook his head. "There're no hard feelings. We have a great business relationship, and I see no reason why we can't continue working together. After all, we were friends before I tried to make it into something else."

Breeze hugged Edmund, and when he kissed her, it was a tame, tender kiss signifying their friendship.

CHAPTER FIFTEEN

Breeze tore open the Federal Express package and pulled out a videotape that had "demo" scrawled on the front. She ran down the stairs, out the rear door, passing the pool, and down the short path before opening the door to Lex's custom-designed recording studio. With headphones on, Lex was lost in the symphony of sound, concentrating on his work. Breeze tried to get his attention, but Lex didn't acknowledge her presence until Breeze stood beside him and tapped him on the shoulder. Lex held up his left hand with his index finger extended, signaling that he would be done in a minute.

Breeze showed Lex the tape in her hand, pointing to the label. Lex nodded his head and started pressing buttons on the console, ending his session.

"Sorry to disturb you, but I couldn't wait," Breeze said excitedly, after Lex removed the headphones.

In the viewing room, Lex picked up the remote control hidden in a vase on the table and pressed a button. On the blank wall facing him, two cabinet doors slowly slid open, revealing a large projection screen television, a stereo system, and several VCRs. Breeze handed him the tape, and he pushed it inside the VCR. Lex pressed the appropriate buttons, and the TV came on. He sat down on the sofa next to Breeze.

"I hope you like it," Breeze said, as a large can of Coca-Cola appeared on the screen.

The sixty-second commercial reenacted Breeze and Lex's first meeting. Scenes flowed in rapid succession—a wedding; the bride walking down the aisle; the bride and groom kissing; the reception; the wedding cake. The camera zooms in on the band, waiting for the singer to arrive. The leader of the band announces, "We need a singer." When no one volunteers, he picks Breeze out of the audience to sing for them.

Breeze hesitates. She takes a sip of Coca-Cola, and runs on the stage. Then she sings Coca Cola's theme song, "Coca Cola Classic, Can't Beat the Real Thing."

"What do you think?" Breeze asked when the screen went fuzzy.

He chuckled, "How does the saying go? Does life imitate art or does art imitate life?"

Breeze giggled. "Something like that."

"I think it's a good concept. It tells a story, and people seem to like that."

"That's what I thought."

"Does anyone know that it was based on real life?"

"I didn't tell them where I got the idea. I just told them I had a wonderful idea, and they were sold on it."

"You're going to sell them a lot of Coke."

"Are you finished working?" Breeze asked seductively.

Rubbing his hands over his face, Lex released a tired sigh. "For a little while, I guess."

Breeze stood in front of Lex, ran her fingers through his hair, and in a throaty voice suggested, "Let's go skinny dipping." She didn't wait for Lex's reply; she began moving her body in soft, rhythmic movements, dancing to sensual music that only she heard.

Lex stared at Breeze as she writhed her body before him, her hips grinding erotically. He thought of the last few weeks: There were some definite advantages to living with a woman.

"Oh, I like how you distract me." Reaching his arms out to bring her near, he growled, "Come here, baby."

With a teasing, sexy smile, Breeze said, "No!" She backed away from him and slowly began to remove her clothes. She lifted her blouse over her head while rocking her hips back and forth, exposing a sheer lacy bra. Her hands slid past her breasts and down her lean stomach, stopping at the top of her skirt. With both hands on the skirt waistband, she moved the skirt down her thighs, past her knees to the floor. She stared at Lex for a second before stepping out of the skirt and picking it up. She waved the skirt in the air before throwing it at him.

"Breeze!" Lex said when the skirt landed on his head.

"Take off your clothes!" Breeze demanded. "Fair's fair."

Lex lustily gaped at Breeze in her see-through bra and G-string panties. He removed his shirt and pants, his eyes never leaving Breeze's beautiful body.

"Come here," he demanded huskily.

Breeze backed away from him, moving towards the door.

"I'll meet you at the pool," she said before throwing her bra and panties in his direction.

Lex quickly removed the rest of his clothes, and followed Breeze outside. She was swimming around the pool, darting back and forth.

"Come on in," she taunted, "the water's warm."

Lex eased into the water and swam across the pool to Breeze. Just as he reached her, she swam away, teasing him with "catch me if you can." As Breeze swam around the pool, Lex tried to catch up with her, but every time he came close, she would swim underwater to the other side of the pool. She ended up on the shallow end of the pool, waiting for Lex to find her.

When he swam over to her, finally capturing her in the corner, he said, "I got you now!"

"Breeze, are you awake?" Lex whispered as he slid into bed beside her.

Breeze shifted around, turning towards him, and sleepily opened her eyes.

"Sorry to wake you, baby, but I feel like talking."

She lifted her head to read the digital clock on the nightstand. Yawning, she said, "It's 2:30 AM"

"I just finished working on the song for M.J. It's gonna hit big. I guess I'm kind of wired."

"Lex, you're going to have to start taking better care of yourself. Don't you have an early meeting?"

"Yeah," he said nonchalantly.

"How can you survive on so little sleep? I'd be miserable on three or four hours sleep."

"I'm used to it." He turned toward Breeze, his head resting on his hand, and said, "You know, Breeze. I was nervous about living with you. I know it was my idea, but I've always been on my own. I had no idea what it would be like living with a woman. Living with you, now that you're here, I wouldn't want it any other way."

"I was afraid, too, Lex. Afraid that what we experienced in Aruba was an illusion and that it wouldn't work for real. I knew I was taking a big chance living with you." She pressed her body closer to his. "I don't feel as afraid anymore."

"Afraid of what?"

"There are still situations that we haven't faced together. And I don't know how you'll react to some things."

"That's because we're still getting to know each other. But you know what makes me feel better about it?"

"What's that?" Breeze asked, her head tucked in the crook of Lex's arms.

"We love each other. We have something special. So no matter what we face, whether we've faced it before or it's something new, we love each other no matter what. As long as we're committed to that love we can face anything together."

"You're right, Lex. I think that's why everyday I'm less and less afraid."

Lex slid the *Essence* magazine across the kitchen table towards Breeze who was eating fruit salad for lunch.

Breeze laughed aloud at the front cover. She was as brightly colored as the colorful Jacob Lawrence painting hanging behind her. The painting was done in sizzling reds, neon purples, dazzling yellows, and brilliant blues, as was Breeze's hand-painted face and body.

"It's something to laugh at, all right," Lex said with a scowl of displeasure. He laid the stack of mail on the table, sorting it into two piles.

Breeze arched her eyebrows. "You don't like the way I look?" She put the fork down and pushed her food away. She brought the magazine closer to her for a better look.

Beads of perspiration glistened on Lex's face from playing several sets of tennis. He was dressed in sneakers, white shorts and a T-shirt. "No! You look like a clown."

"No I don't," she said defensively, throwing Lex a piercing glare. "I'm made up to look like a piece of art. That's why the picture was taken next to a Jacob Lawrence painting. All the photos were shot with me standing next to art."

"Do you think the public is going to understand that?" He opened the refrigerator and took out a pitcher of ice water. He carried the pitcher over to the tall white cupboards where he pulled out a gold-rimmed glass and poured water into it.

The large kitchen sparkled in black and white— gleaming white appliances, glass cupboard doors, white cabinets, and black-and-white tiled floor. An island in the center of the kitchen featured copper-bottomed pots and pans hanging from an overhead frame; a Cuisinart on the counter; a hardwood rack holding knives and a butcher's round; and a double-sink of stainless steel.

"If they don't, they don't." Breeze shrugged her shoulders. She was hurt by Lex's disapproval. "You don't have to be so harsh."

After gulping down the much-needed water, Lex said, "I shouldn't have been so blunt, but I was just being honest."

"I thought you would like the picture."

"Why?"

"I look so different that you probably didn't recognize me. That should intrigue you."

"Why?" Lex asked again, while pouring another glass of water.

"I know you're used to having different women. From what I hear, you have never been a one woman man."

"Breeze, what are you talking about?"

"I'm just saying, if you've got to have variety," she picked up the magazine and held it up, "this is a different me."

Lex walked back over to the table and sat in the chair next to Breeze. "You're the only woman I want." He trailed a finger from the top of her forehead to the tip of her nose.

"Can you be faithful to one woman?" Breeze asked seriously.

"What is that supposed to mean?"

"I just want to know what I've gotten myself into." She stuck her fork into a chunk of red, ripe, juicy watermelon.

"Somebody's been telling you stories."

"Yeah, so...Are they true?" She bit into the watermelon.

"Look, Breeze, I've had my share of women, but that was before you."

"People don't change that much."

"I have never felt the way I feel for you. I was searching for that feeling. But, baby, I never felt it until we met again."

"Deep in my heart, I feel that you will be true, but I know how women are in this business…and Lex, you have such a playboy reputation that…"

"That was before you. What about you and Edmund?"

Her brows drawn together, she responded, "What do you mean?"

"I know there was something going on between you. I could tell when we signed the contract for your album."

Loaning back into the chair, Breeze explained, "There has never anything between Edmund and me but friendship and business. Business first, I might add."

"I got a strong feeling that he liked you more than that, Breeze."

"Believe me, nothing happened between us."

They were silent a moment, both thinking about how much their lives had changed.

"Breeze, Chanelle isn't pregnant. She lied. I knew she was trying to play me."

"And she's not going to come knocking on this door?"

"I told her she was not welcome here, and I'm not going to work with her." Helping himself to some of her fruit salad, Lex said, "Listen, Breeze, we've got to leave the past in the past.

We can't let it come between us. I ran around with different women, but I don't anymore. Please believe me,

I'm committed to this relationship. We've got to leave the past behind."

"You're right, dealing with the present is tough enough."

Lex leaned over and kissed Breeze on her lips. "I've got to get dressed, Sunshine, or I'll be late for my meeting."

"Lex, don't forget. Rayna's coming to dinner tonight."

Breeze was dumbfounded when Rayna introduced her to Troy Baxter. Over the phone, Rayna had said, "My first boyfriend. I'm almost thirty years old, and I finally have a boyfriend. Ain't that a trip?"

"Maybe you're tripping now?" was Breeze's sarcastic reply.

Troy Baxter was tall like a basketball player, 6 feet 10 inches, with long arms and skinny legs. An earth-tone brown hand stretched out to shake Breeze's hand, and an even-toothed smile warmed away any uneasiness.

Smiling, hoping to conceal her surprise, Breeze muttered, "Delighted to meet you." She noticed the splattering of brown freckles across his cheeks on his good-looking face.

"Good to meet Rayna's baby sister," Troy greeted.

Dressed in a red-and-white polka-dot dress with matching shoes, Rayna gushed excitedly, "Breeze, I have to tell you all about the audition."

"I take it that it went well."

"Of course it did!" Rayna bragged.

They followed Breeze downstairs to the entertainment room where the movie she had been watching was still playing.

"I like this set up," Troy said.

"Troy is an electronics freak. Everything in his house is wired and connected to some kind of crazy gadgetry. You can lie in the bed and say 'lights on,' and the lights come on. Girl, it's a trip!"

"Lex is on his way. He just called from the car. He should be here shortly. He's stuck in traffic. I thought traffic in New York was bad. I hate driving here. Cars are everywhere," Breeze said.

"Troy, you have a seat there," Rayna directed, pointing to the loveseat diagonal from the screen.

"Can I offer you something to drink?" Breeze asked, standing behind the bar.

"Troy doesn't drink," Rayna stated proudly.

"Oh," Breeze said. "How about a soda or some lemonade?"

"Lemonade," said Troy.

"I'll get it for him," said Rayna. She opened the small refrigerator underneath the bar and took out a tall pitcher of lemonade.

"Rayna, are you all right?" Breeze asked, shocked that her don't-have-time-for-no-man sister would wait on a man. Rayna laughed at Breeze's strange expression. "What can I say, Sis," she shrugged her shoulders, "I'm in love."

"For the first time," Breeze commented.

"Believe it or not, girl," she nodded and smiled sweetly.

"I'd be lying if I told you differently."

Troy stayed in the viewing room watching a movie while Breeze showed Rayna around her new home.

"If I get this part, it will totally change my career. Leading lady in a movie. And I have such a good feeling about it. Word is Denzel Washington has already signed on."

"Go 'head, girlfriend," Breeze said.

"Breeze…picture it: I'll be nominated for an Oscar and I'll make history. I'll be the first black woman to win the best actress award. I'll get up there and say 'Thank you very much. It's about friggin' time.' " Breeze and Rayna cracked up laughing as they entered the kitchen.

"My crazy sister," Breeze said. "Troy is not what I expected you to fall for."

"I could tell when I introduced you."

"I expected to meet a comedian or a musician like Daddy maybe with long dreadlocks or something. Or an actor, maybe. Not a suit-wearing businessman."

"Yeah, I know. I'm surprised myself. When I first met Troy, I kept telling him, 'It's not going to work,' but he just wouldn't listen. Thank God. I needed a man like Troy. Someone to keep me straight. All I ever dated were actors or musicians, but nothing good came out of it," explained Rayna.

"You never can tell what's going to happen in life, can you?"

"Sure can't, B.B. How do you like living with Lex?"

"Sometimes I wish we could go back to paradise."

"Is something wrong?"

"Not specifically. We love each other. It's just living together is so different."

"Too real for you?"

"Yeah, maybe that's what it is. We've had to make adjustments. Lex stays up all night working, and I like to go to bed early. I guess you just have to realize that it's not about just what you want, but negotiating two people's needs."

"That's tough to learn," Rayna confessed. "Believe me, I'm fighting it all the way."

"Rayna, I've learned something about myself that I didn't know before, and I'm not really happy about this discovery."

"What's that?"

"I can be one jealous witch!"

"Jealous?"

"Lex was seeing Chanelle Diamond before we hooked up. The first night I moved here, she came over and claimed to be pregnant with Lex's child."

"I know you wanted to kill her."

"I was cool. I wasn't going to let her know that she upset me, but I wanted to strangle her. Rayna, I've never felt that way before."

"I know I'd do some serious ass kicking if another woman tried to come between me and Troy."

"I know that Lex hasn't been celibate, but ever since she came strutting in here, I've felt so jealous and insecure. I'm trying to get to a place where I don't feel like running anymore."

"What happened? Is she really pregnant?"

Shaking her head, Breeze said, "No, she was just trying to blackmail Lex into producing some songs for her. Her career is on the decline, and she figured that Lex could get things rolling."

"I know you were relieved."

"Yeah, things are complicated enough." Entering the dining room, Breeze said, "I saved the best for last."

"The house is as beautiful as I expected. Lex has good taste, and I can see your touches in the place. Even the table."

"That's what I wanted to show you. I did the place settings, the napkins, everything."

"You, Breeze?" Rayna asked, walking around the table.

"I'm trying to be a little domestic. You know I'm a disaster in the kitchen. You should have seen the kitchen when I tried to bake an apple pie for Lex. I ended up going out and buying a pie. I didn't tell him at first, but he knew."

Laughing, Rayna said, "The table looks fabulous. What are we having?"

"It's a surprise. I won't tell any lies, I didn't make it. I selected the meal, but the cook, Raoul, prepared the dinner. All I have to do is warm everything up."

"I hope Lex gets here soon. I'm starving," Rayna said.

"India wants us to meet her tomorrow at the bridal boutique for a fitting. Can you do it around eleven?"

"I'll be there."

CHAPTER SIXTEEN

"Here, this is for you," Lex said, handing Breeze a small box delicately wrapped in shiny gold paper. He kissed her softly on the lips and caressed her body with his deep, dark brown eyes. Breeze met his caressing eyes with a sensual smile as she lowered the *Los Angeles Times*. Loaning back against the chaise lounge, there was delight in Breeze's eyes.

"Ohh," she said teasing, "I'll just sit and look at the wrapping. It's so pretty."

"What's inside is even prettier," Lex taunted, sitting on the end of the lounge.

Breeze tore the wrapping paper off the velvet case and caught her breath as she pulled out an incredibly beautiful diamond necklace surrounded by sapphires, the center teardrop shaped stone twinkling up at her in multi-colored prisms.

"Oh, Lex, this is beautiful!" she squealed, admiring the unique design and expert craftsmanship of the necklace. "Here, put it on for me." She handed Lex the necklace and turned around so that he could fasten it.

"I gotta see it," she said gleefully after Lex secured the necklace around her slender neck.

Breeze ran into the bathroom and sat down in front of her dressing table. It was a stunning piece of jewelry, and it lay flat and balanced on her bare skin. She looked into the mirror, turning this way and that, admiring the sparkle of the gems, the glow of the gold.

"It's exquisite," she whispered, her right hand touching the necklace.

Looking at Lex through the mirror, Breeze said, "Thank you, it is the most beautiful thing. I love it."

"It looks beautiful on you."

"What made you buy this?"

"I want to adorn my beautiful woman with beautiful things," said Lex as he stood behind her.

They caught each other's eyes in the mirror and shared a long, lusty stare. Lex ran his fingers slowly down Breeze's neck, trailing sensuously past her shoulders and down her arms. Her eyes closed, Breeze was engulfed by a flood of desire as Lex planted soft, teasing kisses from her neck down to her shoulders.

Lex breathed huskily into her ear, "But nothing is more beautiful than you."

"How can I thank you?" Breeze asked with a smile as wide as the silver moon.

As Lex loosened his bold, colorful tie, he challenged, "You'll think of a way."

She returned his lustful look with a seductive wink and sly smile. "Yes…maybe I will…"

Peeling off his black shirt, Lex excitedly announced, "I'm in the mood to celebrate, baby—the deal went through today." His clenched fists were raised in victory.

Breeze jumped up. "Oh, congratulations, baby. You got your own label!…Chameleon Records."

"Chameleon Records," Lex said, thinking about the meeting with the financial investors for his new record label. He was caught off guard when they suggested signing Breeze to the label. Lex didn't make any promises that Breeze would leave Harmony for Chameleon, but he had a strong feeling that the subject would come up again.

"This is just the beginning," Lex said. "I'm going to be the baddest, the best, and the busiest producer in town." Lex stripped off the rest of his clothes until he was naked. He opened the shower door, turned the water on, and stepped inside.

"Baby...You already are. You already are! Why don't we take a two-day trip somewhere. Okay?" she yelled so he could hear her in the shower.

Breeze headed back towards their bedroom, but a sexy impulse popped into her mind. She took off her clothes but not the necklace. She turned toward the shower and quietly opened the door. The shower was steamy and hot as Breeze crept up behind Lex.

"Let me do that," Breeze offered, rubbing her body against Lex's soapy nakedness, feeling the hot pulsating water pound against her body. She took the bar of soap and washcloth out of Lex's hands.

Feeling Breeze's soft hands wash his back and move down to his legs, Lex was fully aroused. He turned around and said, "The last thing on my mind is getting clean." He took the bar of soap from Breeze's hands and pulled her wet body to his. The washcloth tumbled to the floor.

A wet, wicked exploration of their slick, slippery bodies began, ending with a bolt of pleasure rushing through their bodies.

Breeze left Lex in the shower and dried off in the bedroom before flouncing on the bed. When Lex finished showering, he smiled when he saw Breeze lying naked across the bed, his gift still dangling around her neck.

"What are you reading?" he asked, garbed only in a terrycloth towel wrapped around his waist. Water dripped down his body.

Breeze looked up, whiffed the scent of soap and cologne mingled together, and said, "A screenplay."

"Is it for Rayna?"

"No, it's a part for me."

"For you?" he asked, surprise in his tone.

"It's just a small part in Spike Lee's next movie. Small, but interesting," she answered.

"Are you going to do it?"

She shrugged her shoulders. "I don't know yet...Maybe."

"I really don't think you should," Lex advised.

Breeze replied defensively, "Well, I didn't ask you."

"I just think that sometimes people in our business try to be too many things. Breeze, focus on what you're good at."

"Are you trying to say that I shouldn't develop any other talent besides my singing? Is that it?" She stopped, her voice lowered a pitch. "I'm not supposed to grow and explore other talents?"

"I wasn't saying all that, baby. I just think you should stop and think about what you're doing."

"It's not a big role. And I'm not trying to become the next Cicely Tyson or anything like that."

She followed him into the huge bathroom that had his and her vanities, a separate shower, water closet, and a whirlpool bathtub. The faucets and fixtures were gold. Light streamed in from the skylight above the whirlpool, sustaining the green plants that hung below. She went over to her dressing table and began applying perfumed lotion to her skin. The scent of Opium perfume lingered in the air.

Standing in front of his sink, Lex said, "Well, that's good." He picked up the toothpaste and squeezed a dab onto his toothbrush.

"And if I was, you wouldn't approve?" She slipped a long silk red nightgown over her head.

"If you want an honest answer, no. You should put all your energies into singing. As a matter of fact, I was thinking about you changing labels."

"Oh right...to Chameleon Records."

"Yeah, what's wrong with that?"

"And what about my contract with Harmony?"

"Baby, there's always a way to get out of a contract."

"I'm not leaving Harmony." Breeze said firmly, sitting on the dressing table chair. Her dressing table was neatly organized; jars, bottles, and tubes of makeup precisely aligned.

"Why not?"

"I'm not unhappy with them. Edmund and Jillian have treated me very well, and I wouldn't feel right just leaving them high and dry."

"I'm asking you to," Lex demanded.

Breeze stared at Lex with unsuppressed anger. Storming into her closet, she hastily stripped off the nightgown and slipped on her bra and panties. She yanked an ankle-length cotton dress off a hanger and pulled it over her head. She brushed her wet hair back with her hands before placing a tan straw hat on her head.

Breeze said furiously, "First you're going to tell me that I shouldn't go into acting, and now you're trying to convince me to leave the people who made me a star. Maybe we should have left our romance in Aruba because I sure don't like the way it is here!"

"Breeze, what are you doing?" Lex asked angrily as he watched her grab her keys and purse.

"What does it look like I'm doing? I'm leaving."

"Where are you going?"

Breeze slammed their bedroom door in angry reply.

It was 2:15 AM and Breeze still hadn't returned home. Lex was worried, angry, and confused: worried because he hoped nothing had happened to her, angry that she had abruptly left him, and confused because in all the hours that passed, he didn't understand why she was so upset.

"I may have been a bit overbearing, but for her to leave…" At 7:00 AM, he was ringing the doorbell at Breeze's condo repeatedly until she finally buzzed him in. She'd bought the condo for visiting family and friends so they wouldn't infringe on Lex. He never expected he'd be visiting her there.

"What do you want?" Breeze asked groggily when she opened the door in a short peach gown. After a sleepless night, she was not in the mood for a confrontation.

"I want to talk to you," Lex said, pushing his way past her.

"Lex, just give it a rest. I don't want to talk to you," she said, her anger resurfacing.

"I came to apologize," Lex said as he followed Breeze down the hall out to the kitchen. Pictures of Hollywood legends hung on the wall.

"Breeze, I realize I was wrong, and I want you to know that."

Her arms crossed over her chest, she stood like a statue in front of the refrigerator door. "Damn straight you were wrong. I've been handling my career just fine without you."

"I know, Breeze, I was out of place." His arms spread outward, he stepped over to stand in front of her. "I'm just used to women who expect me, or want me, to guide them. It's hard for me to admit, but I'm not used to being on equal footing with a woman I'm involved with." His expression softened, and his voice reflected respect. "You don't need my guidance."

Glaring at him, she said, "I need your support."

Lex wanted to take her into his arms, for her to look at him with the love that usually shined out at him. The only way that glow of love would return to her eyes, he knew, would be to come to an understanding about their professional lives. A kiss and passionate lovemaking were not the answer. He belatedly realized that Breeze had strong feelings and that she was a far cry from the naive girl he knew a long time ago.

"I understand that. And I was very wrong and I hope you will forgive me."

She gave him a serious look and sternly said, "As long as you understand that I'm very serious about this. I value your opinion, Lex, but I need to know that you will support me even in things you don't agree with."

"I will, Breeze. I promise you." He stood a few feet away from Breeze, his back to the sink and cabinets.

"Remember when my first album came out? There was no picture on the cover, and it was called…"

"*Introducing B.B.* Everybody was going crazy trying to figure out who you were."

"It was my idea to debut anonymously."

"I always figured that was Edmund's strategy." He cleared his throat, "I guess I figured wrong."

"Not only about that…"

"I understand what you're saying. I don't have to play Dr. Doolittle with you." Noticing the tired look on Breeze's face, his eyes playfully warm, he asked, "How'd you sleep last night?"

"I slept like a baby," Breeze said pertly.

A smile edged the corners of Lex's mouth. "Are you going to come home?"

"Maybe!" She moved away from the refrigerator to the large picture-glass window. From the penthouse view, she saw a dense cloud of fog, swelling from the rush hour traffic building below. The sun was rising to make its claim on the morning sky.

"Breeze, whenever we have disagreements we have to talk them out, not run away," said Lex.

"I know, Lex, I know. I was just so angry with you. But you're right: We can't solve our problems apart."

"In this business, we're going to be in the spotlight. People are going to always be around, wanting something, demanding our souls. Some won't even care what they do to us to get what they want. We have to be open with each other, Sunshine. We have to stay close," Lex said.

Lex stood behind Breeze, and put his arms around her. Watching the sun rise higher in the sky, they embraced—a warm, understanding, tender embrace.

The real estate agent whipped through the seven lanes of traffic like a race car driver, ignoring the honking horns and angry gestures. Speaking fast and hard in a New York accent, the middle-aged, blond, blue-eyed woman, shifted gears, guiding her Range Rover to the fast lane. "The new listings come out tomorrow," she explained, "but I still haven't showed you everything on my list. You can keep one of these real estate books on the back seat next to Miss Blackwell. We're really not allowed to let people have these, but for you two, I'll make an exception."

India nodded her head. "I like the last office you showed us."

"Wasn't it lovely? It has a lot of potential," Ruth Berger, said.

"But is that a good location?" Breeze inquired.

"It's not a bad location. Now if you want something where the action is, I can show you some office space smack in the middle of Los Angeles in a new development. It's pretty pricey."

"They weren't kidding when they said real estate was expensive out here," India said.

"You ain't seen nothing yet. I can take you around tomorrow if you still want to look," Ruth offered.

"That's what I came here for."

Ruth pulled into the parking lot of her office building and parked the Range Rover. She reached into her briefcase for her appointment book and quickly scanned it. "How about ten o'clock?"

"That's fine. I'll meet you here," India said.

"When are you going to let me show you some houses, Miss Blackwell? There are some fabulous homes here." Her words were emphatic, her voice persuasive.

"We'll probably start looking in a couple of months."

"Keep me in mind," Ruth suggested.

Breeze and India got out of the real estate agent's car and walked over to Breeze's car, a black four-door Mercedes Benz. Breeze backed out of the parking space and turned onto the main street into the flow of traffic.

"You know I hate driving here," Breeze said. "It's a war zone."

"You'll get used to it."

"So what did you think of the offices we saw?"

"I liked the first place and the last place the best. The other offices were too big or too small." India shrugged her shoulders, "I want to see some more offices before I decide."

"What are you going to name your business?"

"Girl, I've been so busy working on the wedding that I haven't come up with a name yet. I don't want to use my name or anything common. I want something different, but it just hasn't come to me yet."

"How's Mother doing?" Breeze asked.

"She's fine. Fussing about the wedding, but enjoying every minute of it."

"She hasn't mentioned Albert lately," Breeze said.

"That's because she isn't seeing him anymore," explained India.

"What? Why didn't she tell me?"

"She didn't tell me voluntarily. I had to pull it out of her."

"What happened?"

"I don't know, but I think it has something to do with Omar."

"What does Daddy have to do with it?"

"Mother and Albert went to some reunion thing, and ran into him."

"Daddy was there?"

"He was playing the music."

"Oh…So what happened?"

"I don't know what happened there. I can't imagine them fighting or anything, but a little after that Albert stopped seeing Mother."

"Maybe Albert realized that she was seeing him because he looked like her ex-husband."

"Probably. And you know what else?"

"Omar has been calling Mother."

"She hasn't been hanging up on him?" "They've been talking, girl."

"I don't believe it," Breeze said. "I don't believe it."

"I can't get her to say much. She says they're just discussing the wedding, but I think something else is going on."

"You just never know what's going to happen in life, do you?" Breeze said. Shaking her head with a grin, she pushed a CD into the car's CD player.

CHAPTER SEVENTEEN

"How are we going to know who she is?" Rayna asked Breeze.

They were at Kennedy airport in New York, waiting for India's mother to walk out of the gate. The airport was crowded. It was early evening, the peak period for airline traffic.

"We'll just know."

The plane had landed fifteen minutes earlier, but the passengers on the flight from Trinidad had not yet deplaned.

"I hope she got on the right plane," Rayna snorted.

"So do I."

"What did the detective say? Did he describe her? Show you any pictures?"

"He took some pictures, but I left them in L.A."

"Breeze!" Rayna scolded.

Breeze shrugged her shoulders nonchalantly. "We'll know her."

Rayna said, "I tripped big time when you told me you had found India's mother. I didn't even know you were looking for her."

"India asked me to look for her mother after I got back from Aruba. It didn't take the detective long to find her."

"Have you spoken with her?"

"We talked on the phone two weeks ago. I wanted to fly down and meet her and then bring her back, but I couldn't fit it into my schedule."

"What's her name? What did she sound like on the phone?"

"Her name is Josephine, and she sounded real tired when I talked to her. But when I told her I was calling about India, her voice picked up and she fired away a bunch of questions. Some of her words I couldn't understand because of her accent."

"Josephine," repeated Rayna thoughtfully, conjuring an image in her mind of what India's real mother would look like.

"Everybody calls her Josie."

"What happened? How come she didn't come back for India?"

"I don't know all the details." Breeze stopped and pointed at a tall, thin, regal-looking dark-skinned woman who held her head high. Her jet-black hair was neatly brushed into a knot on top of her head. Her eyes were darting about, searching for someone she was anxious to see.

Breeze and Rayna approached the woman dressed simply in a full multi-print cotton skirt, blouse and sweater. Breeze was struck by the loss in the woman's eyes. Dark pouches beneath her eyes reflected her pain and loss for all the world to see.

"Mrs. Abduhl?" Breeze inquired, wearing her friendliest smile.

Josephine nodded her head politely, acknowledging their introduction. "I'm Josephine Abduhl."

"Welcome back to America," Rayna greeted. Josephine seemed to flinch at those words.

"That depends," Josephine replied, looking around, searching deep into the crowd. "Where is my child?" she asked in a trembling voice.

"India's at home. We thought you would want to see each other at home." Breeze turned to steer them towards the exit.

"She doesn't know you're here."

"I'm going to surprise her?" Josephine questioned, her smooth voice dripped with skepticism.

"You won't be a total surprise. I promised her I would find you."

"You're the one I talked to on the phone?" her cool, black eyes examining Breeze closely.

"Yes, ma'am. India's like a sister to me and Rayna. She's been a part of our family ever since we moved to Philadelphia. I was about eight, and Rayna was probably ten when she became a part of our lives."

"How come you got such strange names? You're the wind," Josephine said to Breeze. She shifted her gaze to Rayna. "And you're the rain."

Rayna responded, a warm smile on her face. "Our father named us. He's a musician, and I guess he wanted us to have unusual names."

"That's what they are." She stepped in closer and looked deep into Breeze's face. "When can I see my child?"

"We'll take you to see her right now," Rayna said enthusiastically.

"How long is it going to take?"

Breeze looked at her watch. "About forty-five minutes to an hour."

Josephine looked at her watch. "I've waited twenty years, I guess I can wait another hour."

Breeze pulled her Mercedes Benz in front of Lillian Blackwell's house, a traditional two-story brick home, with four large bedrooms, a finished basement and plenty of land for gardening. Lillian grew vegetables in the backyard and flowers in front of the house.

In the hour's drive from the airport, a tense air of expectation had dominated the conversation, but the last half hour had passed in silence.

Josephine was nervous when she climbed out of the car and walked up the driveway. She admired the beautiful flowers and landscaping. Lillian opened the door and greeted Josephine with a stiff, assessing gaze of suspicion. Lillian politely launched into an inquiry about the flight; but the stern look on Josephine's face stopped Lillian's chatter. With a nod, Lillian wordlessly led India's mother through the foyer to the family room and into the kitchen where India was busy sorting through her wedding invitations and marking off the list of folks who had mailed back the RSVP cards.

"India!" whispered a quivering, uncertain voice.

India looked up from what she was doing and was rendered speechless when she saw the woman she instinctively recognized as her mother. She saw traces of herself in the shape of Josephine's face, her shiny black hair, and her long nose.

"Mama?" India questioned. She stood up from her chair, moving in slow motion. She had dreamed of this reunion a thousand times, but in the face of reality, she didn't know what to do, she wasn't sure what to say. She moved away from the table, inching closer to her mother.

"Yes, child, it's your mother," Josephine said, walking the distance between them until they stood toe-to-toe. Josephine pulled her daughter into her arms. It was an awkward embrace, charged with a mixture of distorted emotions.

Josephine touched her daughter's face, felt the smoothness of fudge-brown skin like her own, and fingered India's hair, the silky texture very familiar.

"I didn't know you were coming," stumbled out of India's mouth.

"I could tell you were surprised."

"I knew Breeze was looking for you. I asked her to help me find you. But I didn't know she had," explained India. She looked behind Josephine to see if Lillian or Breeze was nearby. But no one was there and it was strangely quiet. They had left her to become acquainted with this stranger, this woman, her mother.

"Come sit at the table with me," India suggested.

Josephine sat down, noticing the invitations and envelopes scattered on the table. Spotting India's name, she picked up an invitation. "You're getting married?" she asked, catching India staring at her.

"In three weeks."

"What kind of man is your fiancé?"

"Zeke's a wonderful man. I've known him for four years; he's kind, generous, and loving. He's Jamaican," she paused, wanting to explain why she connected with a man from the islands, how he seemed to fill in the empty spaces. Instead, she said, "He's a musician, plays the drums. He's good to me, and he makes me happy."

"Looks like you're gonna have a pretty big wedding," Josephine commented, admiring the large kitchen with its shiny appliances, green and yellow flowered wallpaper, bay window, and padded window seat.

"Bigger than I expected."

They were quiet a few minutes, both wondering about each other's life.

"Pretty big house," Josephine said. "How long have you lived here?"

"I don't live here. Mother, I mean Lillian, lives here."

"Has Lillian treated you well?"

"Yes! If she hadn't taken me in after Grandma died, I don't know what would have happened to me. I would have probably ended up in a foster home or an…" She didn't finish her sentence, the memories of her grandmother's death vivid in her mind, as if it just happened. It was something she never thought about, something she refused to think about. It was all too painful. At her grandmother's funeral, all she could think of was: Where is my Mama? Where is my Mama? But there was no answer to that question, so she trained her mind to chase those thoughts away.

The pain of yesterday resurfaced, and it still hurt as fresh as a new wound. India didn't want to launch into a battery of questions about the past. She had wanted to relax with her mother, to take time getting to know her. But those questions were too strong, they were funneling their way from her belly, with a powerful force, about to be gushed up like foul-smelling vomit. India couldn't hold it back.

"What happened to you, Mama? Why did you leave me? Why didn't you come back? Did you forget about me?" India's eyes were fixed on her mother's. Sorrow looked into sorrow.

"I owe you an explanation, child. I know that. I've thought about you every day. Believe me, you have never been out of my thoughts. I never came back for you because I didn't think you would understand the reasons why I left. Every New Year, I would say, I'm going to go get my child, but then, I never did. I was afraid of what I would find. I was afraid of how you would feel about me."

"You knew that Grandmother had died? You knew where I was?" India asked, her dark eyes whirlpools of betrayal. To ease the pain of abandonment, she had imagined that her mother didn't know that Grandmother had died, that her mother didn't know where she was. Eventually, she came to believe her own story; it was a story that she could live with, a story that would let her sleep at night.

Josephine closed her eyes, not wanting to look into her daughter's anguished eyes. She knew that India's pain ran deep, and that she was the source of that pain. But she had to face it so India could be free of it. Opening her eyes,

Josephine looked at India, and admitted, "I knew, child. I knew."

"Then why didn't you come back for me?" India whispered angrily.

"I didn't know your grandmother had died until about a year later. I don't know what she told you about me and your father, but she never approved of me. I was this poor girl from a backwards part of an island, and I was very young. When your father was killed, I couldn't live in her house anymore. She promised me that she would take care of you until I got myself together and could afford to take care of you myself. I never got myself together until recently when I returned to Trinidad. I have done things I'm not exactly proud of and leaving you is one of those things."

India took in every word, desperate to understand why her mother did what she did. As her story unfolded, India suddenly realized that she might not have understood, probably wouldn't approve, but she would have to learn to accept it.

"I came to see you a couple of years after your grandmother died. You were living with Lillian. I watched you from a distance and…you seemed happy. You had two little girls to play with, and you lived in a nice house, had clothes to wear and plenty to eat."

"That's no excuse to abandon your child!" India exclaimed self-righteously.

"I had nothing to offer you!" Josephine charged up from her chair. "I was living on the streets, and I didn't have a place of my own."

"But when you have a child, you're supposed to find a way!"

"I should have, but I didn't." Easing back down into the chair, Josephine admitted, "I wasn't strong enough."

"Maybe you just didn't want to," India accused, giving her mother a cold stare. At that moment, she wished she had left the past buried, that her mother was oceans away from her, nowhere to be found.

"I couldn't. Maybe I took the easy way out. I gave you up. I let you stay with a woman who seemed to love you and could provide more for you than I could." Gently she said, "I'm sorry I didn't come back for you. I'm sorry I hurt you."

An avalanche of tears poured down India's face. She stepped over to the kitchen counter for a paper towel and wiped her tears away. She walked out of the kitchen into the family room, where she stretched out on the sofa and quietly sobbed.

Josephine started to follow her, but she knew there was nothing she could say to comfort her. She had told her daughter the truth, and it was up to India to come to terms with it.

"Girl, you won't believe how crowded it is out there. The church is packed," Rayna exclaimed, after she came into the compact dressing room.

"And they all came to see you get married," Breeze said, placing the elaborate veil that matched the wedding gown on top of India's head and smoothing out the gossamer veil, whisking it so that it would fall delicately on her shoulders.

The silk and satin ivory wedding dress was traditionally-styled with leg-o'-mutton sleeves and a long train, but with contemporary details: low-cut bodice, deep V-cut in the back. It featured millions of tiny pearls in flower shape designs and a long train of intricate lace and pearls.

"You look gorgeous," Rayna sighed. "I can't believe Ma picked out this gown. Girl, it's all that!"

"I was surprised, too. She's gotten kind of jazzy in her old age," Breeze commented. "Are you nervous? Scared?"

"Yes to both," India said, her face glowing joy and excitement.

Rayna and Breeze's bridesmaid gowns echoed India's gown in style, but in different colors: Breeze's gown was a deep purple and Rayna's a soft lavender. Zeke's sister Zenora, the other bridesmaid, wore the same soft lavender gown as Rayna.

"This is supposed to be the happiest day of your life," Rayna said. "So enjoy every moment of it."

There was a light tap at the door, and a voice that announced, "It's time."

India appeared on the arm of Omar Blackwell at the back of the church. The pianist played "The Wedding March." The church stood up to honor the bride who nervously made her entrance.

The church was large, seating over five hundred people, and the aisle to the front of the church seemed a mile long to India with all those eyes watching her. India focused on the people waiting for her at the front of the church.

Zeke, her soon-to-be-husband, was smiling warmly in a dove-gray tuxedo with tails. From the distance, she caught his eye and felt his warm, reassuring love. *A new beginning,* she thought, *with the man I love.*

She saw Lillian, the woman who had raised her, beaming proudly, knowing that all her planning and work had paid off. This was a perfect wedding.

And she saw her real mother, Josephine, uncertainty in her smile but warmth in her eyes. A sudden thought occurred to India: Mama is a beginning, too.

India began walking down the aisle to her future.

CHAPTER EIGHTEEN

Photographers swarmed the church, flashing away at the celebrities—local and national—who came to witness the event of the summer: India Abduhl and Zeke Peart's wedding.

Edmund Mitchelson, Jillian Bayer, and the staff of Harmony records came to the wedding and reception, along with the numerous musicians Zeke had played with over the years. India's schoolmates from her undergraduate and graduate years at Columbia University and other relatives, friends, neighbors, and acquaintances from their childhood and the music business attended the wedding. The bride and groom stood in the receiving line for over an hour greeting their well-wishers.

The reception was a formal sit-down affair at the Hilton hotel; attendees had their choice of lobster, prime rib, or chicken for the main course. There was an open bar, and champagne flowed from a silver fountain. The guests couldn't wait to get a taste of the seven-tiered cake that stood several feet tall.

Laughter abounded, cameras flashed, and the live music, intermixed with prerecorded songs, played on and on. Everyone was having a great time—no one wanted to leave.

"Lillian, you're looking lovely," Omar said.

Lillian's simple response was something Omar had waited for years to see: She smiled at him. A warm and open smile that reached her eyes and spoke from her soul.

"Thank you," she said. Pride and happiness emanated from her. "You're looking pretty good yourself."

"So all your worries were for nothing," Omar said, jingling the ice in his mixed drink. "Everything was perfect. Absolutely perfect. You should be proud of yourself."

"I am," Lillian admitted, observing the festivities.

"Now that it's all over," Omar began. "Are you ready?"

"Ready for what?" she questioned, giving Omar her full attention.

"Ready for me."

"What do you mean?"

"We don't have to beat around the bush."

"Omar, what are you talking about?"

"I'm talking about us, Lillian."

He pronounced her name the way she loved to hear it: Li-li-an, distinct and elegant.

"I know," Lillian said. Her heart pounded as it had the first time she stared into Omar's eyes.

"I'm ready to reclaim it. Are you?" Omar asked, grasping her delicate hand into his.

Lillian smiled at him, and softly said, "Yes."

"Hello, Lex," Lillian said when she finally caught him standing alone. Every time she had worked up enough courage to walk toward him, someone else would start conversing with him.

"How are you, Mrs. Blackwell?"

"I'm doing fine."

An awkward silence passed. Lex said, "The wedding and reception have been a hit."

"I'm very pleased," Lillian remarked with a self-satisfied smile. "The wedding was perfect, everything happened the way it was supposed to. It was spectacular." She cleared her throat and said, "Ah...when will I be planning your wedding?"

Lex was taken aback. This was the first time he had spoken with Mrs. Blackwell in ten years. He assumed that she still didn't approve of him, for she rarely called their house.

"Excuse me?"

"I know you and Breeze are living together, but I really think you two should be married. That's the Lord's way."

"We plan to," replied Lex solemnly.

Lillian sensed a bit of hostility in Lex's manner despite the way he nonchalantly leaned against the wall. She decided to speak her mind. Her eyes batting wildly, she said, "I've apologized to my daughter, but I guess I also owe you an apology." She gestured fleetingly with her hands. "Well, here goes: I was trying to protect my baby. I was married to a musician, and I know what a lonely life it can be. But I was very wrong to interfere with your lives. I am sorry...I didn't do it to hurt anybody...I was just..."Lillian stopped mid-sentence, searching for the right words to express her feelings.

Lex held up his hand in a peace-offering gesture, and grasped Lillian's in a firm handshake. "I accept your apology, Mrs. Blackwell."

Relief washed over her face. Lillian was certain that she was going to end up saying the wrong thing. "It seems that you two are meant to be."

"I love your daughter very much, Mrs. Blackwell. I always have. Believe me, I only want to see Breeze happy."

Lillian's hand tightened in Lex's gentle grip. "Welcome to the family."

Lex was tired of waiting for all the wedding formalities to be observed. He wanted to dance with Breeze.

He walked up to the bridal party table, asked Breeze to dance with him. He offered his arm and escorted her to the dance floor. The music changed just as they reached the floor. Breeze's sultry voice singing "I Believe in Love" floated sensuously in the air.

Breeze giggled, "That's an appropriate song. I wrote that song for you."

Lex looked deep into Breeze's eyes, finding joy and happiness shining back at him in warm brown pools. "I feel the same way," he said.

Their bodies pressed together, moving gracefully to the music, Lex and Breeze felt the rapture of each other, the music, the ambiance of a romantic wedding.

Entranced, they stared into each other's eyes, feeling that all the questions that hung between them were no longer there. There was nothing between them to hold them back, to keep them apart. They were free to love each other, not just for this moment, but for the millions of moments yet to come.

The music stopped, but their dancing continued, waltzing and whirling around the floor to their own music—the rhythm of their hearts. Clapping broke the spell. They finally realized that the music had stopped, and it was announced that it was "time for the bride and groom's first dance." Breeze and Lex bowed, not the least bit embarrassed, and glided off the dance floor.

Breeze headed back to the bridal party's table, but Lex stopped her.

"Come upstairs with me!"

"Lex! I've got things to do here."

"Just for a minute. It won't take long. I haven't seen you in a week, baby."

Lex looked at her with eyes she couldn't deny.

"Just for a little while."

Inside the elevator, as they rode to the top floor, Lex unleashed a flurry of kisses on Breeze's lips, leaving them swollen from his urgent demands. They reached the penthouse floor, and upon entering the suite, Breeze squealed in delight at the balloons and flowers everywhere.

"Oh, Lex, you're so sweet and thoughtful," Breeze said, noticing the bottle of champagne in the ice-filled bucket.

"I know we have to get back downstairs, but there's something here that I want you to find."

An impish smile curved Breeze's lips. "Okay," she said, willing to play this game. She searched in the champagne bucket, her fingers cold from digging through the ice. She opened drawers, looked under pillows, and inspected the flower vase.

The balloons, she thought. Breeze removed an ink pen from the nightstand, and popped several of the balloons. But they just made a loud piercing noise, flew into the air, and slowly fell to the floor.

"Tell me if I'm on the right track," she said, trying to decide which of the many balloons to burst next.

"Perhaps," Lex teased.

She burst a few more balloons, when one of the balloons fell with a loud thud.

"Ah," Lex said. "You found it." He picked it up and removed the tiny velvet-coated box.

Before opening the box to reveal what was inside, Lex said, "I love you, Sunshine. I have always loved you. And I don't want to be without you."

A four-carat, oval-shaped diamond sparkled at Breeze when Lex opened the box.

On bended knee, Lex asked, "Breeze, will you marry me?"

Breeze looked at the man she had loved all her life, the only man she had ever really loved. "Yes!"

He slid the ring on her finger and pulled Breeze into his arms. 'He held her against his chest, his arms wrapped around her. Lex kissed her with all the love he felt in his heart. A forever kiss, a kiss that completely melted the wall around Breeze's heart.

2008 Reprint Mass Market Titles

January

Cautious Heart
Cheris F. Hodges
ISBN-13: 978-1-58571-301-1
ISBN-10: 1-58571-301-5
$6.99

Suddenly You
Crystal Hubbard
ISBN-13: 978-1-58571-302-8
ISBN-10: 1-58571-302-3
$6.99

February

Passion
T. T. Henderson
ISBN-13: 978-1-58571-303-5
ISBN-10: 1-58571-303-1
$6.99

Whispers in the Sand
LaFlorya Gauthier
ISBN-13: 978-1-58571-304-2
ISBN-10: 1-58571-304-x
$6.99

March

Life Is Never As It Seems
J. J. Michael
ISBN-13: 978-1-58571-305-9
ISBN-10: 1-58571-305-8
$6.99

Beyond the Rapture
Beverly Clark
ISBN-13: 978-1-58571-306-6
ISBN-10: 1-58571-306-6
$6.99

April

A Heart's Awakening
Veronica Parker
ISBN-13: 978-1-58571-307-3
ISBN-10: 1-58571-307-4
$6.99

Breeze
Robin Lynette Hampton
ISBN-13: 978-1-58571-308-0
ISBN-10: 1-58571-308-2
$6.99

May

I'll Be Your Shelter
Giselle Carmichael
ISBN-13: 978-1-58571-309-7
ISBN-10: 1-58571-309-0
$6.99

Careless Whispers
Rochelle Alers
ISBN-13: 978-1-58571-310-3
ISBN-10: 1-58571-310-4
$6.99

June

Sin
Crystal Rhodes
ISBN-13: 978-1-58571-311-0
ISBN-10: 1-58571-311-2
$6.99

Dark Storm Rising
Chinelu Moore
ISBN-13: 978-1-58571-312-7
ISBN-10: 1-58571-312-0
$6.99

2008 Reprint Mass Market Titles (continued)

July

Object of His Desire
A.C. Arthur
ISBN-13: 978-1-58571-313-4
ISBN-10: 1-58571-313-9
$6.99

Angel's Paradise
Janice Angelique
ISBN-13: 978-1-58571-314-1
ISBN-10: 1-58571-314-7
$6.99

August

Unbreak My Heart
Dar Tomlinson
ISBN-13: 978-1-58571-315-8
ISBN-10: 1-58571-315-5
$6.99

All I Ask
Barbara Keaton
ISBN-13: 978-1-58571-316-5
ISBN-10: 1-58571-316-3
$6.99

September

Icie
Pamela Leigh Starr
ISBN-13: 978-1-58571-275-5
ISBN-10: 1-58571-275-2
$6.99

At Last
Lisa Riley
ISBN-13: 978-1-58571-276-2
ISBN-10: 1-58571-276-0
$6.99

October

Everlastin' Love
Gay G. Gunn
ISBN-13: 978-1-58571-277-9
ISBN-10: 1-58571-277-9
$6.99

Three Wishes
Seressia Glass
ISBN-13: 978-1-58571-278-6
ISBN-10: 1-58571-278-7
$6.99

November

Yesterday Is Gone
Beverly Clark
ISBN-13: 978-1-58571-279-3
ISBN-10: 1-58571-279-5
$6.99

Again My Love
Kayla Perrin
ISBN-13: 978-1-58571-280-9
ISBN-10: 1-58571-280-9
$6.99

December

Office Policy
A.C. Arthur
ISBN-13: 978-1-58571-281-6
ISBN-10: 1-58571-281-7
$6.99

Rendezvous With Fate
Jeanne Sumerix
ISBN-13: 978-1-58571-283-3
ISBN-10: 1-58571-283-3
$6.99

2008 New Mass Market Titles

January

Where I Want To Be
Maryam Diaab
ISBN-13: 978-1-58571-268-7
ISBN-10: 1-58571-268-X
$6.99

Never Say Never
Michele Cameron
ISBN-13: 978-1-58571-269-4
ISBN-10: 1-58571-269-8
$6.99

February

Stolen Memories
Michele Sudler
ISBN-13: 978-1-58571-270-0
ISBN-10: 1-58571-270-1
$6.99

Dawn's Harbor
Kymberly Hunt
ISBN-13: 978-1-58571-271-7
ISBN-10: 1-58571-271-X
$6.99

March

Undying Love
Renee Alexis
ISBN-13: 978-1-58571-272-4
ISBN-10: 1-58571-272-8
$6.99

Blame It On Paradise
Crystal Hubbard
ISBN-13: 978-1-58571-273-1
ISBN-10: 1-58571-273-6
$6.99

April

When A Man Loves A Woman
La Connie Taylor-Jones
ISBN-13: 978-1-58571-274-8
ISBN-10: 1-58571-274-4
$6.99

Choices
Tammy Williams
ISBN-13: 978-1-58571-300-4
ISBN-10: 1-58571-300-7
$6.99

May

Dream Runner
Gail McFarland
ISBN-13: 978-1-58571-317-2
ISBN-10: 1-58571-317-1
$6.99

Southern Fried Standards
S.R. Maddox
ISBN-13: 978-1-58571-318-9
ISBN-10: 1-58571-318-X
$6.99

June

Looking for Lily
Africa Fine
ISBN-13: 978-1-58571-319-6
ISBN-10: 1-58571-319-8
$6.99

Bliss, Inc.
Chamein Canton
ISBN-13: 978-1-58571-325-7
ISBN-10: 1-58571-325-2
$6.99

2008 New Mass Market Titles (continued)

July

Love's Secrets
Yolanda McVey
ISBN-13: 978-1-58571-321-9
ISBN-10: 1-58571-321-X
$6.99

Things Forbidden
Maryam Diaab
ISBN-13: 978-1-58571-327-1
ISBN-10: 1-58571-327-9
$6.99

August

Storm
Pamela Leigh Starr
ISBN-13: 978-1-58571-323-3
ISBN-10: 1-58571-323-6
$6.99

Passion's Furies
AlTonya Washington
ISBN-13: 978-1-58571-324-0
ISBN-10: 1-58571-324-4
$6.99

September

Three Doors Down
Michele Sudler
ISBN-13: 978-1-58571-332-5
ISBN-10: 1-58571-332-5
$6.99

Mr Fix-It
Crystal Hubbard
ISBN-13: 978-1-58571-326-4
ISBN-10: 1-58571-326-0
$6.99

October

Moments of Clarity
Michele Cameron
ISBN-13: 978-1-58571-330-1
ISBN-10: 1-58571-330-9
$6.99

Lady Preacher
K.T. Richey
ISBN-13: 978-1-58571-333-2
ISBN-10: 1-58571-333-3
$6.99

November

This Life Isn't Perfect Holla
Sandra Foy
ISBN: 978-1-58571-331-8
ISBN-10: 1-58571-331-7
$6.99

Promises Made
Bernice Layton
ISBN-13: 978-1-58571-334-9
ISBN-10: 1-58571-334-1
$6.99

December

A Voice Behind Thunder
Carrie Elizabeth Greene
ISBN-13: 978-1-58571-329-5
ISBN-10: 1-58571-329-5
$6.99

The More Things Change
Chamein Canton
ISBN-13: 978-1-58571-328-8
ISBN-10: 1-58571-328-7
$6.99

Other Genesis Press, Inc. Titles

A Dangerous Deception	J.M. Jeffries	$8.95
A Dangerous Love	J.M. Jeffries	$8.95
A Dangerous Obsession	J.M. Jeffries	$8.95
A Drummer's Beat to Mend	Kei Swanson	$9.95
A Happy Life	Charlotte Harris	$9.95
A Heart's Awakening	Veronica Parker	$9.95
A Lark on the Wing	Phyliss Hamilton	$9.95
A Love of Her Own	Cheris F. Hodges	$9.95
A Love to Cherish	Beverly Clark	$8.95
A Risk of Rain	Dar Tomlinson	$8.95
A Taste of Temptation	Reneé Alexis	$9.95
A Twist of Fate	Beverly Clark	$8.95
A Will to Love	Angie Daniels	$9.95
Acquisitions	Kimberley White	$8.95
Across	Carol Payne	$12.95
After the Vows	Leslie Esdaile	$10.95
(Summer Anthology)	T.T. Henderson	
	Jacqueline Thomas	
Again My Love	Kayla Perrin	$10.95
Against the Wind	Gwynne Forster	$8.95
All I Ask	Barbara Keaton	$8.95
Always You	Crystal Hubbard	$6.99
Ambrosia	T.T. Henderson	$8.95
An Unfinished Love Affair	Barbara Keaton	$8.95
And Then Came You	Dorothy Elizabeth Love	$8.95
Angel's Paradise	Janice Angelique	$9.95
At Last	Lisa G. Riley	$8.95
Best of Friends	Natalie Dunbar	$8.95
Beyond the Rapture	Beverly Clark	$9.95

Other Genesis Press, Inc. Titles (continued)

Blaze	Barbara Keaton	$9.95
Blood Lust	J. M. Jeffries	$9.95
Blood Seduction	J.M. Jeffries	$9.95
Bodyguard	Andrea Jackson	$9.95
Boss of Me	Diana Nyad	$8.95
Bound by Love	Beverly Clark	$8.95
Breeze	Robin Hampton Allen	$10.95
Broken	Dar Tomlinson	$24.95
By Design	Barbara Keaton	$8.95
Cajun Heat	Charlene Berry	$8.95
Careless Whispers	Rochelle Alers	$8.95
Cats & Other Tales	Marilyn Wagner	$8.95
Caught in a Trap	Andre Michelle	$8.95
Caught Up In the Rapture	Lisa G. Riley	$9.95
Cautious Heart	Cheris F Hodges	$8.95
Chances	Pamela Leigh Starr	$8.95
Cherish the Flame	Beverly Clark	$8.95
Class Reunion	Irma Jenkins/ John Brown	$12.95
Code Name: Diva	J.M. Jeffries	$9.95
Conquering Dr. Wexler's Heart	Kimberley White	$9.95
Corporate Seduction	A.C. Arthur	$9.95
Crossing Paths, Tempting Memories	Dorothy Elizabeth Love	$9.95
Crush	Crystal Hubbard	$9.95
Cypress Whisperings	Phyllis Hamilton	$8.95
Dark Embrace	Crystal Wilson Harris	$8.95
Dark Storm Rising	Chinelu Moore	$10.95

Other Genesis Press, Inc. Titles (continued)

Daughter of the Wind	Joan Xian	$8.95
Deadly Sacrifice	Jack Kean	$22.95
Designer Passion	Dar Tomlinson	$8.95
	Diana Richeaux	
Do Over	Celya Bowers	$9.95
Dreamtective	Liz Swados	$5.95
Ebony Angel	Deatri King-Bey	$9.95
Ebony Butterfly II	Delilah Dawson	$14.95
Echoes of Yesterday	Beverly Clark	$9.95
Eden's Garden	Elizabeth Rose	$8.95
Eve's Prescription	Edwina Martin Arnold	$8.95
Everlastin' Love	Gay G. Gunn	$8.95
Everlasting Moments	Dorothy Elizabeth Love	$8.95
Everything and More	Sinclair Lebeau	$8.95
Everything but Love	Natalie Dunbar	$8.95
Falling	Natalie Dunbar	$9.95
Fate	Pamela Leigh Starr	$8.95
Finding Isabella	A.J. Garrotto	$8.95
Forbidden Quest	Dar Tomlinson	$10.95
Forever Love	Wanda Y. Thomas	$8.95
From the Ashes	Kathleen Suzanne	$8.95
	Jeanne Sumerix	
Gentle Yearning	Rochelle Alers	$10.95
Glory of Love	Sinclair LeBeau	$10.95
Go Gentle into that	Malcom Boyd	$12.95
Good Night		
Goldengroove	Mary Beth Craft	$16.95
Groove, Bang, and Jive	Steve Cannon	$8.99
Hand in Glove	Andrea Jackson	$9.95

Other Genesis Press, Inc. Titles (continued)

Hard to Love	Kimberley White	$9.95
Hart & Soul	Angie Daniels	$8.95
Heart of the Phoenix	A.C. Arthur	$9.95
Heartbeat	Stephanie Bedwell-Grime	$8.95
Hearts Remember	M. Loui Quezada	$8.95
Hidden Memories	Robin Allen	$10.95
Higher Ground	Leah Latimer	$19.95
Hitler, the War, and the Pope	Ronald Rychiak	$26.95
How to Write a Romance	Kathryn Falk	$18.95
I Married a Reclining Chair	Lisa M. Fuhs	$8.95
I'll Be Your Shelter	Giselle Carmichael	$8.95
I'll Paint a Sun	A.J. Garrotto	$9.95
Icie	Pamela Leigh Starr	$8.95
Illusions	Pamela Leigh Starr	$8.95
Indigo After Dark Vol. I	Nia Dixon/Angelique	$10.95
Indigo After Dark Vol. II	Dolores Bundy/ Cole Riley	$10.95
Indigo After Dark Vol. III	Montana Blue/ Coco Morena	$10.95
Indigo After Dark Vol. IV	Cassandra Colt/	$14.95
Indigo After Dark Vol. V	Delilah Dawson	$14.95
Indiscretions	Donna Hill	$8.95
Intentional Mistakes	Michele Sudler	$9.95
Interlude	Donna Hill	$8.95
Intimate Intentions	Angie Daniels	$8.95
It's Not Over Yet	J.J. Michael	$9.95
Jolie's Surrender	Edwina Martin-Arnold	$8.95
Kiss or Keep	Debra Phillips	$8.95
Lace	Giselle Carmichael	$9.95

Other Genesis Press, Inc. Titles (continued)

Last Train to Memphis	Elsa Cook	$12.95
Lasting Valor	Ken Olsen	$24.95
Let Us Prey	Hunter Lundy	$25.95
Lies Too Long	Pamela Ridley	$13.95
Life Is Never As It Seems	J.J. Michael	$12.95
Lighter Shade of Brown	Vicki Andrews	$8.95
Love Always	Mildred E. Riley	$10.95
Love Doesn't Come Easy	Charlyne Dickerson	$8.95
Love Unveiled	Gloria Greene	$10.95
Love's Deception	Charlene Berry	$10.95
Love's Destiny	M. Loui Quezada	$8.95
Mae's Promise	Melody Walcott	$8.95
Magnolia Sunset	Giselle Carmichael	$8.95
Many Shades of Gray	Dyanne Davis	$6.99
Matters of Life and Death	Lesego Malepe, Ph.D.	$15.95
Meant to Be	Jeanne Sumerix	$8.95
Midnight Clear	Leslie Esdaile	$10.95
(Anthology)	Gwynne Forster	
	Carmen Green	
	Monica Jackson	
Midnight Magic	Gwynne Forster	$8.95
Midnight Peril	Vicki Andrews	$10.95
Misconceptions	Pamela Leigh Starr	$9.95
Montgomery's Children	Richard Perry	$14.95
My Buffalo Soldier	Barbara B. K. Reeves	$8.95
Naked Soul	Gwynne Forster	$8.95
Next to Last Chance	Louisa Dixon	$24.95
No Apologies	Seressia Glass	$8.95
No Commitment Required	Seressia Glass	$8.95

Other Genesis Press, Inc. Titles (continued)

No Regrets	Mildred E. Riley	$8.95
Not His Type	Chamein Canton	$6.99
Nowhere to Run	Gay G. Gunn	$10.95
O Bed! O Breakfast!	Rob Kuehnle	$14.95
Object of His Desire	A. C. Arthur	$8.95
Office Policy	A. C. Arthur	$9.95
Once in a Blue Moon	Dorianne Cole	$9.95
One Day at a Time	Bella McFarland	$8.95
One in A Million	Barbara Keaton	$6.99
One of These Days	Michele Sudler	$9.95
Outside Chance	Louisa Dixon	$24.95
Passion	T.T. Henderson	$10.95
Passion's Blood	Cherif Fortin	$22.95
Passion's Journey	Wanda Y. Thomas	$8.95
Past Promises	Jahmel West	$8.95
Path of Fire	T.T. Henderson	$8.95
Path of Thorns	Annetta P. Lee	$9.95
Peace Be Still	Colette Haywood	$12.95
Picture Perfect	Reon Carter	$8.95
Playing for Keeps	Stephanie Salinas	$8.95
Pride & Joi	Gay G. Gunn	$8.95
Promises to Keep	Alicia Wiggins	$8.95
Quiet Storm	Donna Hill	$10.95
Reckless Surrender	Rochelle Alers	$6.95
Red Polka Dot in a World of Plaid	Varian Johnson	$12.95
Reluctant Captive	Joyce Jackson	$8.95
Rendezvous with Fate	Jeanne Sumerix	$8.95
Revelations	Cheris F. Hodges	$8.95

Other Genesis Press, Inc. Titles (continued)

Rivers of the Soul	Leslie Esdaile	$8.95
Rocky Mountain Romance	Kathleen Suzanne	$8.95
Rooms of the Heart	Donna Hill	$8.95
Rough on Rats and Tough on Cats	Chris Parker	$12.95
Secret Library Vol. 1	Nina Sheridan	$18.95
Secret Library Vol. 2	Cassandra Colt	$8.95
Secret Thunder	Annetta P. Lee	$9.95
Shades of Brown	Denise Becker	$8.95
Shades of Desire	Monica White	$8.95
Shadows in the Moonlight	Jeanne Sumerix	$8.95
Sin	Crystal Rhodes	$8.95
Small Whispers	Annetta P. Lee	$6.99
So Amazing	Sinclair LeBeau	$8.95
Somebody's Someone	Sinclair LeBeau	$8.95
Someone to Love	Alicia Wiggins	$8.95
Song in the Park	Martin Brant	$15.95
Soul Eyes	Wayne L. Wilson	$12.95
Soul to Soul	Donna Hill	$8.95
Southern Comfort	J.M. Jeffries	$8.95
Still the Storm	Sharon Robinson	$8.95
Still Waters Run Deep	Leslie Esdaile	$8.95
Stolen Kisses	Dominiqua Douglas	$9.95
Stories to Excite You	Anna Forrest/Divine	$14.95
Subtle Secrets	Wanda Y. Thomas	$8.95
Suddenly You	Crystal Hubbard	$9.95
Sweet Repercussions	Kimberley White	$9.95
Sweet Sensations	Gwendolyn Bolton	$9.95
Sweet Tomorrows	Kimberly White	$8.95

Other Genesis Press, Inc. Titles (continued)

Taken by You	Dorothy Elizabeth Love	$9.95
Tattooed Tears	T. T. Henderson	$8.95
The Color Line	Lizzette Grayson Carter	$9.95
The Color of Trouble	Dyanne Davis	$8.95
The Disappearance of Allison Jones	Kayla Perrin	$5.95
The Fires Within	Beverly Clark	$9.95
The Foursome	Celya Bowers	$6.99
The Honey Dipper's Legacy	Pannell-Allen	$14.95
The Joker's Love Tune	Sidney Rickman	$15.95
The Little Pretender	Barbara Cartland	$10.95
The Love We Had	Natalie Dunbar	$8.95
The Man Who Could Fly	Bob & Milana Beamon	$18.95
The Missing Link	Charlyne Dickerson	$8.95
The Mission	Pamela Leigh Starr	$6.99
The Perfect Frame	Beverly Clark	$9.95
The Price of Love	Sinclair LeBeau	$8.95
The Smoking Life	Ilene Barth	$29.95
The Words of the Pitcher	Kei Swanson	$8.95
Three Wishes	Seressia Glass	$8.95
Ties That Bind	Kathleen Suzanne	$8.95
Tiger Woods	Libby Hughes	$5.95
Time is of the Essence	Angie Daniels	$9.95
Timeless Devotion	Bella McFarland	$9.95
Tomorrow's Promise	Leslie Esdaile	$8.95
Truly Inseparable	Wanda Y. Thomas	$8.95
Two Sides to Every Story	Dyanne Davis	$9.95
Unbreak My Heart	Dar Tomlinson	$8.95
Uncommon Prayer	Kenneth Swanson	$9.95

Order Form

Mail to: Genesis Press, Inc.
P.O. Box 101
Columbus, MS 39703

Name _____

Address _____

City/State _____ Zip _____

Telephone _____

Ship to (if different from above)

Name _____

Address _____

City/State _____ Zip _____

Telephone _____

Credit Card Information

Credit Card # _____ ☐Visa   ☐Mastercard

Expiration Date (mm/yy) _____ ☐AmEx   ☐Discover

Qty.	Author	Title	Price	Total

Use this order
form, or call
1-888-INDIGO-1

Total for books	_____
Shipping and handling:	
$5 first two books,	
$1 each additional book	_____
Total S & H	_____
Total amount enclosed	_____

Mississippi residents add 7% sales tax